Sarasa Nagase
ILLUSTRATION BY
Mai Murasaki

New York

I'M THE VILLAINESS, SO I'M TAMING THE FINAL BOSS, Vol. 7
Sarasa Nagase

Translation by Taylor Engel
Cover art by Mai Murasaki

This book is a work of fiction. Names, characters, places, and incidents are the product of the author's imagination or are used fictitiously. Any resemblance to actual events, locales, or persons, living or dead, is coincidental.

AKUYAKU REIJO NANODE LAST BOSS O KATTE MIMASHITA Vol. 7
©Sarasa Nagase 2020
First published in Japan in 2020 by KADOKAWA CORPORATION, Tokyo.
English translation rights arranged with KADOKAWA CORPORATION, Tokyo, through TUTTLE-MORI AGENCY, INC., Tokyo.

English translation © 2023 by Yen Press, LLC

Yen Press, LLC supports the right to free expression and the value of copyright. The purpose of copyright is to encourage writers and artists to produce the creative works that enrich our culture.

The scanning, uploading, and distribution of this book without permission is a theft of the author's intellectual property. If you would like permission to use material from the book (other than for review purposes), please contact the publisher. Thank you for your support of the author's rights.

Yen On
150 West 30th Street, 19th Floor
New York, NY 10001

Visit us at yenpress.com
facebook.com/yenpress
twitter.com/yenpress
yenpress.tumblr.com
instagram.com/yenpress

First Yen On Edition: December 2023
Edited by Yen On Editorial: Leilah Labossiere
Designed by Yen Press Design: Andy Swist

Yen On is an imprint of Yen Press, LLC.
The Yen On name and logo are trademarks of Yen Press, LLC.

The publisher is not responsible for websites (or their content) that are not owned by the publisher.

Library of Congress Cataloging-in-Publication Data
Names: Nagase, Sarasa, author. | Murasaki, Mai, illustrator. | Engel, Taylor, translator.
Title: I'm the villainess, so I'm taming the final boss / Sarasa Nagase ;
    illustration by Mai Murasaki ; translation by Taylor Engel.
Other titles: Akuyaku reijou nanode last boss wo kattemimashita. English
Description: First Yen On edition. | New York, NY : Yen On, 2021–
Identifiers: LCCN 2021030963 | ISBN 9781975334055 (v. 1 ; trade paperback) |
    ISBN 9781975334079 (v. 2 ; trade paperback) | ISBN 9781975334093 (v. 3 ; trade paperback) |
    ISBN 9781975334116 (v. 4 ; trade paperback) | ISBN 9781975334130 (v. 5 ; trade paperback) |
    ISBN 9781975334154 (v. 6 ; trade paperback) | ISBN 9781975334178 (v. 7 ; trade paperback)
Subjects: LCGFT: Fantasy fiction. | Light novels.
Classification: LCC PL873.5.A246 A7913 2021 | DDC 895.63/6dc23
LC record available at https://lccn.loc.gov/2021030963

ISBNs: 978-1-9753-3417-8 (paperback)
       978-1-9753-3418-5 (ebook)

10 9 8 7 6 5 4 3 2 1

LSC-C

Printed in the United States of America

First Act
- Isaac Lombard ... 1
- The Demon King Desires a Friend ... 9
- Almond ... 19

Second Act
- The Demon King and His New Guards ... 29
- As This Is the World of an *Otome* Game, Valentine's Day Exists ... 83
- As This Is the World of an *Otome* Game, White Day Comes Even for Ladies-in-Waiting ... 121

Third Act
- What Manner of Thing Is Love? ... 131
- Love Is Something You Fall Into ... 141
- No One Minds How Often You Fall ... 151

Fourth Act
- Roxane Fusca ... 159
- A Childish Love ... 171

Fifth Act
- Amelia Dark ... 181
- What the Holy Dragon Consort Saw in the Sunset ... 195
- The Imperial Couple's First Day ... 203
- When Happiness Follows Happiness, the Result Is a Parfait ... 239

Afterword ... 247

I'm the Villainess, So I'm Taming the Final Boss

CONTENTS

Aileen Jean Ellmeyer

A villainess who has remembered her past life. Empress of Ellmeyer.

"My husband's happiness and better medical care and education for the people."

"Lay the groundwork for a world where demons and humans can live together."

Claude Jean Ellmeyer

Emperor of Ellmeyer, demon king, and Aileen's husband. The final boss of *Regalia of Saints, Demons, and Maidens 1*.

TOPIC: Future goals

I'm the VILLAINESS, So I'm Taming the Final Boss

Character Introductions and Glossary

The Story Thus Far

When her engagement is broken, memories of Aileen's past life surface, and she realizes she's been reincarnated into the world of an *otome* game as its villainess. To escape destruction, she decides to romance Claude, the final boss! After many twists and turns, Claude becomes emperor of Imperial Ellmeyer, and Aileen becomes his empress. This is the tale of a villainess's fight to secure a happy ending that doesn't exist in the game, conquering all the final bosses that stand in her way.

Claude's Advisers

Keith Eigrid
"Pass the baton to the next generation."

Beelzebuth
"Strengthen the demon king's army."

Almond
"Make air force huge!"

Aileen's Ladies-in-Waiting

Rachel Danis
"Balance work and family."

Serena Gilbert
"Do a job that will put my name in the history books."

Aileen's Lackeys

Jasper Varie
"Speed up reporting of foreign news."

Isaac Lombard
"Set up and monetize a job-finding service for demons."

Denis
"Build a floating palace."

Luc
"Get a medical license and establish a hospital."

Quartz
"Study abroad and found a school."

James Charles
"Research and coordinate with the demon realm."

Auguste Zelm
"Become captain of the Holy Knights!"

Walt Lizanis
"Rid the empire of demon snuff."

Kyle Elford
"Rescue the Nameless Priests."

Elefas Levi
"Revitalize my homeland by developing demon stone and sacred stone technologies."

Claude and Aileen's In-Laws

Lilia Reinoise
"If there is no sequel, make one."

Cedric Jean Ellmeyer
"Make a name for myself in the race."

The Kingdom of Ashmael

Baal Shah Ashmael
"Build a global alliance."

Roxane Fusca
"Research and analyze the histories of all nations."

Ares Emir Ashmael
"Establish a military academy exclusively for defense."

Sahra
"Be a doctor."

The Queendom of Hausel

Amelia Dark
"Be Grace's little sister again."

Demon Realm

Luciel
"Be a god who watches over everyone."

Grace Dark
"Be Amelia's big sister again."

✦ First Act ✦
Isaac Lombard

Lotteries feel an awful lot like destiny.

"So you are my partner."

There's a number seven on the white lottery slip she's holding out to him. The slip Isaac drew has the same number on it.

Agh, he thinks. He's doing his best to keep it bottled up, but his emotions are almost certainly showing on his fast-souring face.

This doesn't seem to bother his partner. "Let's start on the assignment over there," she says, turning on her heel.

Aileen Lauren d'Autriche, huh? This is gonna be a pain.

She's the fiancée of the crown prince, Cedric Jean Ellmeyer. That makes her the country's future empress.

If Isaac's parents knew about this, they'd tell him, *Make friends with her! That's why we're sending you to that ridiculously expensive school for nobles!* But Isaac couldn't give a damn.

In his opinion, the emperor's household can't be as wealthy as they look. Focusing on trade with foreign nations should be more profitable than just doing business with the imperial family. Ultimately, since he's the third son of a count, both the company and the noble title they've purchased will go to his big brothers. Isaac won't inherit anything. His only job is to make like a member of the aristocracy, marry a girl from an upstanding family, and convince them to formally adopt him as their son, boosting the house of Lombard's standing in high society.

"The assignment is, 'Propose a method for dealing with our nation's trade deficit.' Do you have any ideas?"

He almost says, *For starters, reeducate that crown prince you're nuts about and the rest of his faction.* The person responsible for the mess is Cedric and he's right behind them, talking to someone and explaining, "First, mint more currency and give it to those whose earnings fall below a certain amount. By doing so, the economy…"

Still, people say he's pretty good as crown princes go. He sure doesn't look it…

"Excuse me. Isaac Lombard. Are you listening?"

The firm voice pulls his attention back. "Mm-hmm," he hums vaguely before giving her a careless answer. "We could hunt down an alchemist and fabricate gold to make up the deficit."

"I believe finding an alchemist is an impossible task to begin with, but even if it weren't, I can't condone a policy that would be no different from raising taxes."

The stoic answer makes Isaac blink. *What in the…?*

This girl is the daughter of Prime Minister d'Autriche, and from what he's heard, her brothers are brilliant, too. Is this due to their influence?

For the first time, he looks straight at Aileen Lauren d'Autriche. "…Then what about just shrinking the deficit with tax revenue?"

"That won't be a permanent solution. Taking on debt for the sake of investment would be one thing, but that would be something else entirely. While Imperial Ellmeyer has a strong military, we're weak when it comes to commerce. Even in the trade agreements we do have, we only buy, never sell."

"Yeah, because the custom of drinking black tea took root here real fast."

"Quite. The fact that we're constantly importing tea while our cotton fails to sell is painful. This nation is vast, though. We must have something, some cultural export unique to Ellmeyer."

"That's too general. It's not a concrete proposal," he says, cutting her down critically. Then he panics a little. According to the rumors, this girl is arrogant and has a mean streak to boot. If she snaps and complains about him to the crown prince, things could get hairy.

However, Aileen simply nods, her brow furrowed. "Yes, you're right. My brothers said the same thing."

"......"

"In addition, our understanding of foreign culture is still very rudimentary. There really must be something unique to our nation that would find a market abroad, but…"

"Technology." Before he realizes what he's doing, Isaac begins saying what he actually thinks. "As expected of a nation this skilled at waging war, we've got all sorts of technologies. They're generally considered military secrets so we're stingy with them, but we should make them work for us instead."

"Do you mean we should sell weapons?"

"No. Use that technology to develop things the common people can use. Communications systems, railroads, that sort of thing. The possibilities are endless. Once they're widely adopted by the general populace, we're sure to end up with new daily necessities and cultural practices. Then it's a simple matter of snapping them up before anybody else and exporting them. If we refine our shipbuilding techniques, we can trade with nations across the ocean, too."

Isaac's suggestion makes Aileen's eyes widen. "It sounds like a fantasy."

"Making things like that happen is the state's job, though. We need to plan for the future, several years out at least."

"...True."

Aileen looks down, lowering her long eyelashes. As he studies her expression, Isaac has a sudden thought.

One day, this girl will be empress. One of the people who takes ideas that seem like fantasies and makes them reality.

And to top it all off, she fully understands the significance of this.

Abruptly, Isaac discovers his interest has been piqued.

I wonder if most of Crown Prince Cedric's achievements are actually hers, he muses privately while they continue working on their assignment.

When he checks into it later, it doesn't take him long to find out the truth.

"Look... Would it kill you to be a little cleverer about how you get things done?"

"What do you mean?" Aileen responds with a question of her own.

After that fateful assignment, Isaac found a great many opportunities to talk to Aileen. One day, while she's having lunch by herself in the shade under the trees, he calls out to her.

"The show our class is putting on for the academy festival is a good example. You changed it without getting anybody's input."

"We never would've finished that in time. The emperor himself will be attending the festival in disguise, you know."

"Geez, for real? ...What, so this *has* to succeed or else?"

She doesn't confirm or deny. However, lowering her voice to

a murmur, she elaborates. "Master Cedric is kind. Since he's seen the others working so hard, I'm sure he didn't have the heart to tell them it would be impossible to incorporate their feedback. That's why I simply said it for him."

"......"

"It's all right. Master Cedric said he understood."

But does he really?

Aren't you just being used, woman?

Isaac wants to say it, but he bites back the words and gazes into the distance instead.

By the fountain, far from the trees, Cedric is having an animated conversation with his friends. It's a veritable who's who of the school; Isaac spots Marcus Cowell, who's pegged to be the future captain of the knights. That bunch will probably lead the government someday.

The most concerning member of Cedric's group is the student next to the prince: Lilia Reinoise, a baron's daughter.

"That's great if it's true. Can you still say it when you're looking at that?"

Lilia playfully presses a sandwich to Cedric's lips. Next she holds one out to Marcus, who shakes his head, blushing scarlet.

"Lady Lilia is of common birth, so he says her perspective is novel and educational. Marcus is also putting more effort into his swordsmanship practice, because he feels closer to the people he must protect."

"Well, that's good." Isaac couldn't care less about the men's sense of virtue, but he glances at the woman seated on the bench.

Aileen murmurs softly, "...He told me it was nothing."

"Is that right?"

"I trust him."

Well, you shouldn't. The words are on the tip of his tongue. *He's fooling you. Don't you know what the crown prince tells people about the stuff you did for him?* "Even I can't deal with her," he says. "She's always been like that. I'll try talking to her, but bear with it for now, all right?" *And then he turns around and tells you he understands, whispering sweet nothings while he shoves all the dirty work onto you. It doesn't get more two-faced than that.*

He can't bring himself to say it, though.

"Never mind that," Aileen says, changing the subject. Her strength and her smile are dazzling in equal measure. "Are you in contact with Jasper? I've assembled some impressive talent, haven't I?"

"Y-yeah. They're not bad."

"What do you say? Will you be our organizer? If you're with us, our business is bound to be a success!"

Cedric's bound to steal the credit for that success as well.

Isaac clenches his fists, but he's smiling. Cedric isn't the only man who knows how to play it close to his chest, too. "Sure, why not? Count me in. This 'new medicines' business sounds lucrative."

"Spare a little thought for the empire as well, if you please."

"That's not how I roll."

Yes. This isn't how he rolls.

He's never been the type to think, *If I'm involved, maybe I'll be able to protect her a little.*

Abruptly, he feels eyes on him. When he glances up, Cedric is looking their way. It only lasts for a moment, so briefly Isaac thinks he might have imagined it. Then their eyes meet—and it's like a clash of hatred and obsession.

"Aileen Lauren d'Autriche. I'm dissolving our engagement."

Isaac slams a fist into the terrace balustrade. He lets go of the breath he's been holding, tips his head back, and looks up at the night sky.

"I'm sick to death of your deluded belief that I love you."

He chews his lip. The great hall that opens onto the terrace is buzzing with the sudden, dramatic dissolution of the crown prince's engagement.

"Hey, bite your tongue. You set her up for that!"

That triumphant face. The arrogance of his impassive denunciation. Some crown prince that guy is. It should be funny, but it's really not.

I'm the real fool.

He'd realized this would happen. He'd seen this coming for so long. After all, he'd been closer to Aileen than anyone.

He'd even thought about coming up with countermeasures, but he hadn't been able to. Why not? Because Aileen had been in love with her fiancé? No, that wasn't why. Isaac had noticed something else.

The fact was, he hadn't even wanted to prevent it.

"Dammit... Why am I about ready to cry over this?"

She didn't cry.

She'd been dignified and elegant. She'd held her head high to the end. She'd never once looked wretched.

Isaac drains the glass of wine that's been served to everyone with instructions not to stand on ceremony. Then he presses his forehead against the cold balustrade.

Don't do it. Don't do anything while your anger's in control. You're up against the crown prince and the Cowell dukedom. They won't be easy opponents.

They'll probably snatch the business Aileen has started. First, they'll fire the fifth-layer employees. He'd seen that flicker of contempt in the crown prince's expression at the meet and greet. What about Isaac? He's not from the fifth layer, but his aristocratic title is purchased. If he begs, he'll be allowed to stay— Would that be a good move or a bad one?

What would put him in the best position to ruin the prince?

His people are selling us short. It's just like how they're mocking Aileen. Good, that's how I like it.

Calm down, calm down, calm down.

It's not as if they've killed her. She's just been hurt, that's all.

"…She's not cute at all, is she."

If she'd only cried, or gone to pieces, or even clung to his arm…

Starting now, with that wish in a corner of his heart, Isaac plans to atone for his sin of not preparing for this day.

Until the day a man who could make that woman cry appears.

The Demon King Desires a Friend

It's no exaggeration to say that fashion is a young noblewoman's—or really every woman's pleasure. Dressing up is fun, of course. If there's someone attractive to dress up, all the better.

If that someone is her own fiancé, no one could blame her for getting carried away and indulging herself until sundown.

"Master Claude, here. Try this on as well, if you please."

"Aren't we done yet...?"

"Well, it's just that everything looks splendid on you!"

"Which one is next?"

"The demon king's a total pushover," Isaac says, disgusted.

"Oh, it's nice that they're so close," Luc tells him, smiling as if he finds the pair charming. The others who've gathered on Aileen's orders are watching them as they work in a corner of the room.

Quartz murmurs, "...It's been five hours already. It's impressive that he's lasted this long."

"He does look good in anything, huh! It's amazing."

"That's only natural, Denis. He is our king."

"Yes, and thanks to the renovation, we have more storage space. I'll have to buckle down and work hard, too."

"How does the demon king have so few belongings to begin with? No furniture, no clothes... Even your uncle Jasper here has a bit more than he does."

Aileen gleefully presents another outfit, and Claude snaps his fingers. With magic, changing clothes takes no time at all.

A brand-new cravat flutters, and now he's wearing a full formal suit that's a striking midnight-blue. He looks even better in it than Aileen assumed he would, and she's entranced. "Yes, let us go with this one. Traditional styles are fine, but we really must incorporate the latest fashions as well!"

"I see. Then if you're satisfied, it's about time we—"

"A cloak! What shall we do about your cloak? A crown prince must be dignified."

"...Didn't we already choose one a few minutes ago?"

"Oh, but the color of your outfit has changed. We must choose another."

"......"

"Hang in there, Master Claude."

Keith cheers him on from a corner of the room that is practically buried in clothing.

Aileen smiles brightly. "Once we've picked Master Claude's outfit, I'll dress all of you as well, naturally."

Luc is the first to respond, and he gives her a composed smile. "A fine idea. Unfortunately, we won't be able to attend the soiree, so I assure you it's completely unnecessary."

"Thaaat's right! Your uncle Jasper can't go, either!"

"...I'm glad I'm not a noble. Good luck, Isaac."

"I'm not going. There's no way in hell I'm going to the party!"

"Aww! I'd like to go to one! I wonder how the castle is on the inside."

"It's very normal looking, Denis. I like that military uniform thing."

"Yes... Perhaps that would suit you best, Beelzebuth. What shall we do about Sir Keith?"

"I'll just wear my usual. Don't trouble yourself over me!" Keith takes a step back.

Aileen turns to Claude again. "Earrings would suit you beautifully, Master Claude. Let's make them red to match your eyes. Hee-hee! The young ladies will positively swoon over you."

"You wouldn't mind?" Claude sounds skeptical.

Aileen balls her hands into fists. "Of course not! This soiree will mark your debut as crown prince. And this! This face! How could we not flaunt it?!"

"A-ah, yes, of course."

"I can't wait to see everyone grovel, overwhelmed by your beauty."

"I don't intend to make them grovel, but...I am looking forward to the soiree, I suppose."

"Goodness. You, too, Master Claude?"

She'd assumed public appearances weren't something he particularly enjoyed, but had she been mistaken? Aileen looks perplexed.

Claude gives a faint smile. "Well, I think I might be able to make a friend."

Aileen has never heard anything more shocking than this. Even that time lightning struck right behind her three times in a row can't begin to compare.

She's not the only one who feels this way. Everyone else is frozen, too. Someone seems to have knocked over their teacup, but even so, no one makes a move.

Claude continues, sounding strangely animated. "There should be people about my age at the soiree."

"……"

"I've never had a friend before, you see."

"…………"

"It's my first social function in ages. I'd like to meet a human I'll be able to call my friend."

"……………………"

Holding their breath, Aileen and her companions exchange glances.

In this situation, pointing out the facts would be unwise. *But you're the demon king* and *The demon king, make friends?* and *On top of that, you're the crown prince*—

All these statements are accurate, and they're also completely off-limits.

As everyone tries to avoid looking at Claude, Beelzebuth nods emphatically. "If that is your wish, sire, I will help you."

"Ye… Yes, absolutely?!"

"Lady Aileen, your voice just cracked! Please calm yourself, milord. I'm going to tell you something for your own good." Keith is the first to act.

That's a loyal retainer for you. Will he say it? The humans all watch with bated breath.

"First, make sure to greet people properly!"

"Hang on, that's what you're starting with?!"

"W-well, he is correct, Master Isaac. I think…"

"…Greetings are key."

"Y-yeah, they are. Any adult who can't even greet people properly might as well be a kid!"

"Greetings… Greetings, hmm? I see. Come to think of it, at the previous soiree, I appeared from the sky… That was a mistake. No human would do that. That's how the demon king behaves."

What should she say in response? She doesn't even know where to begin. Her beloved fiancé's long eyelashes are fluttering in a melancholy way, yet she's broken out in a strange sweat.

Beelzebuth, on the other hand, is pure and honest. He reacts immediately, his shoulders falling in concern. "...Sire, does being the demon king pain you?"

"No, Bel. I want a friend, that's all."

"...Hey, this isn't the kind of wish that could end up destroying the world if it goes south, is it?"

It isn't clear whether Claude has caught Isaac's mutter, but he looks up. "Aileen."

"Yes?!"

"You've spent more time in high society than I have. Tell me: When making friends, is there anything besides greetings that I need to be careful about?"

Claude has put her on the spot with his sincere question, and Aileen panics a bit. *This is* definitely *the type of wish that will destroy the world if I make the wrong choice! B-but how can I convince him to give up?*

As Aileen's gaze wanders uncomfortably, Isaac whispers in her ear, "Break it to him gently."

"Make sure he gets the message, though." Even Luc is shoving everything onto her.

Jasper nods in agreement like a man with tons of experience. "Well, getting a taste of reality is a step on the road to adulthood."

"The world of adults is a harsh one, huh."

"...I feel bad for him, but..."

Both Denis and Quartz are speaking irresponsibly, too.

Every one of them fully intends to make this a purely Aileen problem. She is Claude's fiancée, so perhaps that's only natural— But how can she tell those sparkling, puppy-dog eyes something so brutal?

No, Aileen, that's no good. Precisely because you are his fiancée, you must make him understand!

A future emperor can't make friends so easily. Particularly not if he's the demon king. And really, with that face, finding a friend is out of the question. It's impossible. No matter how she thinks about it, it won't work.

She must tell him so properly.

Just as Aileen comes to that resolution, Claude breaks into a soft smile, like a flower blooming. "Thanks to you, I no longer have to give up on being human."

"—! ………………………V-very well, Master Claude! Let us find you a friend!!"

"""""Huuuuuuuuuuuuuuuuuuuuuuuuhn?!"""""

A chorus of shrieks breaks out behind her. She glares at them sharply. "Is that clear, everyone? Procure a friend for Master Claude!"

"You can't just *procure* friends!!" Isaac fires back for all he's worth.

Luc begins thinking seriously. "If Denis made a doll that housed a soul, it might work out…"

"I-I'll give it my best shot!"

"…Some say plants grow if you talk to them."

"In other words, milord, when it comes to friends, you have a choice of dolls or plants." There's a distant look in Keith's eyes as he says this.

Beelzebuth scowls. "What's all the fuss about? The king has informed us of his wish. Grant it."

"Aileen," Claude calls, and she turns. Her fiancé, who

habitually does his best to stifle his emotions, is as expressionless as ever. Even so, the night wind blows in softly from the terrace, and the cut flowers in the vase blossom like they're in full bloom again.

"From the bottom of my heart, I'm happy you're my fiancée."

You should go home soon.

The words are like a sweet sigh, and Aileen nods without even understanding what he's said.

He snaps his fingers, and the next thing she knows, she's on her bed in her own room.

…That face really is against the rules.

Mind completely blank, Aileen buries her head in her pillow.

"Master Claude, do you actually want a friend?"

Keith is straightening the bedsheets.

Nightclothes in hand, Claude turns to look at him. "Yes, I do. Why?"

"…Bel. Is he being serious?"

"The king is looking forward to it."

"Making friends isn't what he's looking forward to, though, is it?"

"You're too clever by half. Just take it at face value. It would be fun if I made a friend, wouldn't it?" From behind his spectacles, the other man is giving him an intensely suspicious look. Claude smiles faintly. "If that were possible."

"…Poor Lady Aileen."

"By the way, Keith."

"Yes, yes. What is it?"

"I don't know how to put this on," Claude declares with a straight face, looking at his nightclothes.

Keith's shoulders slump. "You spoiled rich-kid demon king... It's because you always cut corners with magic, that's why! I'm going to train you so that you'll be able to change your own clothes by your wedding night. Lady Aileen will be appalled otherwise."

"But having her undress me is an amusing idea, no?"

"I'll pretend I didn't hear that."

Picking up on the fact that the demon king feels cold, Beelzebuth crosses to the open terrace doors and shuts them firmly.

Almond

For Colonel Almond of the demon king's first air force command, mornings begin early.

This is because he's had more work to do since the demon king he loves and respects got engaged to a human woman.

"**Aileen! Aileen! Cookies!**"

"How many times must I tell you not to emerge at my feet during breakfast?!"

Having crashed the d'Autriche duchy's breakfast table, Almond flaps his wings, bouncing up and down on the floor. On one occasion, he'd flown around scattering feathers and made Aileen so angry she banned cookies for three whole days, so now Almond makes sure his outbursts of excitement stay on the ground.

Giving up, Aileen rings the bell to summon a servant. On that cue, a maid opens the door and brings in a basket. Almond recognizes the round, woven shape, and his eyes light up.

"Thank you for your patience, Sir Almond."

"**Good work!**"

He gives her a sharp salute, and for some reason, the maid who's brought the basket looks away quickly. Her shoulders are trembling. However, promptly assuming a dignified expression, she begins to go over the day's offerings. "Based on the materials you've compiled for us, Duke d'Autriche's chef has devoted every effort to create these cookies. They have been improved according to Miss Aileen's suggestions."

"Improved...?"

"It means they've made them taste better."

What could that mean? A strong shiver runs through him, ruffling all his feathers.

"We would love to get a second opinion from a member of the demon king's air force. On behalf of all the servants, let me express our gratitude for your service in defending our mansion."

"Understood! I can show demon king!"

"Tell Master Claude that I will visit in the afternoon today."

"Message? Pay with cake!"

"Cake for a single message is unreasonable. Besides, I have no time to bake one... Oh, very well, if I must. Next time."

"Promise!"

Almond and the others have been charged with patrolling the d'Autriche estate. If they spot anyone suspicious loitering around, they tell the servants; if they hear a rumor, they inform Aileen. Covert operations, in which they keep their distance so they won't be seen, is currently considered the coolest job by the group.

The perks are good, too. The people of the mansion never fail to express their gratitude, and if Almond takes rubbish back with him as instructed, Aileen's father treats him to unusual sweets and delicacies. The people who make treats for the d'Autriche family have been actively developing recipes to present to the demons on a daily basis. Getting lots and lots of delicious things makes Almond and everyone else happy. It's a job with no downsides.

However, the sweets Aileen makes are irresistible. His first experience with them was awful, and he's also learned that there are plenty of other delicious treats in the world, but for some reason he just can't get enough of them. When he asked the demon king why this was, his master simply said, "That's love."

"I can tell demon King. I take cookies!"

"Yes, be careful on your way. Make sure to show the cookies to the demon king."

"I Know! Later, human!"

He takes the basket's handle in his beak, careful not to spill its contents, and he hops into Aileen's shadow.

This shadow is made from the demon king's magic, and it sends him anywhere he wants to go immediately. He opens his eyes, and he lands at the feet of the demon king—who's in bed, reading a newspaper—with a light thump. There are signs that Keith's already been here. He spots coffee and sandwiches on the nightstand.

"Good morning, Almond."

"Morning, Demon King! Cookies!"

"Yes, bring them here." The demon king, who's still in his nightclothes, folds his newspaper and gently holds his hand over the cookies. He's checking to make sure there's nothing dangerous in them.

"When you're given something to share with everyone, have the demon king check it over properly" is something Aileen has told Almond again and again, after he began getting treats from the d'Autriche family. He obeys her warning faithfully. As the captain, keeping everyone safe is his responsibility.

"It's all right. They're fine."

"Demon King, Aileen will come this afternoon!"

"I see. I'll be visiting the imperial castle in the morning in any case, so I won't be here."

"The castle? Just you, Demon King?"

That castle is a dangerous place. Long ago, the demon king came face-to-face with death there more than once. Just as Almond thinks he can't let his master go to a place like that by himself, the demon king breaks into a kind smile. "It's all right. Keith and Bel are coming with me."

"And me?"

"You and your people have your own work. What are you doing today?"

Almond cocks his head, searching his memory. **"Helping Denis. The wolfman mansion is almost done!"**

"I see. And how are your houses?"

"Comfy! The strategy headquarters come next..." Almond's looking forward to seeing things progress, but just as he's about to get into the details, he falters.

"What's the matter?" the demon king asks, so Almond confesses his worry.

"Demon King, do you have money?"

The demon king freezes with his coffee cup still raised to his lips.

Isaac taught Almond the concept of economics. Almond is aware that, just as he has to work if he wants cookies, it takes money to raise buildings.

Apparently, the demon king is the one who needs to provide that money. Aileen could do it, but that would put the demon king in her debt, and if that debt got too big, Almond and the others might be sold to Aileen. Then they wouldn't be the demon king's demons anymore. He heard this dreadful story from Isaac and Jasper.

All the demons who heard that story were terrified, so Aileen got really mad at Isaac and Jasper. Denis got mad, too; he told the demons, "I wouldn't let that happen." Almond thinks Denis is a good guy.

"...What have Aileen's people been telling you?"

"We might get sold. Then no more seeing you, Demon King..."

"Don't worry. I'd never part with any of you."

Almond's face lights up when the demon king pats him on the head. His master is never wrong.

"Understood! Time for cookies!"

"Yes, make sure to share them with the others. That reminds me, how is the new white one doing?"

"I take care of that one!"

Almond throws his chest out, and the demon king tells him he's counting on him.

As soon as Almond nods, the demon king snaps his fingers. Instantly, Almond and the basket of cookies have been sent to where the rest of the air force is waiting.

This is the meeting place Denis made for them: a space filled with dappled sunlight where Almond's many comrades can gather and rest their wings. The design uses the trees of the forest as they are but is also equipped with conveniences like a roof to keep out the wind and rain. A magnificent tree several centuries old stands at its very center.

This is the spot where he hands out cookies first thing in the morning. The waiting demons' eyes light up, and they start to clamor.

"Cookies! Cookies!"

"Pie! Any pie?!"

"Stay in order! Line up!" Almond tells them, and instead of shoving their heads into the basket, everyone files past, taking one cookie each. Aileen has said before she'll burn them with the sacred sword if they fight over the cookies. Above all, fighting would cause problems for the demon king.

None of them would ever willingly cause problems for their lord.

"Today, I take jam!"

"Chocolate pie for me..."

"Daily special! Daily special!"

The people of the d'Autriche duchy provide treats that fulfill everyone's requests. They also offer to send their personal recommendations, so the demons can choose to be surprised instead of placing an order.

Today's special is sugar cookies with a sprinkling of coarse sugar on top.

After giving it a little thought, once he's eaten his own almond cookie, Almond takes a sugar cookie and flies down to the base of the tree.

A white crow is hiding below, in a little hollow that's hard to spot from the outside.

"**Here's yours,**" Almond says, setting the special cookie down a short distance away.

The crow peeks out and looks at him. He can see pure white feathers and eyes the same red as the demon king's. Just like Almond's.

This is a demon Keith brought back just a little while ago.

"It good. Eat."

"...Humans made that..."

Almond's new companion hates humans.

He heard that after being captured by humans, they had their wings broken and were kept in a birdcage all the time. Their pretty eyes were gouged out as well. When Keith brought the demon home, they were on death's doorstep until the demon king's healing intervened. However, even he couldn't heal a scarred heart. This demon can't even go near the demon king. Evidently, his human appearance is too terrifying. In fact, upon waking, the rescued demon had shrieked and thrashed and was generally a real handful. The demon king used his magic to induce sleep, then carefully brought them here, to a place with no sign of humans. And because Almond's new comrade had been caged for so long, flying is impossible.

Keith blamed himself for this tragedy. Denis made a special bed so their new friend wouldn't hurt themselves no matter how much flailing occurred, while Luc and Quartz told Almond about delicious foods and nuts and berries that might have a calming effect. Jasper brought a blanket, and although Isaac pretends it's no concern of his, he has been reading a book with pictures of creatures that looked a lot like Almond and his comrades the other day.

He's pretty sure all the humans here are being nice to this demon.

The newcomer doesn't even acknowledge that kindness, though. Almond and the others think this is strange.

Aileen gets her sacred sword out if they don't all get along, so no one bullies the newcomer. However, they can't understand how any of them could be afraid of the demon king. Between that and the unusual feather color, the others tend to keep to themselves.

Because of the tricky situation, the demon king has asked Almond to take care of things, so he won't abandon his new comrade. After all, this pure white bird is going to be a member of the air force.

"You want something else? You can't fly. I can get it for you."

"I don't want anything..."

"What? You get it yourself? How?"

"Once the humans are all gone, I'll fly."

The problem is immediately apparent—that'll never happen.

The demon king allows humans to enter his territory now. What the demon king says goes. The white demon must understand that. Even so, the impossible request stands.

"Humans can't be trusted."

The resentful remark makes Almond cock his head.

He'd thought the same way once, and yet he's fine with it now. Why?

Then he finds his answer.

"Eat a cookie."

"No."

"Eat it!"

This flightless recruit does nothing but crouch at the foot of the tree. No new chick is a match for Almond. Using his talons, he grabs the other demon and force-feeds them a cookie. Eyes rolling in consternation, they have no choice but to swallow.

"Good?"

"....."

"If yes, then you're Sugar, starting now!"

The white demon blinks at him.

Gloating triumphantly, Almond boasts. "Almond, me. Sugar, you. All settled!"

"...Sugar."
"Aileen named me. I name you!"

Aileen gave him a cookie, and then a name.

He'd gotten mad because she'd laced that cookie with a numbing agent, but he hadn't disliked the name. Like the bow tie on his breast, it was a magic spell that had lifted him out of the crowd and made him Almond.

"And I protect you! Because I'm captain!"

Aileen had also saved his companion.

That's why Almond had decided it was okay to trust her.

"If you get it, then practice the dance! There's no time! We have to surprise the demon king!"

The demon king's birthday is in a few months.

Aileen had enthusiastically declared they'd celebrate it with a big event. She's promised to provide lots of delicious food and celebrate with everyone all night long in the renovated castle.

When they learned about the custom of giving people presents on their birthdays, Almond and the other demons put their heads together to think of a good gift. Even among the demons, there were divisions along species lines, so they wouldn't be doing this together. They did want to give him something, though... As a result, Almond and the others decided to perform a dance. Apparently humans spin around and dance to celebrate things, so imitating them seemed like a fine idea.

Right now, Beelzebuth is practicing for dear life on percussion instruments Denis made. Denis has told the other humans about the plan, and they're helping with the dance practice. However, it's a secret from both the demon king and Aileen.

Everyone's determined to surprise them.

They're going to make the demon king happy.

As a matter of fact, it's named the Demon King Love-Love Dance.

"You're all white. That means a good position!"

"...I don't think I can do that..."

"We dance and make the demon king happy. Good times!"

Isaac is the one who's been directing them to make sure their dance will look pretty. He said, "This would definitely sell. You could monetize this," so it must really be something. Jasper said he wanted to write an article about it. Luc and Quartz are making floral ornaments for all the dancers so they'll look even better.

There's no way it won't succeed.

Almond hops down to a lower spot among the tree roots.

"Sugar," he calls.

Hearing that name, the white crow looks straight into Almond's eyes, which are an identical red. A timid step forward brings Sugar closer to a new life.

When Almond sees that, he puffs out his chest.

Almond is the captain. His red bow tie proves it.

"I protect! I'm great!"

Sugar, the one he thinks he's protecting, will go on to win a great many achievements, receive a blue bow tie, and threaten Almond's position…but not for quite a while yet.

✦ Second Act ✦
The Demon King and His New Guards

He wants to run for it someday. That's all he's ever wished for.

His mother had left him with the church when he was six. She'd apologized over and over—*"Please be happy, okay? I'm so sorry"*—so at the time he'd thought these things probably happened and there was no sense in complaining, and he'd tried to be strong.

At the church, since he'd had an aptitude for it, he was assigned training that was positively inhumane. He did have food, clothing, and shelter; maybe he should have been content with that.

However, he was nothing more than an "amazing tool" that slaughtered all enemies of the church. Once they couldn't use him anymore, they'd promptly disposed of him. If he tried to sell them out, they'd send assassins after him. If he'd been able to believe he was protecting people—even if he was just a tool or a villain—he could have taken pride in that, but that was an impossible task.

I want to run away. Someday, somewhere, for sure.

That thought has never left his mind— Except Walt Lizanis has become the demon king's underling.

Yup. Looks like I'm toast.

Phrased in the way he's used to, his assignment had begun yesterday. Two days after a demon attack had half demolished Misha Academy, Walt had received his usual written orders from the church. This time, the gist had been "We've sold you to the demon king." It really was a rough world.

He was to be shipped out that day, transportation costs not covered. Walt is currently on his way to deliver himself to the demon king on foot.

All of this is happening because he got curious about a certain student pretending to be a boy. Maybe he has only himself to blame, but the price he's paying is far too great.

"You understand, don't you, Walt?"

"Understand what, hmm?" he responds carelessly.

His traveling companion is also being shipped to the demon king free of charge. The man glares at him with narrow, almond-shaped eyes. Apparently he has a problem with Walt's attitude; Kyle Elford is as serious as ever. Keeping his pace steady, he lowers his voice. "The content of our actual mission."

When Walt stops in his tracks, so does Kyle. They stand facing each other in a deserted corridor of the palace.

"If the church has given us to the demon king, they mean for us to assassinate him. If we can't, we're supposed to do the noble thing and kill ourselves."

"...You're not seriously saying that, are you?"

"Yes, I am. Don't tell me you're still thinking about running away."

Hey, want to run away with me?

It was an invitation Walt had extended to Kyle once, long ago. He regrets it now; it had been a careless move.

Year after year, his comrades were declared useless tools and disposed of, and so the one face he always saw had become a sort of comfort to him. As a result, he'd gotten the wrong idea, and then he'd learned.

In this world, there are people who don't mind being tools. *I'd sure rather not be one.*

The guy possesses a blind belief in the church's supposed ideals, and he carries out his missions dispassionately. He'd kill infants and slaughter demons to make the church richer, firmly believing that was the essence of justice.

He's a fool, and Walt is hopelessly jealous. Jealous of the weakness that let him respond with "What need is there to run?"

Jealous that he's strong enough to accept the fact they can't escape.

Kyle won't run.

That's what makes him Walt's natural enemy. He's sure they'll never see eye to eye. He's not even interested in finding out why Kyle didn't report him for even suggesting running away.

"I know what the church wants. I don't need you to spell it out for me."

"All right, then. We're up against the demon king. Keep your wits about you."

"Yeah, more importantly, don't go holding me back. Also, quit talking already. What if somebody hears you? This is the kind of place where crow demons come flying in to tell you you've been summoned by the demon king."

"I wouldn't make a blunder like that."

"Oh, I see. Well then, let's do our best without getting in each other's way," Walt jokes.

Narrowing his eyes, Kyle murmurs, "Even so, officially, we will be the demon king's guards. We won't be able to get by without cooperating."

"Terrible. No thanks."

"I don't want to, either! This is a mission, though. How much experience do you have with running security?"

"More than you. They were all people I would've loved to kill. If they're telling me to kill the person I'm supposed to guard, that's perfect."

Walt starts walking again, ending the conversation.

A mission where we charge the demon king like suicide bombers? So we're human bombs now, huh? Hilarious. Survive. If it comes down to it, take Aileen Lauren d'Autriche hostage. Then, someday, make a run for it.

...But run where?

"Walt Lizanis, reporting as summoned."

"Kyle Elford, also reporting in."

"I'm glad you're here."

In the dappled shadows under the trees, the demon king slowly turns around.

Black hair, red eyes. Unmistakable features of the demon king. Born with the appearance and fate that the legends foretold, he had once surrendered his claim to the throne. However, upon his engagement to Aileen Lauren d'Autriche, a duke's daughter, he had gained the support of her family, and his position as crown prince had been restored. That is what the general public knows.

However, what the world knows can often differ a great deal from reality. Someone who seems upright may actually be a lecher with a fondness for young boys. That sort of thing is all too common.

Granted, the demon king seems head over heels for sweet Ailey, so this isn't just a marriage of convenience.

Still, he may be kind to the woman he loves, but cruel to others. That's common as well.

Walt knows Ailey is naive, so he could probably take advantage of that; however, if he's careless, he'll doom himself. After all, he's dealing with the demon king.

Looking tense, Kyle speaks to the man. "What did you need, Your Highness?"

"As I think Sugar's told you already, starting today, the two of you are going to be my guards. However, I'm sure you have your own situations to consider. Do you have any objections? I would like to be the sort of king who listens to others."

He's asking for their opinions. Walt and Kyle exchange looks. They have nothing but objections. That being said, they've seen plenty of people get beheaded because they took powerful people at their word and spoke their minds.

As far as church missions go, guard duty is extremely convenient. They'll be able to carry blades, and they'll be allowed to act a little reckless. For that reason, when selecting guards, trust is the most important factor. Assuming someone wants to avoid getting stabbed in the back, it's only natural.

Apparently the demon king doesn't know this.

We're from the church, remember? But he did say he was short on people. Maybe he didn't have a choice.

Poor demon king, he thinks ironically.

Whenever he trusts humans, it always ends in betrayal. The two of them are no exception. Even though arguably, they're more monster than human.

Feeling charmed and rather sorry for him at the same time, Walt nods. "Frankly, I'm not entirely satisfied with the way this happened. Still, I have my orders, and I'll follow them."

"We will perform our duty to the best of our abilities."

"I see. I'm very glad to hear that."

The man's face is expressionless, and he doesn't look the least bit happy. Abruptly, though, a bright spot of color catches Walt's eye. He blinks. *Were there always flowers there?*

"All right, then. Let's get right to it. Come with me. I'd like to go out for a bit."

"Yes, Your Highness. Will this be an inspection of the town?"

"No, we're heading to the imperial capital."

"Huh?"

"Master Claude, there you are!! Freeze, milord! Don't you move!"

The abrupt angry yell makes Claude *tsk* in irritation. "Keith certainly does work fast. Well, let's go."

"B-but that's your adviser..."

"You have a mountain of work waiting for you! What do you mean, you're going out for a bit— Wait, no! You fool of a master!"

Walt hears the sound of snapping fingers.

Instantly, the adviser's cursing recedes, and then both Walt and Kyle fall flat on their rears.

Instead of the lush, peaceful garden, they're in a stone-paved alley. A short distance away, a street teems with people, and they can hear carriage wheels and the clopping of hoofbeats.

"You're supposed to guard me. Even if I forcibly transport you, stay on your feet."

Walt's never been cautioned about anything like that before, so although it makes him sound dim-witted, he asks a question of his own. "...Huh? 'Forcibly transport'? Do you mean teleport?"

"Then— It can't be. Is this the capital?!"

"That's right. I'd like to visit something called a 'café.' It will be a practice run, so that I can invite Aileen next time. I have high expectations for you," the demon king says gravely. He seems to have the wrong idea about what guards are for.

"Kyle, I take it back. We should cooperate."

When they meet in front of the demon king's office bright and early in the morning, those are the first words out of his mouth. Kyle doesn't criticize him for it.

On the contrary, he lowers his gaze, looking haggard. "I'm glad you think so as well. I knew it wouldn't be easy with the demon king, but…"

"Let's work together. I mean, this is never going to work if we don't. We won't function as guards."

"Not to mention we're the ones that adviser yells at."

"Frankly, at this point, it's a matter of pride. This is unacceptable for Nameless Priests."

Exchanging emphatic nods, they turn to face the double doors. Taking a deep breath, they push them open in perfect sync.

"Master Claude, good morning!"

"Please be here today— Yeah, he's not here. I had a feeling he wouldn't be! Kyle, did he leave a note?!"

"Found it! 'I'll be back by the time Aileen arrives.'"

"His life is way too Ailey-centric!"

He hurls the note to the floor.

"Ailey said she was going to take a look around Misha Academy today, didn't she? They're planning to meet up at the soiree this evening! As if they'll let him get away with having no guards until then—he's the crown prince! We're the ones people will think are incompetent!"

"Almond! Sugar! Is anybody there?!"

When Kyle opens the window and calls for them, one of the crow demons who tend to hang around the demon king flies over.

This demon is pure white, a particular rarity among crows. They've been told it met with awful treatment from humans in the past. As a result, it's always hard on them. It gives them a cold glare. **"What, humans?"**

"Sugar, do you know where Master Claude is?"

"You lost him? Worthless. Useless louts. This is the trouble with humans. You should be ashamed of yourselves."

"We are. Deeply. Would you tell us what you know?"

"Here's a reward."

When Walt shows it the candy he's begun carrying around with him, the white crow's eyes widen ferociously. **"I won't be bribed with mere candy!"**

"I—I know, I know! I'll go buy sugar cookies!"

"As long as you understand." With an exaggerated nod, the white crow perches on the windowsill, then speaks as if it's conveying a divine revelation. **"The demon king departed on horseback, bound for the lake."**

"The lake? That's what had him restless the day before yesterday!"

"You have our gratitude, Sugar."

"Sing my praises! Present me with offerings!"

"Sure thing, but later!"

"This is what's wrong with humans," the crow demon fumes, but Walt and Kyle take off running, leaving it behind. In the corridor, they pass James; he's carrying a textbook. His current job is to make sure Auguste passes the Holy Knights' entrance exam.

"What, he got away from you again?"

"Don't say 'again.' If you see the demon king, grab him for us!"

"I can't."

"C'mon, don't be like that!"

"More importantly, if you turn that corner, Sir Keith will catch you."

Hearing the name of the demon king's carping adviser makes them instantly choose a more roundabout route. Something about him is scary even though he is human, like them, and probably not very skilled in combat. More than anything, he's a valuable supervisor who's able to read the demon king the riot act.

"It's kind of late to ask, but you can ride a horse, right?"

"Of course."

Nameless Priests must be able to blend in with both commoners and aristocrats in order to carry out their missions, and so they've been given a wide-ranging education. The only thing they're incapable of is disobeying orders.

That means they're in their element on horseback. When they reach the stable, they choose horses, leap into the saddles, and kick their mounts' sides.

Good grief, he's impossible to guard.

First the demon king had forced them to go to a café with him. The day after that, for some reason, he'd wanted to go buy a snack. Apparently Auguste had recommended the pie in Mirchetta, and it had made him want to try some. They'd told him in a rather exasperated way that he couldn't, and he'd run off. When they'd found him in the park at the end of a frantic search, he'd said, "That took you a while."

The adviser who's served the demon king for more than twenty years had explained, "That's just how Master Claude is.

There's no point in telling him anything. Since that's the case, you're the ones I'll yell at. You've been inadequate guards, and I'm docking your wages!"

It's not fair.

The demon king may have vanished, but if they just leave him to it, both the church and the demon king's people will suspect they're not trying. If that gets them fired, they will have failed in their mission and the church will send assassins after them.

It really isn't fair.

"Oh... Huh. You caught up to me."

The cause of all this unfairness is standing on the bank of a small lake surrounded by trees and greenery.

After tying his horse to a tree, Walt draws himself up to his full height. "Yes, we've caught up to you. What are you doing here?"

"I've discovered I enjoy having you chase me, so..."

For a moment, the idea of assassinating him here and now is genuinely tempting. Kyle has to be thinking the same thing. Veins are standing out on his temples.

"At any rate, let's go back. We'll have Sir Keith lecture you."

"My business here isn't finished yet. You two can go back first. Actually, I insist."

"We can't do tha—"

Abruptly, Walt feels a familiar sensation on the back of his neck. He turns, scanning their surroundings... *Isn't it a bit too quiet?*

Kyle must have felt it, as well. He's searching for something, his eyes sharp.

The lake is surrounded by trees. It's peaceful. However, what's making his skin prickle is—murderous intent. From several directions, at that.

"...Master Claude. What business brought you here?"

Both Walt and Kyle's expressions have changed, but Claude's is as blank as ever. "Let's see... A nice picnic."

As if to shred that answer, an arrow flies at them. Walt's hand snaps out to grab it, but the arrow breaks on an invisible wall right in front of him and falls to the ground.

"That's why I told you to go back first."

The demon king sounds as if he's humoring troublesome children. He steps in front of them, and just then, a rain of arrows falls.

None of them reach him, though. The thin membrane of light that covers Claude, Walt, and Kyle repels every arrow. Even their horses are shielded, and they keep tranquilly munching on grass.

"Wha—? Look, I think you're under attack here, don't you?! Any idea who this is?!"

"Mm, I doubt it really matters."

""Huuuuuuhn?!""

Both he and Kyle utter incredulously. As they do, a masked assassin lunges out of the brush at them.

The demon king snaps his fingers. A hole immediately opens in the ground, and the assassin plunges into it with a roar.

"......"

"For now, I'll send you two back to the castle. I'll deal with this, so don't mention it to anyone."

Those words clue them in.

Now they know why he came here, on horseback, by himself.

He did it to draw these people out. He'd come to this nice, open space to give them the perfect opportunity to kill him.

Kyle seems to have come to the same conclusion. He looks dazed.

When he sees their faces, the demon king's red eyes sparkle. "I'll be back by evening. Be good."

"—Don't screw with us! Hey, Kyle!"

"Please stay with your horse, Your Highness!"

By the time Claude echoes "'Horse'?" they've already leaped into action.

Arrows are still flying at them, so they've got a good idea of which direction to go. Deciding he can leave the left half to Kyle, Walt dives into the brush on the right.

He spots an archer lurking in a tree and knocks him out of it. A fighter armed with a dagger attacks him, but he sends him to the ground with a roundhouse kick. The scary thing is the way they keep appearing, one after another. Did they bring an army or something?

Still, none of them are experts. He deals with them methodically, knocking them out; there's no need to kill them. They seem to be a hired crew somebody cobbled together. As Kyle and Walt systematically clean up, the focus of the attacks shifts to them, but it's not a big deal.

Then a white crow flutters down from over their heads, and the situation shifts. **"What are you people doing?"**

A talking crow. That probably seemed like enough of a reason to attack it. An arrow flies in from nowhere in particular; *tsk*ing, Walt pulls Sugar to him, catching the missile with his free hand. In the same moment, Kyle kicks the archer out of a tree.

"Are you all right?"

"Yeah. Was that the last of them?"

"It looks like it."

"**...You're hurt**," Sugar murmurs. Walt has let go of the arrow, and the crow is staring at his palm. There's a tiny split there, but it heals completely in moments.

"It's fine; this is nothing... Sugar?"

"......"

The demon's usual bluster has vanished, and Sugar is trembling. *Oh*, Walt realizes. This demon had been badly abused by humans. That must be what this is about.

Kyle has joined them. After giving it a little thought, he starts to pet Sugar's head roughly, rumpling its feathers.

"**What are you doing, human?! Know your place!**"

"Hey, you're back to your old self. So what brings you here?"

"**Well, erm... You people are unreliable!**" For a moment, the crow's eyes wander uneasily. Then Sugar stands proudly.

Walt nods. "Did you maybe follow us because you were worried about us?"

"**Worried?! Get over yourselves!**"

"Don't tease, Walt. As long as everyone's safe, that's—"

Spotting a figure in the bushes, Kyle launches himself at it. One straggler is trying to escape.

Still holding Sugar, Walt twists the deserter's arm up, then threatens him quietly. "Why don't you state who you're with before we kill you?"

"Th-they just hired me with gold! I dunno anything!"

"Fine," Kyle says flatly, setting the tip of his dagger against the man's carotid artery.

The man yelps with fear, then starts talking rapidly. "Th-the church!"

"What? That can't possibly be—"

"Kyle, calm down. Listen, fella, what exactly is that about?"

"H-how should I know? The church told us they'd taken steps; they said we just had to attack this place as a group and cause trouble! We didn't think he'd have guards with him!"

Meaning— In other words...

Was the church giving us a hand? Or...

Was it a warning? Had they been testing them?

"Spare me, I'm begging you! Lemme go!"

"—Enough. Get lost."

If the man is the church's pawn, he'll probably be disposed of even if they let him escape. Feeling bitter, Walt gives the man's back a push.

Although the man's face had filled with joy for a moment, it suddenly freezes up. "Th-the demon king...!"

"The church again?"

"Demon King! That was terrifying!"

Sugar flies over and clings to him. The demon king pats the crow's head. Turning pale at the sight of Claude, the man tries to run, but his feet rise off the ground. Then he flies through the air in a beautiful arc before landing in the lake.

Following Kyle's instructions to the letter, the demon king has brought over all three horses. "We need to collect all these people, or they'll be killed," he mutters absently.

"Huh?"

In the time it takes to blink, the bodies of the attackers they'd knocked to the ground bob lightly into the air. The demon king takes a look around, red eyes shining.

When he snaps his fingers—a sound they've already grown used to—all the attackers vanish.

Sugar is trembling with emotion. **"All the villains disappeared! Demon King, that's just like you!"**

"Wh-where did you send them?" Kyle sounds rattled.

The demon king responds casually, "For the moment, the foot of a volcano that's crawling with demons. The church shouldn't be able to get at them there."

"Um, no, but they won't be able to get home either, will they?!"

"It's fine. If it comes down to it, they'll be able to live off the land."

Was that the problem? Walt wonders. *Still, if it's a choice between that and getting killed by the church, they've got a better chance of surviving this way.*

...Although it does seem like that's a strange thing for him to be concerned about.

No, forget that, focus on the demon king! If he knows the church was behind that, he'll naturally suspect us, and—

"Sugar. You go back home ahead of us. Everything you've seen and heard here is a confidential matter between you, me, Walt, and Kyle."

"A confidential matter...!"

"You can keep it that way, can't you?"

Sugar responds with a crisp salute. **"Understood! Leave it to me."**

"Very good."

He snaps his fingers, and Sugar disappears.

The demon king turns back to them. Kyle's face is set, while Walt is waiting to see how this plays out. "You two did well. Thanks to you, both the horses and I are fine."

When he tells them that, straight to their faces, all the tension drains out of him. Next to him, Kyle looks a little deflated.

"You're strong, and you were a big help."

"Thanks... We're not as strong as you are, though. I have the feeling we actually got in the way."

"No, not at all. Guards are nice to have."

"Pardon me for asking, but what did you think guards were for before now?"

Kyle's question is dead serious, and Claude thinks about it just as seriously. "...Curiosities?"

"Are you kidding?! You're a crown prince, remember?! For the love of—!" Forgetting himself, Walt fires back with a genuine retort. He rakes his bangs up in frustration, then crosses his arms. "All right, Master Claude. You mean the first thing we're going to have to do is teach you what it means to have us guard you, right?"

"Have I done something wrong?"

"...Frankly, yes. Many, many things." The fact that Kyle's added this quiet comment means he's probably at wits' end.

Standing up straighter, he begins to advise him. "To begin with, in the event of an attack like this one, check us before you do anything. For guards, being protected by their lord or allowing him to serve as a decoy for them is a failure. To put it bluntly, it's an embarrassment. Make sure you remember that.

"Oh, and also, you really need to end these things at the source. Don't just toss them into a hole and leave them there. Sometimes things just can't be done, but deal with them as best you can.

"In addition, you mustn't give us the slip and sneak out. We're the ones Sir Keith yells at when you do."

"All very true. I'll be as flexible as possible, though. I know you want to have fun."

"Walt! Why, you—"

"Hey, even the demon king has to feel stifled sometimes. The best guards are a little considerate."

"But what if something happens?!"

"We'll cross that bridge when we get there. You're too inflexible."

"You're not serious enough!"

"You two certainly get along well."

""What exactly are you seeing here?!"" they retort at the exact same time before catching themselves.

Ever so faintly, Claude smiles. "That's fine. As I said at the beginning, I'm not a king who refuses to listen to others. — Within reason, that is."

"Huh?"

"Does that mean you don't listen?"

"That's a good question. For now, let's go home. Since I have guards, I'd like to ride back and enjoy the scenery."

He tosses the reins casually, and they scramble to catch them. Claude vaults lightly onto his horse, then looks down at Walt and Kyle. "Oh, right, I just remembered. About that business with the church earlier. Do you think you two will be able to do something about it?"

He's speaking with a much more familiar tone now; a notable sign that he feels closer to them. Walt and Kyle exchange glances.

Whether or not he's aware of their situation, the demon king smiles. "I wouldn't mind dealing with it myself, of course."

"No, we'll handle it," Kyle says hastily. He could hardly say anything else.

"I see. I'll leave it to you, then."

"Wouldn't that mean trusting us too much, though? What if we betray you?" The words are out before Walt's realized he's going to say them. He thinks he sees Kyle glare at him briefly, but the other man says nothing.

The demon king responds quietly, "If I couldn't trust or value you, what kind of king would I be?"

He gulps. The feelings that well up after that are—a little frustration, probably, and deep emotion. *I see, sweet Ailey. So this is the sort of man you like, hmm?*

He's not sure why the thought occurs to him, but it does. He swallows it down, along with something bitter.

Valuing someone. Trusting them.

Something he'd thought was completely foreign to him, something he assumed he'd never reach, is right here. He wants to make sure he doesn't forget it.

"Besides, even if you've betrayed me by accepting secret orders from the church, I won't be angry with you. I'd actually sympathize."

"Huh? Why—?"

"How exactly are you planning to win a fight against me?"

Walt and Kyle immediately go silent. Gazing at them as if he's amused, Claude tugs on his horse's reins. "We're going home. Follow me."

"—Yes, sire."

Walt's always wanted to run for it. To flee somewhere.

Maybe it's finally time to decide on a destination.

If his soul has turned that way for even a moment, then...

* * *

Dear Bishop,

How are you, Your Excellency? I am fine.
The other day, we had tea in the imperial capital with the demon king. Walt moaned that doing so as a group of only men was hell, but in order to get as much information as possible, we kept him company voluntarily. The demon king liked the strawberry tart I recommended so much that he bought some to take home.
At a certain dinner party, we kept a watchful eye on the demon king in an attempt to learn about his relationship with humans. However, perhaps he is still wary of us as well, because he said the roast beef was delicious and made us keep bringing him additional servings. Walt ended up helping him pick out a sauce to put on the meat. I thought it was really unforgivable, but in retrospect, it may have been part of a strategy to make the demon king careless. I will apply myself as well. However, I can confirm that the trusting relationship we have built is solid enough that the demon king personally shares his roast beef with us.
The demon king does not seem to suspect us. Lately, he seems to feel he can take us with him anywhere. He wanders off more than one would expect. He likes to travel incognito, and he's always strolling through the lower levels of the imperial capital undisguised. He believes no one notices him, but with a face like his, of course everyone is well aware of his identity. He stands out, so I can't recommend targeting him. If we take our eyes off him, he vanishes, and there's no telling where or when he'll turn up. As a result, Keith, one of his advisers, gets angry with us: He claims it's our fault that the demon king wanders off, because we aren't managing him properly. It's really deplorable.

The demon king is able to teleport himself and anything he sees. Several times, I have seen men charge at him with blades, only to fall into holes that weren't there a moment before and disappear. Walt and I have told him that he should let us capture them, and we are now dealing with such matters ourselves. For some reason, the demon king looks extremely happy as he watches us work. It makes us feel very awkward.

We have also learned that the demons will be our allies if we give them sweets. Walt has begun to carry candy around with him and is using it to gather intelligence. The demons consider their king's orders absolute, so even though we are Nameless Priests who have killed countless demons, they trust us... Simply because the demon king does.

Possibly as a result, our former target James hasn't expressed any resentment. On the contrary, as he watches the demon king run us ragged, he seems to pity us...

The demon king flies through the sky, is served by demons, and wields tremendous magic. However, I am convinced that he is merely human. In that case, might it not be possible to reach a compromise with him? After investigating the demon king and his surroundings for half a month, I am writing this letter because I wish to recommend a diplomatic approach.

There have been several attacks. Were they the work of the church? If so, you must have been informed of the results. It would be very unwise to make an enemy of the demon king.

As I said earlier, the demon king has begun to trust us. No doubt this letter won't even pass through a censor. If you wish it, Your Excellency, I would gladly mediate a reconciliation.

Please do take my proposal under consideration.

Yours sincerely, Kyle

★ ★ ★

"Oh, Walt. Have I caught you on your break?"

He's just folded the letter he's been peeking at when someone calls out to him, and he can't pull on his usual joking smile fast enough. He hastily slurps his soup, buying time to pull himself together. "Right. I'm on lunch. Kyle's guarding Master Claude."

"And how is it? Guarding Master Claude, I mean."

"It's fine, just fine."

When he raises his cup of black tea to her, Aileen laughs a little, her golden locks swaying. She's probably well aware they're having a hard time.

...*She doesn't seem to know the demon king was attacked, though.*

If she knew, he's pretty sure she'd get angry and shout at the demon king. Claude must be hiding it. The fact that he knows this and can guess these things makes him feel oddly superior.

He hides his smile by pretending to take a sip of tea.

"My, did you just laugh?"

"No, no. And? What did you need?"

"You were brooding and looked unusually serious, so…"

"Sure you weren't imagining that?"

"Is something troubling you? The church, for example."

Due to his job, he's pretty good at keeping a straight face no matter what happens, but this time, he stares back at Aileen.

He's thought there was something different about this woman for quite a while. Now he's positive it isn't because she was pretending to be a boy when they first met or because she's the demon king's fiancée.

She knows something. Something even Walt doesn't know about.

Aileen seats herself across from him. Narrowing her eyes, she peers into his face. "As I'm sure you know, the church is bound to discard the two of you after it's finished with you."

"...Come on, Ailey, the church sold us to you. That's nothing to do with us now."

"I won't order you to align yourselves with us. One can't count on loyalty when it's forced. Still, with Master Claude's support, you'll be able to buy time." Softly, Aileen covers his hand—which is still holding his fork—with her own. "By which I mean, please don't do anything desperate. Ensure that both of you will remain safe."

Feeling her warmth soak into his cold hand, Walt manages a smile, although it doesn't go past his lips. "You talk as if you're worried about us."

"I am. If anything were to happen to you, it would grieve Master Claude."

Somehow, he's able to imagine that, and he can't just laugh it off.

She continues, "If there's a favor you'd like to ask me, then ask it. If you're going to act spoiled and expect me to guess, I won't be able to help."

She has a point.

Realizing he's stopped breathing, he draws a deep breath. "Helping someone who doesn't want help is meddling, though."

"If you're prepared to endure any ire as a result, then it's fine," Aileen says firmly. "I'll help you because I want to do so. You should also do as you please."

When he hears that, for the first time, the realization hits him. *Oh. Is that what I want, to help him?*

The other guy doesn't even want to run, but he wants to help him get away.

That idiot. He hasn't even realized his own quiet wish, and he's confronted them with it directly. Even though there's no way that would work on that crowd.

"...I see. That's just like you, Ailey."

"And? What is it you'd like me to do?" Aileen cocks her head, waiting. She looks as if she's enjoying herself.

Walt rakes his fingers through his hair and gives her a wink. "Sadly, nothing."

"After a conversation like that? Stubborn, aren't you? Asking for help is a kind of strength, you know."

"Are we done here? There's something I'd like to talk to Master Claude about."

Aileen looks miffed.

It's gratifying, and he laughs in spite of himself.

"...You intend to rely on Master Claude? That seems as if it might be against the rules."

"Nice. I love not playing fair."

"If you do rely on him, treat him with care." Aileen rises to her feet and folds her arms, looking down at him. "Common sense only works on him occasionally."

"Yes, we're on the same page there," he says with a heartfelt nod. Aileen gives him a cheerful smile, then bids him goodbye and turns on her heel.

That's a good woman.

She looks happy because the demon king has more people who understand him. That really isn't fair. She's gone and made him think she's cute.

Not that he has the courage to pick a fight with the demon king, of course.

He clears away his lunch tray, then heads for the office to take over for Kyle. On the way, he sees humans running around, busy with the work of rebuilding. Now that he's paying attention, he gets the feeling there are a lot fewer nobles around.

Come to think of it, the demon king pushed some reforms through, didn't he? James will pick up where he leaves off one day…

Walt doesn't think the demon king will manage to become emperor this easily. Humans tend to make poor choices. It won't matter how good his policies are. Humans will believe lies are true, and they'll never doubt they're in the right. They can overthrow their lords in the name of justice and kill for the sake of peace.

On top of that, this is the demon king. Throwing their lot in with him will be like going to sea in a sieve.

"Kyle, you're off."

"Right."

But as long as he feels he'll have no regrets when they sink, then… "Master Claude. Do you have a minute? There's something I need to tell you."

After he's sure Kyle's left the room, Walt goes to stand in front of the desk.

Claude's scribbling his signature on documents with a quill pen. "It can't wait?"

"The two of us are betraying you."

Claude snaps his fingers, and the documents vanish. The quill drifts off, settling into an inkstand by itself.

Slowly narrowing his red eyes, the demon king smiles.

"Let's hear it."

He's started to think this is correct. He's had to. If he doesn't, he's sure he won't be able to stay on his feet. Not when he doesn't have the courage to suspect he might be serving the wrong masters or harboring the wish to run away.

"The church has proposed a confidential talk...with you? The demon king?"

"Right. I'm sorry to spring this on you so suddenly, but it's tonight. Since the church is headquartered in Mirchetta, they're eager to do this while I'm here, so there's really no way around it. They've specifically asked me to bring the two of you as my guards. Will you come?"

"Of course. It's our job." Walt shrugs.

Kyle shoots him a glare for his lack of manners and nods. "If those are your orders."

"That's settled, then. I've already told Keith, but be sure not to let anyone else know. That includes Aileen, of course. It is a confidential talk, after all."

The demon king seems to be enjoying himself a little. Kyle has been guarding him for more than two weeks now, and in that time, he's become all too aware that the demon king is unexpectedly naive and tends to be rather careless. He frowns slightly. *I hope he hasn't let the unusual term "confidential talk" go to his head. He does understand how important this is, right?*

Walt seems to be worried about the same thing. He sighs. "Please don't let your guard down, Master Claude. You're dealing with the church. They haven't even told you what they want, have they?"

"Walt! We shouldn't go into the conference with a suspicious attitude," Kyle scolds. "They may want to make peace."

"What? You know something about this?"

"O-of course not!"

The other man gives him a dubious look, and he avoids his eyes awkwardly. There's no way he could tell him.

This talk is the result of a letter Kyle sent to the bishop—his foster father, to whom he's indebted—in secret. After reading the letter, the bishop began to consider rebuilding the church's relationship with the demon king. Kyle has received a confidential letter from the bishop that said *You're entirely correct. We would like to speak with the demon king, and we request your cooperation.*

However, the church isn't a monolith, and the bishop is merely the leader of one faction. Since this isn't the will of the entire church, their talk must remain a secret. No one could blame the demon king for being suspicious. Kyle and Walt have standing orders to assassinate him, and there's no sign of those orders being rescinded anytime soon.

Still, this isn't a bad deal for the demon king, either.

Everyone knows that the Holy Knights, who are under the direct command of the emperor, are officially in charge of subjugating demons. There's no way for them to cover the provincial areas, though, so all routine demon-slaying is handled by the church. If Claude reaches a compromise with the church, he'll be able to work out an arrangement regarding that end of things.

When Claude Jean Ellmeyer was born as the demon king, the demons calmed down, but they haven't stopped causing damage entirely. In the first place, many demons appear to be ordinary wild animals. Some demons haven't abandoned their hostility toward humans, while others have been driven into a fury by human poachers and attacked villages. Cooperating with the church will make it much easier to resolve those problems.

If the demon king really wants demons and humans to coexist, these negotiations are important, and yet he can't sense any nerves or enthusiasm from the man. Kyle is the one who's nervous.

If these negotiations fall through, we'll—
He steals a glance at Walt.

He's sure Walt wants to stay here. The only way for him to do that without becoming a traitor is for the church and the demon king to reconcile. When Walt acts pessimistic about the negotiations, since Kyle is the one who set them up, it makes him feel almost panicky.

"Your concern is completely natural, Walt, but the letter does technically say what they want."

"Oh yes? What is it?"

"It's a secret."

"It is, huh? Well, sure, it's probably nothing to do with your guards..."

"However, if they propose a reconciliation, I intend to accept."

Kyle's eyes return to Claude. The demon king is resting his chin on his hand, smiling faintly.

Walt looks disgusted. "It's sort of impressive that you can expect something like that after fielding all those assassins the other day."

"Walt! Would you stop talking as if—"

"Should I assume you think this confidential talk is a trap, Walt?" Claude asks.

Walt narrows his eyes, then sighs. "That's the normal thing to think. You handled those assassins as if you were really used to it. You must do it all the time. In other words, the church has been making constant attempts on your life for ages."

"And if they have?"

"Then there's no way they'd compromise now. You don't have

to walk into their trap for them. I know you're strong, but carelessness can really cost you."

"It's fine. You two will protect me. Am I wrong?"

He's said it with a straight face, and even Kyle freezes up. An odd sort of embarrassment wells up inside him. *This man really does…*

He genuinely trusts them.

Walt gazes off in a random direction, and when he does respond, he sounds sulky. "…Yeah, sure. That makes extra work for us, though."

"Put up with it, please."

"So you've got no plans to be cautious in the first place, is that it?"

"Walt… I know what you're trying to say, but you're being rude," Kyle says.

"Although I'm sure the situation's complicated, the church is basically your family. I'd like to get along with them," the demon king says mildly.

That reason makes Kyle's heart constrict.

He's never once thought of the church that way— Oh, but he might have wished they were his family. That's probably true even of Walt, who wants to run away.

If the church had been gentle and kind, a place they could love, they could have been so happy. If only it hadn't been something they'd had to resign themselves to, believing it was their only option… They really do think that way.

"If you say so, Master Claude, then I've got no objections. Although I do think you're being naive."

"I do mean within the range I can tolerate, of course."

Claude says that frequently, but he can tolerate an awful lot. At the very least, Kyle has never seen him get angry in earnest.

Well, no, when he found out Ailey's identity, he did get...angry, but...

He's not sure he really understands that range of tolerance.

In any case, the demon king is going to accept the church's invitation, and that's a relief.

Now as long as the negotiations with the bishop go well, we'll be set.

They won't have to try to assassinate this man anymore. Walt may even be able to stay here.

...Although Kyle still isn't sure what he wants to do.

"By the way, what should I take as a hospitality gift?"

"Huh? A hospitality...gift?"

Does he mean a bribe of some sort? He hadn't taken the demon king for the sort of person who'd try to butter them up, so he asks without thinking.

Tossing the paper with the date and time of the confidential talk onto his desk, the demon king smiles. "As I said, the church is basically your parents. I'll need to greet them properly. It's my duty as your master."

Walt and Kyle sigh in unison.

As usual, the demon king isn't quite in step with the rest of the world.

"Is he going to be all right like that...?"

"Oh my, is something worrying you?"

Apparently he's spoken aloud by accident, and Aileen responds from the other side of the standing screen.

The demon king's confidential talk with the church is only a few hours away. However, he has orders not to tell Aileen about it.

Pulling on an outfit that's just been tailored for him, Kyle emerges from behind the screen. "No, it's nothing. —The size is fine. It's a perfect fit."

"It certainly seems to be. It suits you nicely. I knew it would." Aileen smirks.

Feeling uncomfortable, Kyle looks down at his new uniform. Aileen had them custom-made for Claude's guards. Since guards need to attend soirees and society events, Denis has designed the uniforms to be symmetrical when he and Walt stand next to each other.

Since they are the crown prince's bodyguards, the cut of the clothes is similar to knights' uniforms. There's even a short cape. The fabric is of the finest quality. These are clothes that are meant to be seen, and Kyle is perplexed. "This isn't the sort of thing guards should wear, though. They stand out."

"They're meant to. Hee-hee! If I put Master Claude in the center, then placed James and Auguste there with you, I'd practically have the perfect lineup…! I'd expect no less from *otome* game love interests: This season's soirees are as good as mine."

"…What are you talking about? At any rate, guards shouldn't stand out."

"Gracious, if you two fade into the background, Master Claude will simply stand out all by himself. I want you two to make him fade just as much as you can. If I put him out there on his own, things will get completely out of hand."

"I…I suppose…so?"

In a weird way, her argument is persuasive, and it unnerves him. Aileen closes in, managing to intimidate him even though she's shorter than he is. "We don't do things the way the church does. You are Master Claude's guards. That means you aren't allowed to do anything disgraceful. Your every gesture will affect his reputation. Is that clear?"

"...I...believe so."

"Good. No doubt you will join Master Claude in public more and more frequently. Make sure you behave yourself. Particularly when it comes to your relationships with women."

"Relationships with women?! Me?!" Kyle is shocked.

Aileen nods soberly. "I'd imagine Walt has plenty of experience, but I'm concerned about you. You seem as if you'd fall quite easily."

"Wh-wh-wha...? D-don't be rude! I'm older than you are."

"All I did was dress up a little, and it made you stand there like a slack-jawed scarecrow."

"You took me by surprise!" he retorts, flushing bright red.

With a short laugh, Aileen sweeps her hair back. "Every young lady in the capital can manage that level of coquetry."

"Are you claiming it's normal for the young ladies of the capital to pass themselves off as men?!"

There's just no way that's true. Kyle's remark seems to have hit home. Clearing her throat, Aileen tries to gloss over the matter. "That aside, while it's true that I am beautiful, I am not unrivaled in that department. Take care not to be deceived by looks—"

"That's not true. You were lovely."

Aileen blinks at him.

Feeling awkward after the fact, Kyle averts his gaze. "I'm not very familiar with the capital's young noblewomen, but you are, erm... I think you're beautiful. Like a jewel."

Aileen crosses her arms, gazing at him steadily. Then she

laughs a little. "I take it back. Kyle, you're really a bad man, aren't you? You've just shown me how you deceive women."

"Don't be rude. I wouldn't be as careless as Walt."

"Gracious, I was complimenting you. That was a wonderful romantic advance. Thank you."

She's called him a bad man, but if he's flustered her at all she doesn't show it. Even though the demon king simply whispering that she was adorable had shaken her so badly she'd almost fled.

"That will be your basic uniform, and I'll have a few others made up for you."

"You're making more? Isn't that wasteful?"

"Not at all. I'm repeating myself, but you are Master Claude's guards. Important companions."

"…'Important companions.'" He isn't used to hearing those words, and he repeats them in spite of himself.

"That's right," Aileen laughs. "Our bond was forged by those duck costumes."

"…I would like to pretend that incident never happened."

"You can't change the past. Accept it like a man and focus on the future," Aileen says firmly. It's as if she's noticed Kyle's hesitation.

If today's talk changes the relationship between the demon king and the church, his position will change, too.

Kyle doesn't know if the church will tell the demon king about their secret assassination orders. However, if they rescind those orders, it's very likely that Kyle will return to the church. In any case, once Claude knows the truth, he may not want them near him anymore.

A needle of pain runs through his heart, startling him.

What was that? he wonders, but decides not to give it too much thought. The job at hand is more important.

"Kyle, it's time. Master Claude is waiting," Walt calls out to him.

"...Right."

"My, my, you're going out with Master Claude? You've grown quite close, haven't you." Aileen looks curious.

Walt, who's come to retrieve Kyle, smiles and covers for them. The demon king's orders prevent them from telling Aileen about the talk. However, deep in Kyle's heart, there are other reasons he doesn't tell her: his modest pride as a guard, and a sense of superiority.

"Yes, it's one of his usual impulsive outings. He's started to warn us in advance, at least; that's progress."

"Master Claude is leaning on you far too much. Sir Keith was grumbling about it. He said he's started telling him, 'I'll be taking Walt and Kyle with me, so it's fine.'"

"We're the demon king's guards, not his minders," Kyle grouses in spite of himself. Walt shrugs, agreeing with him.

Gazing at the two of them as they stand side by side, Aileen smiles. "Hee-hee. You two look even more splendid together."

They exchange glances, and then Walt tries to turn the remark into a joke. "Then what about a date one of these days, my sweet Ailey?"

"If there's any chance we'll manage to outwit Master Claude, then yes, I'll go with you."

"I suspect he'd erase us first."

"Master Claude would do nothing of the sort."

I'm not so sure, he thinks, but swallows the question. Walt's probably done the same thing.

The demon king is too capable. If something bars his way, he might physically remove it from existence.

"To begin with, Master Claude is the one who'd grieve the most if you were gone. It would give me no end of trouble as well." She laughs. Has she caught on?

...*You, who led us astray with words like that, are a bad woman.*

If this talk doesn't go well, and they're ordered to kill the demon king after all, what will he do?

Will he be able to shake off Aileen's smile and turn his blade on the demon king, after the man has said he values them?

—Even though that isn't the sort of thing he should be thinking when they're already inside the mansion where the talk will be held.

"Do you think they'll like the sugar cookies I brought them?"

"Master Claude... Wouldn't you usually bring, you know, a painting or jewels? Something expensive?"

"That would be too normal."

"Oh, so we've come full circle and cookies are extraordinary now? Hmm, that idea hadn't occurred to me..."

"Sugar recommended them. I'll allow no objections."

While Claude exhibits tyranny fit for a demon king, they're shown into the mansion's parlor. There's a long table that looks as if it could seat ten, with a fire burning bright red in the fireplace beyond it. The room their young guide has shown them into is empty but well-maintained.

"Wait here, please."

"All right."

The boy leaves, and then Claude, Walt, and Kyle are the only ones in the large parlor.

Even though he's being made to wait, Claude's mood doesn't

sour. He takes a seat in the chair that's farthest from the door, rests his elbow on its arm and his chin in his hand, and closes his eyes. For a little while, the only sound is the ticking of the clock on the wall. Then, signaling the hour of their meeting, a bell begins to chime.

That's when it happens.

"——?!"

There's a strange sensation at the base of his neck, and Kyle claps a hand to his throat. He doesn't understand what's happening until he makes eye contact with Walt and sees that he's holding his throat, too.

It's proof that they are tools.

A spell they can use to destroy themselves if necessary is grafted to the throats of Nameless Priests. The demon snuff they've been given has made them accumulate an enormous amount of magic, and that magic can be detonated, turning them into powerful human bombs. Those spells have just been remotely activated.

His feet won't move; it feels as if they've been sewn to the carpet. The sound of the clock must be laced with a binding spell. With every peal of the bell, he loses more control over his fingers and arms. He's becoming a mere tool. So is Walt.

They'll be used to slaughter the demon king they lured here.

Oh… So the bishop's abandoned me…

He'd always been prepared to be disposed of at any time. That was how he'd been raised, so he'd assumed that was how he'd die. All of his comrades had gone that way. He can't flee when no one else has.

So why has he screamed, as if he doesn't know when to let go?

"Master Claude, run! Leave us and get out, now—!"

Protecting you is my job, so please, at least at the end…

A moment later, a deserted mansion on the outskirts of Mirchetta explodes in a blast that briefly banishes the dark of night.

He coughs violently, which helps him realize he's still breathing.

Leaping flames and black smoke are rising in front of him. He can hear the burning mansion gradually collapsing. On his knees in the grass, Kyle sets a hand on his chest and takes another tentative breath.

He's alive.

"...Master Claude?! Walt! Where are you?!"

"Alive, although that is completely not what I expected," Walt says and raises a hand.

He's behind him and a bit to the side, still sitting on the ground; he might not be able to get up. Kyle feels extremely drained, too.

"Why aren't we dead? I thought they were getting rid of us..."

Saying it aloud makes the reality feel heavier. They've been cut off, used against the demon king as human weapons. They'd been tricked into leading him here, oblivious to the fact that they were going to be used, then destroyed.

It wasn't supposed to be like this..., he thinks, then laughs at himself for it. He'd forgotten he was a tool. Somewhere along the way, he'd begun to hope for a future where the demons and the church could make peace with each other, one where he wouldn't have to kill the demon king.

The result was this hellish scene.

"The demon king must have saved us." Walt's laid-back remark makes his heart feel as heavy as lead. "Still, that was nasty. Nobody told me the suicide spell could be activated by somebody else."

"...Walt. You seem fine."

"Well, I feel like crap. Frankly, I'm impressed I'm not dead."

"That's not what I meant! They've gotten rid of us! What are we going to do n—?"

"We're finally free."

Free, Kyle echoes silently, not quite understanding.

Walt laughs at him, looking relieved. "That means you, too, Kyle. Serves you right."

"Wh-what are you talking about?"

"Now you can't use your 'It's for the church' excuse. That side of you always made me sick. Well, I was dragging my feet, too, I guess." As Walt speaks, his eyes are on the inferno that used to be a mansion. "Now we're no longer chained to the church. In that case, I'm serving Master Claude."

"......"

"What about you?"

"...I'm...a man of the church. I don't know any other way to live."

"Even though you screamed at the demon king to run?"

Right. That one moment.

If he were really thinking only of the church, that wasn't a thing he should have wished for. What he should have done was make sure the demon king was killed in the explosion, even if it meant clinging to him.

...But he hadn't done it.

"I thought...Ailey might cry..."

"Nah, she'd probably go berserk and try to kill us, don't you think?"

"Also, I thought at least at the very end..."

What if he could truly be a guard?

What if every single thing about those days had been real?

It was what he'd always wished for. Even if he'd never been aware of it.

Big tears spill over. Shocked, Walt pulls back. "What the— Are you kidding me?! Who in their right mind would cry now?! Knock it off! Having men sob at me is the opposite of fun."

"Where's...Master Claude...?" It's been so long since he cried he can't even remember the last time, and it's hard to breathe. "Will he forgive me? He won't think it's too late, will he?"

"...I dunno?"

"You're supposed to say it's going to be fine!"

"You're a surprisingly big pain in the butt, you know that?! Actually, forget it, where did the demon king go? I can't imagine he got caught in the explosion, but—"

"Did you call for me?"

Claude appears out of nowhere right in front of them, and they almost scream. Kyle's tears immediately dry up, while Walt narrows his eyes. "What's that in your hand? Don't tell me..."

"The cookies. My gift. I saved you two and brought you out here, but I forgot these, so I went back in for them. Look: They caught fire a little, but they're still fine."

"You went back into a burning building? Are you an idiot?! What if something had happened?!"

"Are you suggesting that something could happen to me?"

"Argh!" Walt covers his face with a hand.

Kyle says quietly, "Maybe you wouldn't be harmed, Master Claude, but that doesn't mean it's all right for anything to happen to you. Please refrain from doing anything dangerous."

Claude falls silent. Just as Kyle begins to worry he's spoken out of turn, a scatter of little flowers blooms at Claude's feet.

Thinking it's odd, he looks up. Claude is wearing a mild smile. "Guards are anxious types, I see."

"Yeah, that's our job," Walt says. He's already decided to pledge his loyalty to Claude. The guy's always several steps ahead of Kyle.

I'll just have to admit it already.

Squeezing his hands into fists, Kyle forces his tired body to kneel. Bowing his head, he gazes at the dark shadow on the ground. "Master Claude, there's something I must tell you."

"Go ahead."

"The church gave me orders to assassinate you. I was also the one who suggested that they hold these talks... Although I never dreamed that we would be the weapons they turned on you." With a self-mocking smile, he brushes his throat with his fingertips. "I was the one who put you in danger. All the responsibility is mine. Walt had nothing to do with it."

Walt calls his name, trying to shut him up, but Kyle ignores him. "And so please, let me be the only one you punish."

"The church wasn't targeting me this time. They were after you two," Claude says firmly. Kyle looks up. "I assume they didn't want me to have access to your knowledge. Besides, they're aware that you're excellent guards. They'd never simply leave you with me."

"...Even if that's true, the fact that I betrayed you wouldn't—"

"However, you recommended that the church make peace with me, and you tried to save me."

He bites his lip. As he's trying to decide how to respond, the gentle voice forgives him. "It just didn't go well this time, that's all. There's no need to torment yourself over it. In the first place, it was Aileen who forcibly took you from the church. There have been a few misunderstandings."

"You think assassination orders and blowing us up counts as 'a few misunderstandings'...? I mean, okay, whatever."

"Besides, Walt had already told me the church had ordered you to assassinate me... In strict confidence."

"Huh...?" he says weakly.

Walt's already hauled Claude up by his shirtfront. "So what are you doing blabbing secrets like that, hmm?!"

"He said he'd swear loyalty to me if I protected you from the church, Kyle. Then he told me everything."

"Look, would you quit telling *him* everything?! I said it was confidential, remember?!"

"Walt, you..." Moving unsteadily, Kyle manages to get to his feet.

Walt looks away. "I just wanted to get the jump on you, that's all."

"Hearing that made me really sad."

"?!"

The conversation has taken an unexpected turn, and both he and Walt turn to look at Claude.

Claude doesn't look sad at all, but his shoulders droop a little with what's probably dejection. "I thought, 'He won't pledge his loyalty to me because he wants to?'"

"You just made an incredibly needy request like it was nothing! Listen, Master Claude, telling somebody you'll serve them in exchange for a favor is normal, all right?"

"So you won't serve me if I don't do anything? Am I that unappealing a master?"

Loyalty that asks nothing in return is an insane demand, but when his handsome eyebrows draw together sadly, a terrific sense of guilt and anxiety wells up inside Walt. The demon king's beauty is a sin.

"Walt! Look, apologize to Master Claude!"

"No, you apologize, too! And actually, Demon King, sometimes you're really immature...! Even though you're being all dashing in front of sweet Ailey."

"That's only natural, isn't it?"

The man's expression is perfectly composed, and both Kyle and Walt groan.

He's completely messing with us, isn't he?

Once they realize that, everything else seems ridiculous.

This man is sure to accept them, guilt and agony and all.

That's the sort of master he is.

"Now then. Is that all you wanted to tell me? I'd like to be a king who listens to people."

He'd said the same thing back when he first spoke to them about being his guards. Kyle and Walt exchange looks. Then they kneel before their lord, side by side.

The blazing flames are as beautiful as the fires of hell.

"Walt Lizanis. As promised, I pledge my loyalty to you. Please use my life long and well."

"—Kyle Elford. I, too, pledge my loyalty. This time, of my own free will."

"Very well."

He hears the demon king snap his fingers, and instantly the blazing mansion is gone.

Or rather, they are; they've been whisked away to some other place.

He hears an owl hooting. The road is paved with stone, and

there's a bell tower so tall he has to look up to see all of it. That tower is very familiar.

It's the church's cathedral.

A statue of the Maid of the Sacred Sword gazes down at the demon king.

"The church's invitation said, 'We need to discuss what to do with Walt and Kyle.'"

This is news to Walt and Kyle, and their eyes widen. The demon king turns away from them; he's still holding the scorched hospitality gift. "I'll have to greet them properly. I mustn't be rude."

His red eyes flash, and lightning strikes the tip of the bell tower.

At the report that the mansion designated as the site for the confidential talk has gone up in flames, the tension in the conference room dissolves.

All the bishops in the duchy of Mirchetta have assembled in this room. Flames flicker on silver candlesticks, stretching their shadows.

"What's happened to the demon king, then?"

"We don't know about him, but it's safe to assume that Walt and Kyle are gone. It was a tremendous explosion."

"I see... Still, there's no knowing how long it may take to cultivate such talent again."

"That's precisely why we couldn't leave them with the demon king. Those two knew too much."

"My, my. How heartless of you. You raised Kyle yourself, Bishop Elford."

The sarcastic bishop next to him has come all the way out here just to see how things go. Bishop Elford's smile slowly deepens. "It was for the sake of the church. The boy understood that. It's how I raised him."

Besides, he's already been more than useful enough. The bishop gloats to himself. *Now my promotion to cardinal is all but secured.*

Not only does he have the achievement of raising a brilliant Nameless Priest to his name, but he's boosted his own status by using him as a pawn.

Cardinal Lizanis, Walt's guardian, was always a guardian in name only. He left Walt to his own devices, treating him like any other Nameless Priest, so he isn't likely to be held responsible for the current problem. Even tonight, he'd said only that it was fine to dispose of him in accordance with church regulations, and he's made no attempt to learn whether it was done.

However, in order to make Kyle his pawn, Bishop Elford had treated him as his own son. If the demon king had managed to use Kyle, he would have been blamed. The status he'd secured for himself would have crumbled on the spot. No matter what it took, he'd needed to keep that from happening.

Besides, he would only have been able to use Kyle for another two or three years anyway.

The average life span of a Nameless Priest was a scant twenty years, and even the longest-lived only made it to twenty-five. In their later years, they lost their sanity and became useless, which was the natural price of excessive exposure to demon snuff.

Taking all these things into consideration, disposing of him before he harmed the church had been the right choice.

He does feel it's a pity, of course.

He'd raised the boy carefully, and he'd been an outstanding tool. If only he hadn't caught the demon king's eye, he could have used him for several more years— He sighs. Just then, lightning streaks through the cloudless sky, and an impact shakes the room.

"Wh-what was that? Lightning?"

"Where did it fall?"

"Calm yourselves, gentlemen. It's only a thunderbolt—"

Lightning strikes above them, blowing the cathedral's arches away with a roar. The wind of the blast snuffs out all the candles.

"I hope you'll excuse me for calling so late."

In the blustering wind, a voice speaks.

Even their numbed eardrums pick up that voice. They open their misting eyes. Someone is descending through the half-destroyed ceiling, black hair and cloak streaming behind him. The figure's dirty shoes touch down right on the snow-white cloth that covers the clerics' long table.

Lightning from a cloudless night sky and glittering red eyes.

"The demon king…!"

"Why is he here of all—?"

"I was under the impression that you wanted to speak to me about my guards. While I was waiting, the mansion where we were scheduled to meet exploded, so I decided to come and see you directly."

"Kyle… Walt Lizanis…!"

Two figures have landed on the table after the demon king,

and the bishop calls their names without thinking. Why are they alive? The demon king doesn't answer this feeble question. Instead, he takes a look around the table.

"Which of you is Bishop Elford?"

A frightened squeak escapes him. The demon king seems to have heard it. He walks up to the table toward him.

Silver candlesticks topple. Dishes fall off the table and shatter. With every step the demon king takes, the priests and bishops on either side of the table start from their chairs, or their legs give out and dump them on their rears. The demon king doesn't even glance at them.

Then he's right there, looking down at the bishop.

"I apologize for not greeting you sooner. This isn't much, but do take it. It comes highly recommended."

A scorched box floats lightly from the demon king's hand. Before Bishop Elford even has time to refuse it, it falls into his petrified lap.

"By the way, speaking of Kyle and Walt: They almost exploded for some reason, so I rewrote the spells you'd placed on them. I suppose even the church accidentally miscopies spells."

"A-accidentally...?"

"Of course. Or are you saying you tried to blow up my guards without my permission?"

Lightning flashes behind the demon king. It casts his face into shadow, hiding his expression. His red eyes seem to be laughing, though.

"Let's move on to the main topic, then. Would you formally transfer Kyle and Walt to my service?"

"......"

"I know. However, I can't have them stay registered as

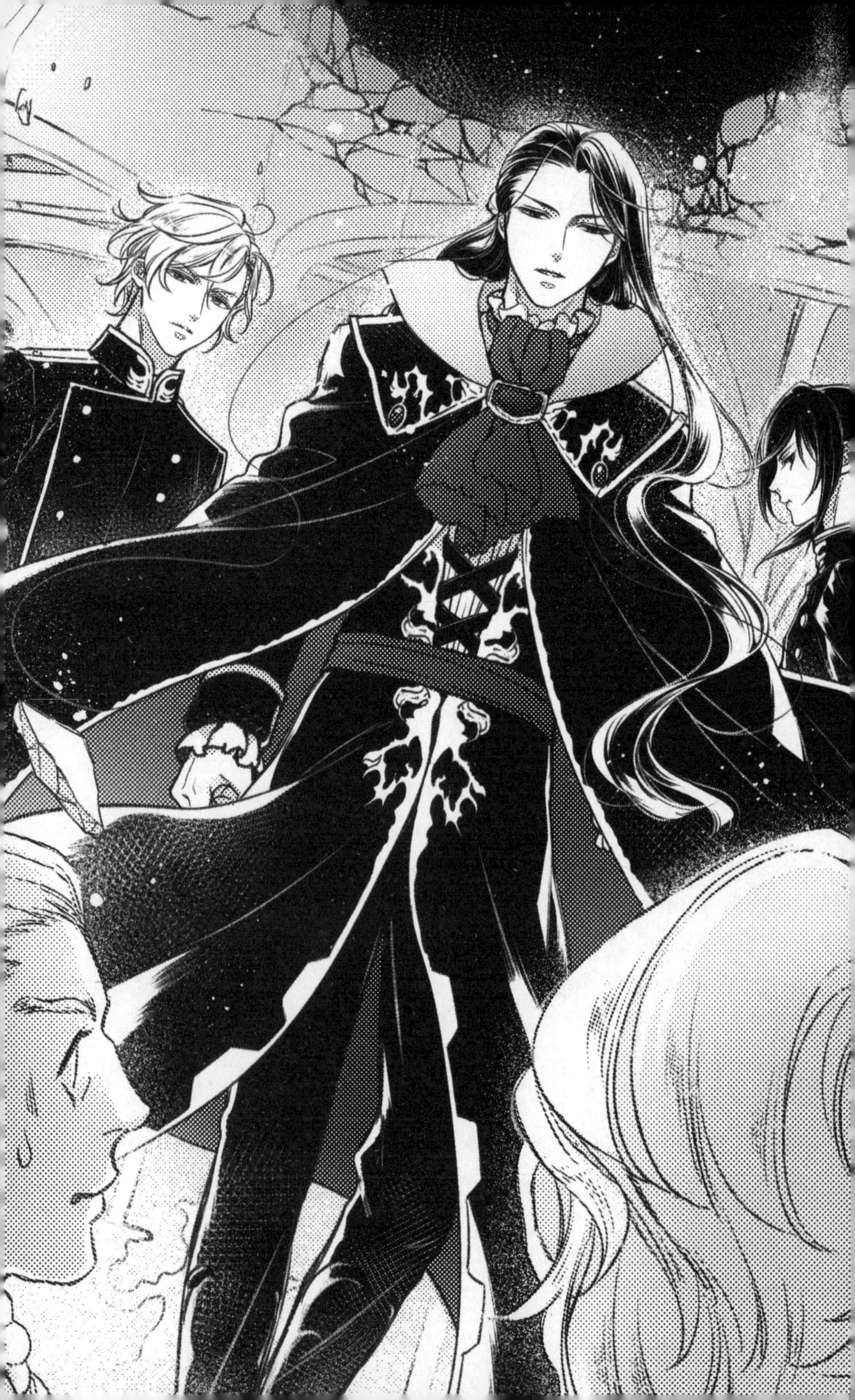

Nameless Priests. Naturally, I consider the church their family home, and I'll send them back for visits. I'd like you to let them come and go as they please."

"...Wh-wha—?"

"Thank you. I'm told you were very kind to Kyle. You don't need to hesitate: I owe you this much consideration. However, do remember that their lives and the right to give them orders belong to me."

If they allow all of this, those two will be spies. He wants to say it, but the demon king's red eyes are even more intimidating now, and the bishop's tongue tangles, leaving him speechless.

"Thank you for being understanding. Don't worry. I will treasure both Kyle and Walt."

"...Somebody has to say it, so it might as well be me: Master Claude, this isn't actually a conversation you're having..."

"I'm reading their minds. Or are you suggesting they'd refuse me? Perish the thought."

Lightning strikes again, then keeps on striking, all around the building.

The demon king mutters to himself nonchalantly. "What odd weather we're having. I do hope it clears up soon."

Screams and the noise of people falling out of their chairs echo from all over the room, but it's as if the demon king can't hear any of it. He simply waits for a response. Even if his surroundings were reduced to a blasted wasteland, he'd probably just wait for a reply, his expression unchanged.

That's when Bishop Elford makes up his mind.

"A...as you wish."

"You have a good foster father, Kyle."

When Kyle lets his gaze leave the demon king, for just a

moment, his eyes narrow. However, he promptly lowers them. "Thank you for your understanding, Your Excellency. Please don't worry. I'll serve Prince Claude with all my heart."

"K-Kyle... F-first you fail to die, and now you betray me?! After I raised you—!"

Before Kyle can answer, lightning strikes directly in front of the bishop.

Instantly, his heart quails and his throat goes dry. Fearfully, he looks up at the demon king. For the first time, the man is smiling.

"Phrasing it this way may get me a reputation for arrogance, but— How long do you intend to keep me standing?"

The demon king is looking at the chair where the person of highest rank would sit.

The chair the bishop is currently occupying.

Those red eyes are demanding he surrender it voluntarily. Or rather, he's laughing at him because he knows the man will fold.

He clenches his fists, then responds with trembling lips, "—I beg your pardon. Please, sit here."

"Thank you."

The demon king settles into the chair Bishop Elford has given up. Walt and Kyle jump down from the table to stand on either side of him.

"Now then, let's talk. I would like to be on friendly terms with the church, at least within the range that I can tolerate. Oh, that's right: I'll need to go greet Cardinal Lizanis later. Make sure he knows I plan to stop by."

The demon king's words make the men gulp or exchange looks.

Bishop Elford hangs his head, squeezing his hands into fists. Is the fact that Cardinal Lizanis will be dragged into the mess as well the one small saving grace in this fiasco? No, there's no way that will be the end of it.

For the church, dawn is still a very long, long way off.

✦
♛
✦

"What on earth happened? Explain yourself, Master Claude." Folding her arms, his master's fiancée draws herself up to her full height.

Claude feigns ignorance. "What are you referring to?"

"Last night! The sudden explosion of a mansion outside the city, and the news that lightning somehow struck the church's cathedral in Mirchetta—in isolation, mind you—many, many times and half destroyed it!"

"That's awful. I should pay them a condolence visit," Claude tells her, straight-faced.

Behind him, Walt comes very close to cracking up, but he manages to fight it back. On Claude's other side, Kyle looks perfectly composed; Walt can't be the one to give everything away.

Smacking both hands down on his work desk, Aileen leans in toward Claude. "It was you, Master Claude. Wasn't it?"

"Keith, get us some tea. Aileen is here, so that's enough work."

"No. All those documents need to be dealt with by the end of the day."

"……"

"By the end of the day."

"This is more important than documents. Master Claude! An explanation, if you would. Depending on what you say, I may get very angry! What happened? Don't tell me Walt and Kyle were targe—"

"Aileen." Claude leans in to meet her and whispers, "You're adorable when you're mad, too, but you shouldn't be preoccupied with men who aren't me."

"Wha...? Nobody is talking about that!!" Voice cracking, Aileen flees from the desk all the way to the wall.

Is she bright red because she's angry, or is it embarrassment? Walt has no idea. However, from the fact that she's almost in tears, he can tell she's fundamentally bad at this sort of thing. *The demon king's a nasty guy. He's doing that on purpose.*

The fact that Aileen digs her heels in and schemes anyway is probably one of her charms. She gives Walt a sharp glare, and he kind of likes it. "Fine. Walt, Kyle, you explain!"

"The church has it really rough, getting hit with such weird weather."

"I hear it's fairly common for lightning strikes to be localized. It may have been related to the building's construction."

"You intend to take Master Claude's side?! Sir Keith, say something!"

"When one has served Master Claude for long years, one stops caring about little things like sudden lightning strikes," Keith says impassively.

Aileen is practically boiling over with frustration.

Walt is quietly impressed. Keith knows that Claude was summoned by the church, and that he, Walt, and Kyle went to a confidential talk with them. However, he hasn't attempted to ask about the situation. Either he already knows about it, or he's decided it's too trivial to bother with.

"I see… So every single one of you claims nothing happened last night!" Aileen is trembling, fists clenched.

Claude takes a sip of the tea Keith has served him. "If you're so concerned about what I did last night, visit my bedroom tonight."

"Enough! I understand! Do as you see fit."

Turning away in a huff, Aileen leaves the office, slamming the door behind her.

Kyle winces at the noise, then whispers in his ear. "Are you sure that's okay, Master Claude? I think you've made her angry."

"I think you're right. I'm definitely the only thing on her mind now. She's probably so annoyed that she'll go around investigating my movements. Just thinking about it makes my heart fill to bursting with affection."

"He means every word… Heinous!"

"Even so, milord, you need to finish that work today."

"……"

Claude sighs at his adviser, who refuses to be sidetracked.

"You should hurry and find fiancées, too. When you do…"

Claude blinks. Walt and Kyle brace themselves. There's no telling what he's just thought of, but they're certain it won't be anything good.

"…then I'll be able to attend your weddings. That sounds like fun. You should both hurry and get married."

"For a reason like that?!"

"Besides, you'll definitely bring some sort of useless wedding present…"

"If you finish this work by the end of the day, I'll think of a way to get these two married as soon as possible, milord."

"Will you really, Keith?"

"Uh, listen, Sir Keith, wait on that, okay? Don't make life decisions for us over stuff like this!"

"We don't even have anyone to marry!"

"Why not just grab whoever's available, then promptly break up with her? I'd like to help you through a divorce, as well."

"Guards aren't toys, Master Claude..."

Kyle slumps over as if he's fighting back a headache. Beside him, Walt has a sudden idea. As Claude picks up his quill, finally in the mood to do some work, Walt smirks at him. "Master Claude, you know who's likely to get married long before either of us? Isaac and Rachel."

Claude turns toward him, still holding his pen. At the same time, the flowers in the office's vase all begin to bloom at once. It's as if spring has arrived.

"I'll have to lend my support. I'll definitely provide advice."

"Are those two in that sort of relationship?"

"Kyle, you sure are dense. Isn't it obvious? It looks like it's still a one-sided crush on Rachel's end, but with the demon king on her side, she'll have a huge advantage!"

"Keith, do you have any good ideas?"

"Once you finish this job, I'll think about it for you."

"...It has to be done today, no matter what?" Claude knits his eyebrows in consternation.

Keith nods, smiling. "By the end of the day."

"But the happiness of people close to me is at stake..."

"What are you saying? You just want to get rid of men who are close to Lady Aileen as quickly as possible."

"Keith... You have the wrong idea. I want to be invited to someone's wedding just about as much as I want that."

Walt doesn't think that's the sort of line that should be

delivered in such an authoritarian way, but the only response he can manage is an apathetic smile. *A wedding, hmm...? I've never actually been to one of those, either.*

Claude and Aileen will probably get married before Isaac and Rachel do. That means the first wedding he attends will be his own master's.

Walt knows he'll be protecting Claude on that day, too. Claude will be the one protecting Aileen. Walt will probably see her in her wedding gown and feel sort of sad and lonely, but proud.

Yeah. That's not bad.

Up until yesterday, he hadn't even been able to picture a future like that.

"By the way, Walt and Kyle, how are you feeling? Since it's you, I doubt it will take you long to get used to it, but..."

"...What are you talking about?"

"I told you already. Last night, I rewrote the spells the church had cast on you."

Come to think of it, he had said something like that.

Walt and Kyle have a bad feeling and brace themselves, as Claude goes on breezily. "I made it so you'll hear a bell whenever I want to summon you. Now I'll be able to call you any time at all, morning, noon, or night."

"Huh?! Why would you do a random thing like that?!"

"Because being able to call you when I'm lonely is convenient."

"Seriously, what do you think guards are?!"

"Remove those right now, please!"

"Why?" he asks, and they hesitate.

It feels as if things might get scary if they answer this wrong.

They're silent for several seconds. The whole time, Keith is trying very hard not to laugh. Kyle looks up suddenly. "...Th-that's it. Did you cast that spell on Sir Keith as well?!"

"Keith comes even when I don't call him. In fact, he comes when I specifically tell him not to."

Claude sounds sulky, and suddenly Walt knows what the right answer is. Sighing, he speaks up as if this isn't important at all. "Listen, Master Claude. We'll come even if you don't call us, too."

They are his guards, after all.

"It's our job to protect you," Kyle adds, looking a little disgusted.

"...Really?"

"Yes." They both nod in unison.

"Really," Claude says, one more time.

"Good answer," Keith comments quietly. Sighing with relief, Walt exchanges a glance with Kyle.

The road to becoming the demon king's guards is a long one. No doubt there are all sorts of hardships in store.

However, they've been able to choose their own future, and that's unmitigated happiness.

I want to run for it, someday, for sure.

He doesn't think that way anymore.

"In that case, I'll rewrite the spells so that you'll be able to talk with me at any time."

""Please just don't, sir. Please.""

...Probably. Fairly certain. Almost definitely.

As This Is the World of an *Otome* Game, Valentine's Day Exists

Come to think of it, wasn't cocoa quite valuable? Aileen wonders. The d'Autriche kitchen is currently filled with the sweet fragrance of chocolate.

That means chocolate is valuable as well. As a rule, it should be something only the upper classes can obtain, so why is Valentine's Day popular even among commoners?

The world of an otome *game is a formidable thing indeed.*

Reservations aside, the custom exists in this world, so there's nothing to be done about it. In that case, one should make the most of it. Before she'd recovered her memories of her previous life, Aileen had taken part in this event as a matter of course. Developing doubts at this point would be ridiculous.

"Lady Aileen. I believe we're all ready."

"Yes, Rachel, it looks as if we are."

The two of them are gazing at a mountain of chocolate: all of their finest creations in one place.

Once she packs her handmade truffles into cardboard boxes or paper cups, then fills her basket with them, she'll set off. Her list is a long one this year.

Isaac and the rest of her original circle go without saying, and now her fellow duck squad members have joined them. She's made some for Beelzebuth and Keith as well, naturally.

After all, I am Master Claude's fiancée!

This will be her first Valentine's Day with a fiancé who returns her affections. Of course she's enthusiastic about it.

She hasn't forgotten about Rachel, either. They're saving the petite heart-shaped chocolate cake they made for themselves for the end of the day.

"Once we're finished handing these out, we'll eat this together."

"Yes, Lady Aileen."

"By the way, Rachel, where are Isaac's? Yours all look like romantic chocolates, but they're for friends…aren't they?"

Rachel's chocolates are astonishingly similar. They're all carefully wrapped, but while each looks like chocolate destined for a lover, the quantity and size are all the same.

"Oh," Rachel says with a smile. "Goodness, Lady Aileen. Isaac and I aren't like that."

"Perhaps not, but…"

"That means it's all right to give him the same chocolate as everyone else. Besides, he seems to be aware of my feelings for him, and so…"

Isaac is very observant, and Aileen suspects this may be true. Then Rachel gives her a smile that doesn't make it past her lips. "He'll be braced for romantic chocolate. If what I give him is clearly the same friendship chocolate I give everyone else, he'll no doubt be confused. It's the most effective approach."

That's the villainess of Game 2 all right. Isaac is unexpectedly naive, and the day when he stumbles into a clever love trap is apparently not far off.

★ ★ ★

Second Act

After she and Rachel part, Aileen's first stop is Auguste—who's practically dead from studying for the Holy Knight's entrance exam—and his tutor James.

"How is it that you can remember the wrong answers but never the right ones?!"

"I just can't get them to stick! It's no good, I'm dying... It's hopeless, and so am I..."

"Hee-hee. Why don't you two rest for a little while?" Aileen peeks into the room.

When Auguste spots her, he breaks into a smile. "I smell chocolate. Is this for Valentine's?!"

"Correct."

"Hooray! Let's take a break, James!"

"Listen, you..."

"Oh, do let him. A little sugar will help him work more efficiently."

Aileen sets a truffle down in front of each of them. At the sight of the chocolate in its little box, Auguste's eyes light up. "Wow, it's handmade!"

"Our relationship has just begun, so there's only one this year. Next year, you shall have two."

"What are these, sweets for children? Well, I suppose Master Claude won't glare at us over this." James tosses his truffle into his mouth.

Aileen laughs. "My, so you don't want Master Claude to dislike you?"

"...! I didn't... That isn't why I said that."

"Yeah, James likes the demon king an awful lot!"

"Auguste, finish that entire workbook today, or I'll kill you."

"Huh?! Why?!"

"I see I'll have to give poor Auguste a little extra. Here, say 'Aaaah.'"

Auguste looks blank. Then he plucks the truffle from Aileen's fingers.

She blinks at him in surprise, and he grins. "I only take things that way from girls who like me back."

"—Very nice. That's an admirable principle of conduct. You mustn't mislead girls, though."

"I wouldn't do that."

"...I'm not so sure," James mutters. He's almost certainly onto something.

Auguste is the main hero of *Regalia of Saints, Demons, and Maidens 2*, a character who should have been the Holy Knight. While she'd rather he found a sweet, wonderful girlfriend instead of causing any romance-related drama, she knows that isn't likely.

"Well, I have other stops to make, so I'll be off."

"Mm-hmm, have a good trip."

"...Don't cause too much trouble for Master Claude. He's feeling nervous."

James is a worrywart. Aileen responds with a knowing smile and turns to leave.

After they've watched her go, Auguste mutters to James, "I've been wanting to ask for ages: Do you like Ailey or something?"

"I'm not childish enough to pick a fight with the demon king."

"Geez. You of all people are saying that after you fought him so hard before?"

"Shut up. What about you?"

"Mm... I'm not sure. Maybe I do? It doesn't feel quite like that, though."

"...Just don't fall for a troublesome woman. I won't help you."

Auguste tosses his truffle into his mouth.

Will there ever be a day when the sweetness of chocolate has no bitter edge?

When Aileen steps into the hallway, she runs into Jasper coming around the corner. "Exquisite timing. Our relationship is in…its fourth year, isn't it? There, four chocolates."

"Hey, Valentine's Day, huh? That's real nice of you. Guys my age don't usually have much going on occasions like this." Jasper laughs.

Aileen can't help herself. "Don't you have anyone special?"

"Well, your uncle Jasper got his heart broken when he was younger, and it just hasn't healed up yet."

"I can introduce you to someone, if you'd like—but offering would be meddlesome, wouldn't it?"

The sorrow she's seen in Jasper's eyes makes Aileen lower her own for a moment.

They've known each other long enough that some things don't need to be said.

"…Might I ask one thing? What sort of person was the wicked woman who broke your heart?"

"Oh, let's see. She might've been a bit like you, Miss Aileen."

"A beauty, then." Matching Jasper joke for joke, Aileen smiles back at him.

Seeing Jasper pop a truffle into his mouth, she takes a step back. "I have more to deliver, so I'll be going. Make sure to savor those."

"Miss, just a word of warning: Don't make the demon king mad."

"Master Claude isn't so narrow-minded." Chuckling proudly, she waves, then continues down the corridor.

Picking up a truffle between his thumb and forefinger, Jasper mutters. "...I do think that if I were ten years younger... But that kid *is* the demon king. I can't compete with that."

Besides, even if he were ten years younger, he probably would have made the same choice.

That's why he simply wishes for Aileen's happiness, just as he did for that other woman.

When she peeks into the conference room on the assumption that someone is likely to be there, she finds an unexpected pair. "Denis and Isaac? It's rare to see you two alone together. What are you doing?"

"Lady Aileen! Um, you see, I'm going over the renovations for the demon king's castle with Isaac."

"I see. May I interrupt you for a moment?"

"Go for it," Isaac says carelessly, and she enters.

Denis rapidly rolls up the blueprints he'd spread out on the big table, tidying them away. "We've got tea. Would you like some, Lady Aileen?"

"Oh no, don't trouble yourselves."

"It's fine, it's already here! I was just thinking we should take a break; Isaac's been sort of useless for a while."

"My, whatever's the matter, Isaac?"

"Nothing."

Isaac's propped an elbow on the table and is resting his chin in his hand. In contrast to what he's said, he looks as if he's in a very bad mood.

Denis briskly pours a cup of tea from the pot sitting on a corner of the table and hands it to her. It's already quite cool, but an herbal fragrance rises from it. Seating herself at the table, Aileen takes a sip, then blinks. "This is delicious. Denis, you really are clever."

"Oh, the tea's not mine. Rachel came by and made it for us a minute ago! We got chocolate, too; she said it was for Valentine's Day."

Denis puts two sets of chocolates right in the middle of the table, side by side. Just as she'd seen in the kitchen, they're identical. Then he leans in close to Aileen's ear and whispers, "We both got the same chocolate, and Isaac's been sulking ever since."

"Gracious." Aileen looks at Isaac, covering her mouth with a hand.

Isaac scowls. "...Whatever that was about, Denis, Aileen didn't need to hear it."

"He acted normal while Rachel was here, but he's been thinking ever since she left, and we haven't gotten anything done."

"Denis! Quit whispering like that. You have no idea what you're talking about!"

Denis might be small, but he has plenty of courage. He lets Isaac's glare roll off him with a smile.

Meanwhile, Aileen is desperately stifling a laugh. *Rachel... It's going just as she planned. That girl is frightening.*

Aileen's shoulders are quivering, and Isaac's eyebrows come down. "What's so funny?! And what do you need anyway?"

"I came to give you your Valentine's chocolates. Denis, we've known each other for five years, so here are five."

"Huh?! Is that okay?! Thank you very much."

"It's three years for us, Isaac, so these three are yours."

"...Isn't the demon king gonna get mad if you do stuff like this?" Isaac asks, eyeing the three chocolates she's set down in front of him as if he has mixed feelings about them.

Denis, who's eaten one of his already, argues vigorously, "The demon king's getting romantic chocolates, so it's not about numbers for him!"

"Well, yeah, but still..."

"So, like I was saying, you can't tell how a girl feels by how many chocolates she gives you! I really don't think you need to worry, Isaac."

"Denis, you've got the wrong idea here! I don't even care about this!"

"It's true that I got five chocolates because I've known Lady Aileen longer, but even if you only got three, you're her right-hand man and everybody knows it! Right?!"

"......"

There's no telling how much of this Denis is actually doing on purpose, but he's really something.

Thanks to that, Isaac starts moping in earnest.

Her subordinates are hopeless. Biting back laughter, Aileen takes pity on him. "So these are the chocolates Rachel gave you. These are yours, Denis, and those are Isaac's? The ribbons are different colors."

"Yes, she said mine was pink and Isaac's was orange."

The chocolates are the same size, and they're wrapped the same way, but the ribbons that close the bags are different colors. Rachel's chocolates, neglected in the center of the table, are clearly marked. There's no way to get them mixed up this way.

"When a girl gives you something, provided it isn't dangerous, do make sure you eat it."

"Of course!"

"Also, thank her properly with a return present on White Day."

"Oh, right! Let's see, what should I make...?"

"What a pain."

Denis is already enjoying himself, while Isaac looks thoroughly disgruntled. It's quite a contrast. She can't stop smiling.

Isaac picks up one of Aileen's chocolates and eats it, then finally looks at her. "What, is Valentine's Day fun for you this year or something?"

"Yes. Last year I had my hands full courting Master Claude and had no energy to spare, while the year before that..."

She'd attempted to give Cedric a homemade chocolate cake. Lilia had a particular talent for making sweets and cooking in general, so Aileen had the d'Autriche cook instruct her, so that her offering wouldn't be inferior. She'd improved her skills by testing them on Isaac and the others, and then—

"This year should be fine."

"I bet the demon king's waiting for you."

These two had seen the results of that earlier attempt with Cedric.

Aileen puffs out her chest. "Naturally. After all, I incorporated a very special essence."

"Ooh, you mean love?!"

"How could one possibly incorporate a thing like that? No, it was something more reliable."

"Huh?"

"Wait just a minute, you're still doing that?! What did you lace it with?! Whose idea was it?! Was it Luc?! Did Quartz help out?!"

"Oh, that's reminds me: I must give Luc and Quartz their

chocolates as well. I still have many stops to make," Aileen says, rising from her chair.

Isaac, who's back to his usual self, sighs. "Don't come crying to me later."

"That won't do. If something happens, you're going to deal with it for me."

"I'm fine with it. I want to build ice mansions and things!" Denis's eyes are sparkling.

Pretending she hasn't heard him, Aileen leaves the room.

Isaac watches her go as if he's not sure about this. Then he picks up one of Rachel's chocolates. Denis seems to be planning to eat all his chocolates right now; he's popping them into his mouth one after another.

It's not like it was on my mind, and I wasn't exactly hoping for anything.

He had been wondering, absently, how to brush off something like that if she gave it to him. He always does his best to keep romance out of his work life. That means he couldn't be happier with this outcome. He's also glad that Aileen has a fine lady-in-waiting who keeps her work and her personal life separate.

It's just that, since he'd been on his guard, it's thrown him a little off-balance.

Since the distraction has kept him from worrying about whether Aileen will make it through this Valentine's Day safely, it's probably all for the best.

Telling himself that this is just chocolate from a random coworker, he tosses it into his mouth. As he bites down, he tastes a fragrant note of orange peel. He'd thought it was just a plain truffle, but she's gotten a little creative.

The thought that he's been worried over nothing makes the

tension drain from his shoulders. It's also extremely unlikely that Aileen will end up in the sort of situation she lived through two years ago. Cold herbal tea sounds good right about now, and he raises the cup to his lips.

"The chocolate Rachel made was good, wasn't it? There were nuts in it. I like that."

"...Wasn't it orange peel?"

"Huh? These have nuts. Yours have orange peel, Isaac?"

"......"

Without answering, he quietly sets his cup back in its saucer.

The truffles were exactly the same, but they'd been clearly marked by their ribbons. All she'd said was, "They're for everyone who's helped me." For better or for worse, his sharp mind kicks up something fairly close to the answer.

That woman...! No, hang on. If everyone's had different centers, she wouldn't have said it like that.

Isaac likes oranges. However, Denis just said he likes nuts.

Perhaps she's made it look as if they're all the same, but the flavors suit their recipients' preferences. It wouldn't have been odd for her to be considerate like that. It's too early to assume she made something different just for him.

That means playing it cool is the appropriate reaction right now. He reaches that conclusion almost instantly; however, Denis apparently knows zilch about guys' sensitive hearts.

"That's great, Isaac! Yours were special after all!"

"...I bet not. She might've done that for everybody."

"Huh? Let's go around and ask, then! That way we'll know for sure!"

"Whoa, whoa, whoa! Forget it, seriously, we don't have to do that!"

"Huh? But aren't you curious?"

Isaac has no answer for that. This time, he drains his tea.

Were the fillings different for everybody, or just for him? He'd be lying if he said he didn't want to know. However, as Denis says, the only way to find out is to go around and ask. If he does that, it's bound to get back to Rachel.

Dammit! Why did the woman have to pull something like this?!

How can he outwit her and find out the truth? He should examine all the options before making his move.

Quietly, in the distance, Denis murmurs, "It looks like I'm going to lose Isaac again. He's thinking too much."

It had happened with Aileen as well: Isaac's clever, and he tends to land in nasty situations by overthinking things.

Denis decides that if a girl he likes ever gives him chocolate, he'll just be openly happy about it.

Taking Isaac—who's using his excellent brain on something pointless—as an example of what not to do, Denis simply enjoys his last chocolate.

Now then, where should she go next?

As Aileen hesitates in the great hall that serves as the palace's entrance, a pair wearing Misha Academy uniforms walk in.

"Walt and Kyle. You're students today?"

"Yup. We had several things to set up as student council members. We can't bring back regular classes yet, but the principal-slash-demon king says to at least make the graduation ceremony happen."

"On top of that, we can't use James and Auguste for odd jobs. They're in the home stretch right now."

"Hee-hee. You rarely sound like it, but you're kind to those two."

"Well, my sweet Ailey? It's Valentine's Day, isn't it? I'm always open to getting romantic chocolates." Walt winks at her. He's already holding a paper bag that's nearly bursting with chocolates. Apparently he landed quite a haul at the academy.

"I certainly hope you aren't causing trouble with any of the girls."

"Of course not. You're the only one I'm interested in. There's nobody else."

"If you do anything to make a girl cry, I'll personally break you."

Walt tenses, the sultry smile freezing on his face. "...Break my, um, what? My heart?"

"Here you go. We just met this year, so you get one each. Next year you'll get two."

"Wow, is that an unsexy way to give somebody something. Be a little more, you know..."

"Th-thanks, Ailey," Kyle says shyly, while Walt keeps complaining. He's accepted the chocolate politely, with both hands.

Aileen feels her heart skip a beat.

Kyle gasps, blinking. "N-no, you're Lady Aileen now, aren't you? I'm sorry; I'm not used to that yet."

"Kyle... Perhaps I'll give you Walt's chocolate as well."

"Huh?! Wait just a minute, sweet Ailey! Listen, Kyle, that's not fair!"

"Not fair? You're not making any sense."

"Argh, I hate this. What happened to the guy who was all cold at school and turned down *everything*, huh?"

"It's crueler to be nice when you don't actually care about the girl."

Walt flashes a thin smile. "There's no way the girls who brought these were that serious, either."

"Oh, Walt, don't think that way."

"Well, even if they were, it's not like we have much time."

Due to her knowledge of the game, Aileen understands that Walt is referring to their lives. Nameless Priests all have short life spans.

The church had trained these two as human weapons and treated them as tools, and they can't seem to shake the habit of tormenting themselves. Thinking it won't do for people who serve Claude to act like that, Aileen draws herself up to her full height. "Walt. Kyle. You are Master Claude's precious to—favorites."

"You almost said *toys!*"

"It's fine; there isn't much difference. You two pledged your loyalty to Master Claude, and he's already used a cheat to resolve the problem so that you'll be able to live properly. For ages now, your bodies have been—"

"I've got a bad feeling about this, and I don't want to hear it!"

"I-I'll refrain as well."

The two of them back away, plugging their ears. Feeling weary, Aileen decides to leave it alone. They just don't know when to give up.

"Pull yourselves together. Master Claude is serious. He's asked me to arrange marriage interviews for both of you."

"Wha—? That joke's still going?!"

"Lately I've learned that once Master Claude says something, he stops listening."

"Since I have the opportunity, let me ask you: Is there a type of woman you prefer? It would be better to have me search for them than Master Claude, wouldn't it?"

She's spoken out of kindness, but Walt and Kyle exchange looks.

"...I'd say it's six of one, half a dozen of the other."

"What we'd really like is the option of finding them ourselves."

"You mean you'd like to marry for love? That would be fine, but... I'm not certain any ordinary women would volunteer to wed the demon king's guards." Aileen begins thinking about it.

Walt speaks up hastily. "No, come on! Sure, our job's sort of unique, but the take-home pay is generous, and we'll be the emperor's guards someday! I shouldn't be the one saying it, but our looks are good, too. We're fine real estate!"

"...I'm not fond of that mindset, but, erm, if we were able to marry, I also feel that we would be reliable enough to protect and provide for our families."

"Even if Master Claude began meddling from the sidelines?"

In more ways than one, there's no telling what the demon king may do. As his guards, these two feel that more keenly than anyone, and they both fall silent.

However, Aileen mercilessly drives them into a corner. It's important to face reality. "Not only that, but consider his face. I'm worried he may charm every girl you take a fancy to."

"I-it's true that Master Claude's looks are unrivaled, but—"

"Once he becomes emperor, both his rank and his finances will be guaranteed. In addition, Master Claude is kind and broadminded, and while he does have his faults, those are lovable as well. He's polite, accomplished with both pen and sword, worthy of respect, and then there's that exquisitely perfect face..."

"First you start gushing about your lover, and then you mention his face twice?"

"With a man that wonderful right next to you…it may not be possible for you…to genuinely marry for love…"

Aileen's apprehension makes both Walt and Kyle fall silent.

She thumps both of them lightly on the shoulders. "Well, try your best. I'll give you chocolate every year."

Wishing the unresponsive pair good fortune, Aileen softly moves on.

Left behind, still holding their chocolates, the two of them murmur to each other.

"Let's…give some thought to the future."

"That's a good idea."

This is no time to wax sentimental about how protecting their lord's fiancée is also part of their job. After hearing something like that, they'll build happy families and live surrounded by adorable children even if it kills them. While they absolutely do not want to hear the details, apparently the demon king's messed with their life spans, which means they now have a future.

That said, they suspect that not many brides would be happy to have the demon king in attendance at their wedding.

Aileen is walking down the corridor, her basket substantially lighter, when she hears a disturbance in the courtyard. As she gets closer, she's able to make the voices out clearly.

"There, that's good enough. Dig any more and you'll go too deep. All right, these seedlings are next."

"Luc and Quartz…and even Almond and company. So this is where you are."

"Lady Aileen."

Surrounded by demons—albeit small ones—Luc straightens

up, smiling. He's still wearing his white lab coat. Although Quartz glances at her, the botanist promptly returns his attention to the freshly tilled soil and begins to plant seedlings, showing the fidgeting demons how it's done.

"What are you doing?"

"Teaching the demons to garden."

Gardening demons. Her eyes widen, but even the perennially noisy Almond is gazing steadily at Quartz's hands.

"**What goes here?**"

"Strawberries."

"**They grow tomorrow?**"

"After lots of tomorrows, they will."

"**Will the demon king eat them?**"

"Yes. We can all harvest them together."

Quartz's terse explanation makes the demons' eyes sparkle.

Slipping unobtrusively out of their circle, Luc comes over to stand by her. "The demons who are closer to animals took an interest in it. They asked how they could grow strawberries and other types of fruit."

Ah. In other words, they're hungry.

"In the forest, the demons are trying their hand at growing flowers, too. They're keeping it a secret from the demon king."

"My... Are they meant to be a present?"

"Apparently so. They'd like to make a bouquet."

"If they manage it, I expect we'll have some abnormal weather."

Claude may be so deeply moved that the sun will set in the east. Luc nods; there's a distant look in his eyes. "I'm concerned about the effects on the other plants. We've implemented as many safeguards as we can, but..."

"They're causing you two quite a lot of trouble. Isn't this obstructing your research?"

"It's all right. When the plants got sick and withered, they came to us and made a huge fuss about it, but it's a whole lot of fun. Quartz may not look it, but he's very happy."

"Quartz, Quartz! A bug! Kill?"

"...No, it's fine. That's a good one."

"A good bug! No killing!"

"Cover those lightly with dirt. Don't dig too deeply over there, Ribbon."

"Yip!"

The young man with the eye patch is surrounded by demons. Although he looks a bit ominous, he's actually kind, and she can see why the demons like him.

"I shouldn't stay long; I don't want to get in your way. Here you are, your Valentine's Day chocolates. You get five."

"Ah, yes, thank you very much. I'm afraid my hands are rather muddy at the moment, though..."

"That's fine. I'll leave it in the gazebo for you. Yours as well, Quartz."

When she calls to him, he nods slightly in acknowledgment, although he doesn't rise to his feet or leave off working. However, the demons are extremely fond of sweets, and they mob her.

"Chocolate! Chocolate!"

"Yip-yip-yip-yip-yip-yip!"

"Oh, for heaven's sake, be quiet. Rachel and I made enough for all of you. We've left it with Sir Keith."

"Keith!!" the demons yell and then race off en masse. They must already know where he is.

As the horde charges away, kicking up a cloud of dust, Aileen shouts after them, "Now see here! You haven't finished your work, have you?!"

"...It's fine. They were only helping out. They'll be back." Quartz stands up, brushing the dirt off his knees. He looks at the chocolate Aileen has left in the gazebo, then back at her. "...What about the demon king's?"

"His will be last. It's romantic chocolate, after all."

"...Are you happy?"

The question is abrupt, but she knows what is behind it, and she gives a genuine smile. "Very."

"...That's good."

"But even back then, I wasn't unhappy. I had all of you."

If she'd had no one, Aileen would only have remembered being hurt, and it might have warped her. Because the others were there, she's able to think *This year for sure!* and dive in enthusiastically.

"I intend to further deepen the bond between Master Claude and myself this Valentine's."

"...If that's what you want, I'm not sure you should have laced that with..."

"If I want to be certain of winning him, it's necessary. There's still much I don't know about him."

"...I see."

"Lady Aileen. Do give me a report on the effects."

"But of course."

Aileen shakes hands with both of them firmly, then turns on her heel. Her next stop is Keith, whom the demons have gone to find. Her skirt swishes jauntily as she walks away, so she's evidently enjoying herself.

The sight makes him rather sad, but it's a genuine relief as well.

"I do hope it goes well for Lady Aileen."

"You do? Really...?"

"Well, why not? If he makes her cry, we'll just have to end him ourselves."

"...That drug is still in development. I don't think we could do it for sure just yet."

"More importantly, don't you think we should kill Prince Cedric fairly soon?"

Quartz doesn't respond. Luc realizes he's ready to kill the man whenever they decide to do it.

"Master Cedric wouldn't accept it.

"He said I must have had our chef make it. That it was disgraceful to act as if I'd made it myself.

"I couldn't tell him.

"I couldn't bring myself to say that I'd practiced making sweets for ages and ages, so that I wouldn't lose to Lady Lilia..."

They never want to see Aileen look that way again.

Aileen follows the demons' tracks until she finds them lining up in a corridor, waiting to receive their chocolate.

"All right. Almond, pass this out to everyone who's still in the forest, please. Have Master Claude send you."

"Understood! Understood!"

"You're next, Sugar. This is for the demons in Mirchetta. They may not want it, so ask for takers first, if you would."

"Leave it to me."

"Everyone who's lined up, take one each from Bel. No getting back in line: one per person! I'll be reporting to the demon king about anyone who breaks the rules."

As expected, the demon king's adviser is good at handling the demons. Beelzebuth begins passing out chocolate as instructed.

Impressed by the organization, Aileen steps into the room they've designated as the distribution point. "Sir Keith, you really are clever at that. However, Master Claude may defend any demons who cheat instead..."

"That's fine. If he does, I'll make him work enough to make up for it."

He's good at handling the demon king, too.

Folding her arms, Aileen observes his technique. *I must become at least as good as this man at taming Master Claude.*

Master Claude's adviser is the one who knows him best. The years they've spent together give him a sizable advantage, but she doesn't intend to back down.

"Sir Keith, I won't lose to you. Please accept this chocolate, and consider it a declaration of war."

"I'm not really sure what you mean by that, but I'll gladly take it if that's all right."

"Beelzebuth, I've brought some for you as well. Will you accept it?"

"For me? Oh, this is that Barentainz thing, isn't it."

"My, you knew about it." She's impressed.

Instantly, Beelzebuth looks proud of himself. "Of course. After all, every year, the king—"

"Bel," Keith says.

Beelzebuth, who's drawn himself up to his full height, freezes that way.

The fact that Keith has clearly stopped him from saying something doesn't escape Aileen. She gives him a slow smile. "'Every year, the king'...what?"

"He's looking forward to it. After all, this is milord's first Valentine's Day with a fiancée."

By *first*, does he mean having a fiancée or does he mean celebrating Valentine's Day? She gives Keith a meaningful look, hoping he'll pick up on her implicit question, but he simply stays silent, his smile as steady as ever. Taking that as a cue, Beelzebuth quietly sidles away and resumes handing out chocolate to the demons.

When she gives it careful thought, she realizes she should have guessed when the demons—who are normally naive to the ways of the world—knew that it's customary to get chocolate on Valentine's Day.

In other words, that is where things stand.

Keith seems to have read her mind. He gives her an affectionate smile. "I have faith in your capacity for tolerance, Lady Aileen."

"Yes, I was wrong to even question it. He does have that face, after all."

"He does indeed."

"Beelzebuth."

"Wh-what?" When Beelzebuth turns back apprehensively, Aileen lightly tosses a chocolate into his mouth. He looks boggled but manages to chew it.

"You are a demon as well, so you also have that sort of face."

"?"

"Stay a good boy, won't you? I find you quite soothing." She pats him on the head, then turns to Keith. "Do you suppose Master Claude is in his room?"

"Hmm, probably. He should be returning soon."

"I see. I'll be going, then." Firing herself up, Aileen walks away, heels clicking loudly.

Finally managing to swallow the chocolate, Beelzebuth turns to Keith. "The king summoned you. Don't you need to go?"

"It's fine. It's hard every year, and we'll need Lady Aileen to help as well."

"Human women can't be blamed for swarming around the king, but…won't Aileen be angry?"

Beelzebuth and the other demons all look uneasy.

Keith responds briskly, "If she is going to wed milord, she'll need to deal with that much and more without turning a hair."

"…Is that how it is?"

"Yes, that's how it is. In any case, milord will be satisfied as long as he gets chocolate from Lady Aileen. Good grief, even I'd like to get at least one romantic chocolate from a fetching young girl."

"In your case, it'll never happen. The king wouldn't allow it."

The demon has spoken without hesitation, and Keith stares back at him soberly. It isn't just Beelzebuth; the demons around them are nodding in agreement, too.

Keith's smile deepens. "All right, everyone, I'm confiscating those chocolates."

"Why?!"

"Sister-in-law, sister-in-law!"

"Who just called me 'sister-in-law'? I'm holding the entire group responsible, so you'll have no sweets tomorrow, either."

"Tyranny! Tyranny!"

The demons may screech and howl, but in the end, they throw themselves on Keith's mercy.

The demon king's "sister-in-law" is strong. Perhaps even stronger than the king himself.

She's finally down to her last one, the object of her romantic affections.

Outside the double doors, she draws a deep breath. *Finally, a love who loves me in return... It would be no exaggeration to call this my first Valentine's Day.*

No matter what, she will make this a success. She isn't quite sure what will qualify it as "a success," but she will make it succeed and laugh off all the unpleasantness in her past.

She grasps the door handle. Women must be bold.

"Excuse m—"

"You're late, Keith. If we don't hurry and clear this away, Aileen will come—"

She and her beloved fiancé gaze at each other across an enormous heap of gifts.

In the next moment, lightning strikes.

She squeezes her eyes shut on reflex. When she opens them, the pile of presents has vanished. Like magic.

"Oh, Aileen. I'm glad you're here."

The demon king smiles, as lovely today as ever.

That said, Aileen had gotten a good look at that mountain, and she howls. "You just hid those!"

"I don't know what you're talking about."

"I saw that heap of chocolates! Where did you steal those from?!"

"A heap of chocolates? It might have been a hallucination. There's nothing here."

"Master Claude."

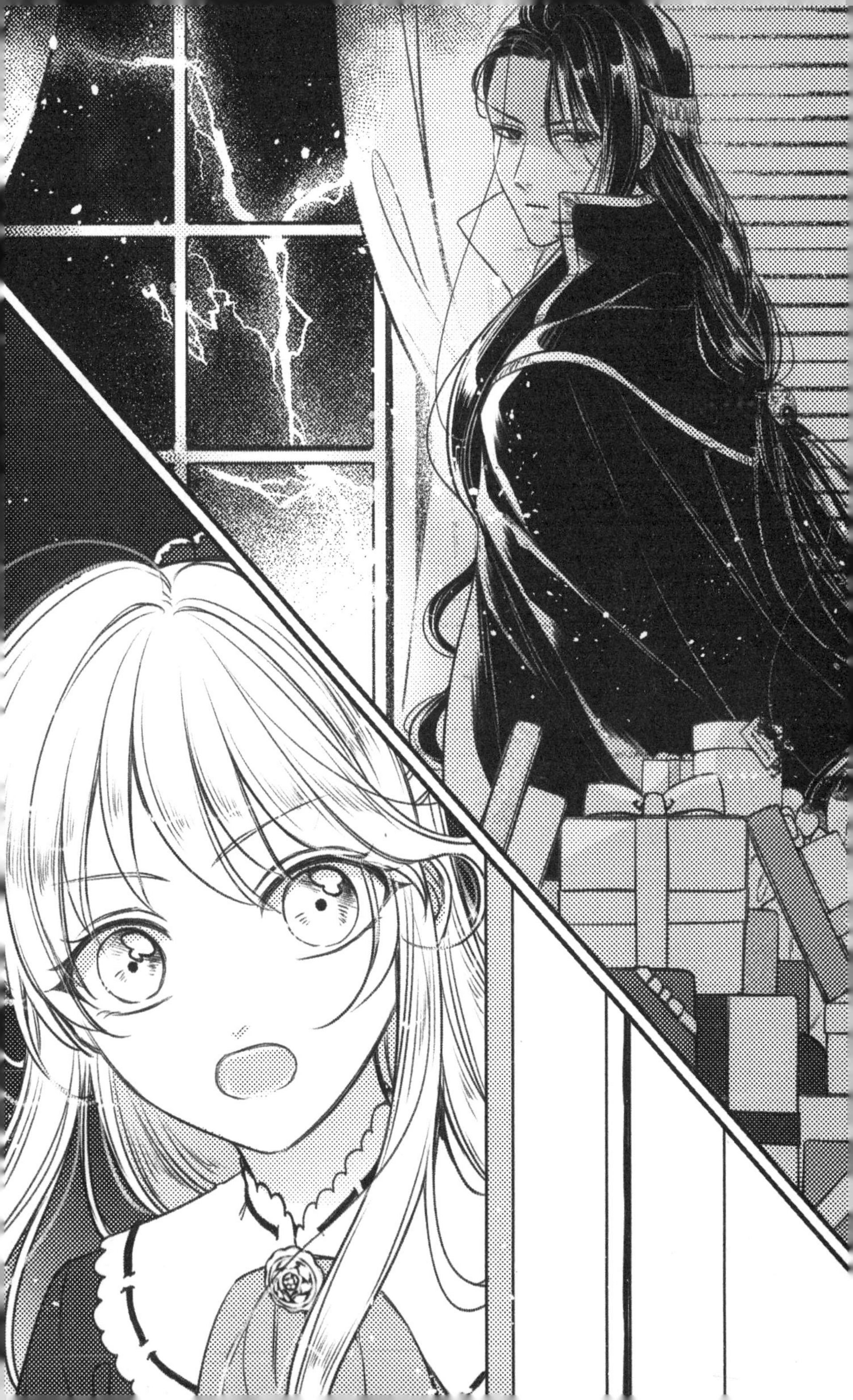

Claude is feigning ignorance, and she grabs his jaw, glaring up at him. The handsome demon king gazes right back at her, but Aileen isn't fooled.

"The window's rattling, Master Claude." Of course, what's ferociously buffeting the window is a sudden agitation-powered gale. "You won't deceive me. Now produce what you've hidden."

"I…I'm not hiding anything—"

"Produce it, or I refuse to give you my chocolate!!"

Once again, lightning strikes from a clear blue sky.

"There's nothing on my conscience," the demon king says, uncharacteristically making excuses. "I just thought that, if they concerned you, it would be a pai— I would feel bad about it."

"You were about to say it would be a pain, weren't you?"

Even when she glares at Claude, his handsome features stay composed, but a small, restless whirlwind is sporadically manifesting at his feet. Apparently he's feeling unsettled.

Aileen is standing tall, directly in front of her fiancé's chair. "Master Claude. Just so you are aware, if I visit your bedchamber in the morning and discover two or three naked women lying around, it won't startle me."

"I'd really prefer it if you were startled by things like that."

"My point is that the very worst thing is keeping secrets! A veritable mountain like this, when you have a fiancée— This is a brazen challenge of my position!"

She points sharply at the mountain of chocolate, which Claude had magicked away to some unknown hiding place a few moments ago only to bring it out again.

Some are decorated with adorable ribbons in all the colors of the rainbow. Others are well-made confection boxes crafted from high-quality paper. Still others are handmade creations wrapped in plain brown paper. There's no common theme. She even sees sweet rolls with chocolate kneaded into the dough.

I can't even begin to guess at their ages or social class!

The pile is being sorted by individuals Aileen has summoned. Irritated, she crosses her arms. "Where on earth did you get all of this, Master Claude?"

"They hand it to me when I walk down the street."

"And what street is that?!"

"The ones in the lower layers of the capital, Lady Aileen. It's like this every year. He's a pitiful prince who sneaks in unannounced, so everyone is very kind to him," Keith tells her. He's sorting packages deftly, as if he's very used to this.

Walt, who's following instructions from Keith, nods as if that makes sense to him. When he'd first seen this mountain, he'd looked hurt by the vast difference between it and what he'd received, but he seems to have recovered. "That's true. When Master Claude makes an appearance in the lower levels, he tends to get quite a lot of stuff wherever he goes."

"Come to think of it, many elderly people worried about whether he was eating properly."

"That's because he's been paying visits there for fun since he was small. I've even made the rounds to tell people, 'If an individual of this description causes any problems, please contact me at the abandoned castle.'" Keith smiles, a distant look in his eyes. He's clearly had it rough.

Settling back in his chair, Claude sighs and crosses his long legs. "They don't know who I am, but they're all kind, and they tell me to come through on Valentine's Day."

"……"

It's probably useless to point out that they almost certainly do know who he is, so no one does.

Claude seems to want to explain properly. He goes on, resting his chin in his hand. "As thanks, I had the demons do various things, such as repair their roofs at night or rid their farm fields of pests. Then, for some reason, I kept getting more and more…"

The demon king has turned into an elf or a fairy.

"Lately, people often include requests for favors or advice in their gifts. I'll look those over later, so be careful not to destroy them. They're the precious voices of our citizens."

"Master Claude…"

She hadn't expected this. As she's gazing at him in astonishment, Jasper smiles wryly. "If he's doing stuff like this for them, no wonder the farther down the layers you go, the more demon king supporters you find."

Luc, who's from the fifth and lowest layer, looks perplexed. "But we've never heard about… Oh, maybe it's only the women."

"It is Valentine's Day, after all. This crochet was definitely handmade by somebody's grandma… Hey, Demon King, is it okay if we look through the letters in these?" Isaac waves a letter that's still in its envelope.

Claude nods. "That's fine, but you're helping with this?"

"It'll be a good source of information for the Oberon Trading Firm. Okay, let's divvy them up. Everybody note down what's in each gift and the giver's name, then bundle that with the letters. Letters with urgent content go in this box. You help, too, Duck Squad."

"Who's a duck?!"

"What's a duck squad?"

James immediately gets mad. Next to him, Beelzebuth tilts his head in confusion.

Auguste laughs. "I'll help for a few minutes. Should this go over here, Keith?"

"Yes, thank you, that's a great help. He gets this much every year..."

"...Aren't you going to give return presents? I could get you flowers, at least," Quartz suggests.

Luc adds, "Medicines we're testing might be good as well. It wouldn't be easy for them to complain."

"Isn't that human experimentation...?"

"Here, over here! Demon King, what are you going to do with these chocolates and presents?"

"I donate what people give me to a children's care home. Handle them gently."

"Okay!" Denis responds energetically.

Everyone sets to work efficiently. Watching them, Claude murmurs, "There are many children who look forward to the chocolate and presents. When I thought of them... Even though I have you this year, I couldn't refuse. I'm sorry, Aileen."

"N-no, no!" The sincere apology has caught Aileen by surprise, and she hastily shakes her head.

She finds herself fidgeting a little.

She'd be lying if she said she thought nothing of this vast amount of chocolate. She'd initially entertained thoughts of telling the givers to meet her behind the gym after school, but now...

"I think what you're doing is splendid, Master Claude. I'm quite proud of you."

"Are you? I thought you were disgusted with me for failing in my social obligations."

"N-not at all! I myself was walking around distributing chocolates to other men."

That thought makes her feel horribly embarrassed about having yelled at him. *Being angry that Master Claude received so much... Why, that's simple jealousy.*

"It's all right. I know you're the most faithful of women."

"Master Claude..."

"Hey, there are other people here."

"Telling him is useless, Master Isaac. He's doing this right in our faces on purpose."

"Th-that's right, I'd nearly forgotten. I'd made a chocolate cake for you as well, Master Claude."

During the fuss, she'd neglected her romantic chocolate cake, but now she hugs its box to her chest. She gazes at Claude, her heart beating a bit faster with nerves. "Um... I know you've received many other chocolates, but would you accept it?"

"Of course. I'd be glad to."

"It, um... It is homemade, but..."

Claude has eaten sweets Aileen has made before. However, confessing she'd made this particular chocolate cake herself had taken courage, even though she knows Claude would never doubt her.

Rising to his feet, Claude gently pulls Aileen into his arms. As she's blinking at him, he gives her a blissfully sweet smile. "I'm very fortunate to have a fiancée who's good at making sweets."

Aileen can't find the words to respond to that. Her cheeks flush.

Like chocolate, the past is sweetly melting away, leaving just a trace of bitterness.

"Master Claude, I love y—"

"Lady Aileen! This letter says, 'Break up with your fiancée.' What should I do with it?"

"Denis! Timing, my guy! You're asking that right now?!"

"Huh? I wouldn't do that on purpose. I'm not Isaac or anything."

Denis puffs his cheeks out, obviously sulking. As everyone stares at him, aghast, Aileen slowly turns. She's going to be the wife of this wonderful man. Of course, her elegant smile never falters.

"What is that woman's name?"

"Um, it's mrff, whadda hyu ooin, Yaspa?!"

"Read the room, youngster! Okay?! You're taking years off your uncle's life over here!"

"Well, never mind. Jasper, thoroughly research her identity later. Master Claude?"

"Wh-what is it?"

"I will personally select that woman's White Day return present. You don't mind, do you?"

She doesn't need a response to that. It's as good as done.

Aileen smiles brightly, and Claude sighs.

✦

♛

✦

Aileen has been standing tall with her arms folded, keeping a sharp eye out for any other indecent messages. However, when Claude tells her, in a coaxing voice, that he'd like to hurry and eat her chocolate cake, she begins fidgeting again. "Very well, I'll go get it ready," she says, and leaves the room.

The way she intends to do this herself, instead of asking her lady-in-waiting, is too precious. Settling himself into his chair, he murmurs to himself, "My Aileen really is adorable."

"I've never seen a guy use all the chocolate he got from other women to boost his own rep."

As he'd anticipated, Isaac is the one who picks a fight with him.

Opportunities like this don't come around often. He looks up, meeting the other man's eyes, planning to have a proper talk with him. "You are Aileen's treasured right-hand man, and I respect you. It's the same for the others."

"...Well, gee, thanks."

"However, I'm quite certain that people can survive losing a hand."

Aileen's precious companions fall silent.

Recrossing his legs, he rests his chin in his hand. "Are there any questions? I'd like to be a king who listens to the people."

"No, sir, none..."

"I see. It really is important for men to talk things out every so often. Now I won't have to do anything immature, such as steal the chocolate Aileen gave you."

"I'd like to tattle on him to Lady Aileen."

"...Same here."

Luc and Quartz glare at him from beneath half-closed eyelids. Claude smiles back. "You won't tell on me to Aileen. I'm the only one who can heal her trauma."

Claude doesn't know what Aileen's past Valentine's Days have been like. All he knows is that the wound Cedric inflicted on her is a deep one; there was something odd about the way she informed him that the chocolate cake was homemade.

Second Act   115

"Did you feel the way I handled that was satisfactory?"

Isaac and the others, who are all glaring at him, respond in different ways. Some smile tightly, others give up, and the rest grow sentimental. All of these reactions are based on their feelings for Aileen.

Claude permits that. He is the one at the pinnacle of her love, so it's only polite.

When he waits, keeping his cold eyes fixed on them, Isaac shrugs and answers tersely. "It was perfect."

"Hearing that from you is a relief. I'll keep giving it my best."

"Huh? For some reason, I'm getting worried about Ailey..."

"Are you stupid, Auguste? Stay out of this. You'll die."

"That's right, let sleeping demon kings lie."

"...I don't understand the situation to begin with..."

"Oh, that's right. Walt and Kyle. Just so you're aware, there are chocolates for you buried somewhere in that pile as well."

Walt and Kyle, who've been whispering together, turn around.

Auguste speaks up. "Lucky! I didn't even get to go outside today... Oh, but you didn't either, huh, James?"

"I didn't want any in the first place. I don't like sweets."

"You ate all of Ailey's chocolate, though— Why did you hit me?!"

"Don't say things like that in front of Master Claude!"

"'Buried'? They really are buried, Master Claude; there's no way to tell where they are. If you took them for us, you should at least set them aside," Walt complains, looking up at the mountain of gifts.

Kyle tilts his head. "Why did they give you some for us?"

"Because people often see you with me. They told me to give it to 'my light and dark attendants.'"

"You just said 'often,' didn't you, Master Claude. So you've walked around with these two enough that they're being targeted for valentines. I see..." Keith's eyes sharpen, and Walt and Kyle flinch, backing away.

Claude sighs. "It's fine. There's nothing wrong with that. Let them have Valentine's Day, at least. It isn't as if they accepted the gifts personally."

"Wait just a minute, Master Claude! Don't tell me you're not planning to give them to us. That's mine, isn't it?!"

"If you've accepted them, you really must let us see what they are. We won't be able to thank their senders otherwise."

"What are you talking about? I refuse to acknowledge any woman who sets her sights on you without my permission. I will select the women you associate with."

Walt and Kyle fall to their knees. James seems to sympathize with them; he frowns. "It's good that you're so fond of them, but that seems as if it might be excessive interference."

"It's fine, James. I'll find you someone, too, so that you won't fall in love with my Aileen."

"That is not what I'm talking about...!"

"Um... You're not planning anything like that for me, are you?"

"In your case..."

Gazing at Auguste, who's looking around at the others uneasily, Claude narrows his red eyes. "...I suspect there's no need. Even if I leave you alone, you seem likely to have plenty of trouble with women."

"Huh?!"

"Do you have prophetic visions, Demon King?!" Denis's eyes are sparkling.

Keith forces a smile. "Technically no, but milord's instincts tend to be on the mark."

"Me! What's going to happen to me, Demon King?! Please check!"

"You're fine. You'll be happy."

"Woo-hoo!" Denis throws his hands in the air and does a little jig.

Beelzebuth smiles happily. "That's terrific, Denis. The king's words are never wrong."

"Uh, in that case, maybe your uncle Jasper will ask, too."

"For the most part, the rest of you will have it rough."

The whole group looks aghast, which makes for quite the funny scene.

No matter how you think about it, there's no way they'll be rewarded. Not when they're serving someone else's fiancée with such devotion.

Instead of getting sarcastic with them, Claude begins to relate what his instincts tell him. "As an aside, in terms of woman trouble, Auguste is at the top of the list. Next is—"

"Why?! Why am I that far up?!"

"Don't worry, I'm speaking of the future. Currently, Isaac is in top place."

"I didn't ask, don't tell me, I don't believe it anyway!!"

"Uh, milord, milord. They'll stop working entirely, so that's enough of that. The rest of you, don't worry about it too much, all right?" Keith claps his hands lightly, taking control. He smiles sarcastically. "Besides, having woman trouble isn't so bad. I don't have a single romantic story to my name, you know. Lady Aileen and Rachel gave me chocolate this time, but who knows how many years it's been since the last time... Even Bel gets chocolate through milord's connections, and yet..."

"? What are you saying? People send you chocolate every year, too—"

"Bel."

He's stopped him too late.

Keith, who's twice as sharp as average when it comes to Claude, as well as more formidable than the others, slowly looks his way.

Furtively averting his eyes, Claude takes a sip of cold tea.

"...Sire?"

"My tea is cold, Keith."

"Master Claude. You know what will happen if you aren't honest, don't you?"

He does, so he sighs. Then he looks him straight in the eye. "What choice did I have? If you got married, who would take care of me?"

Silence falls. Then his adviser's anger flares. The ones who stand between them are, naturally, Claude's guards.

"E-e-e-e-easy, easy, easy, Sir Keith, just calm down, okay? Geez, come on! Master Claude, apologize!"

"I don't wanna."

"Are you a child?! Well, I certainly raised you wrong, didn't I!!"

"No blades! Please, please don't use a blade! If you bare steel, as his guards, we'll have to get involved!"

"Man, there had to be a better way to do that. Your uncle Jasper really feels for you, guy."

"...That adviser's going to go bald one of these days."

"Shall we make him a potion that's effective against baldness ahead of time, Quartz?"

Claude's surroundings have grown considerably more colorful. Keith has completely snapped, while the demon king's two guards are desperately trying to stop him. Beelzebuth is flustered. James is appalled. Auguste is dejectedly muttering about woman trouble, and Isaac and the rest are watching him in disgust.

And most of all...

"What on earth is all this commotion?! What did you do, Master Claude?!"

Astounded, Aileen rushes in. That's all it takes to make Claude's lips soften into a smile.

Happiness is days like this one.

"It's nothing you need to worry about, Aileen. More importantly, do you have any requests for your White Day present?"

"Huh? ...I—I, um...erm... If it's a present from you, Master Claude, then anything's..."

"It's pretty amazing that you can focus on love in a situation like this!"

"What's this White Day business?! I don't suppose you'd give me back my Valentine's chocolates, you incorrigible master?!"

The people around him are yowling about something or other, but Claude keeps his eyes on his sweet fiancée and promises her something special.

Of course, he's picked up on the truth serum she's laced that chocolate cake with. He doesn't know why she'd do a thing like that, but it's not as if it will work on him anyway. In order to set an example, though, he'll need to punish her.

This probably calls for an ice mansion, doesn't it?

White Day is sure to be lively—in more ways than one.

As This Is the World of an *Otome* Game, White Day Comes Even for Ladies-in-Waiting

Under a clear sky that heralds spring's arrival, on a lawn bright with new growth, there stands a very chilly mansion.

"Master Claude... What is this?"

"Your White Day return present. Spend the day here, alone with me." The demon king flashes her a breezy smile.

Rachel's mistress responds awkwardly, "I...haven't, uh, done...anything..."

"You're not to blame, of course. I'm the one who made you uneasy. I had no idea my past relations with women concerned you so much that you'd put truth serum in my Valentine's Day chocolate. And so this is proof of my love for you," the demon king tells her, his voice dulcet and bewitching. "You doubted my love because that love was lacking, and I've repented."

"N-no, I'm— It's enough! I—I only added the truth serum on a whim because I thought it might reveal some weakness, or an embarrassing episode from your past..."

A sudden blast of wind that feels like spring buffets them from behind.

The demon king's aura has grown more intimidating. Aileen's smile tenses, and she shrieks. "I—I wanted to know more about you!"

"I see. In that case, you really must spend the whole day in that mansion with me. I want you to feel my love from head to toe. Or shall I whisper sweet nothings to you all day in my office?"

"I'll enter the mansion!"

Her discerning mistress boldly starts toward the mansion of ice.

As the demon king watches her walk away, the corners of his lips rise in satisfaction.

Seeing this, Rachel is certain the choice was a trap. Her mistress is bound to totter back home this evening, delirious from the heat of the demon king's love.

Unexpectedly, her eyes meet those of Claude's adviser. "This is pretty ominous for White Day, isn't it? I'm sorry."

"No, I think it's very like Prince Claude. I'll accept as many of the others' return presents as I can on Lady Aileen's behalf. I'm sure he won't mind if she looks them over together at a later date."

Rachel has picked up on Claude's reason for shutting Aileen inside the ice mansion. Keith's eyes widen, and then he smiles faintly. "That's a great help. He really did just want time alone with Lady Aileen, though. I'm truly glad she's so tolerant— Oh, that's right. Here."

He drops an adorably decorated paper bag into her hands. The cord that binds the mouth of the bag has several different types of small, dainty flowers tied into it.

"You and Lady Aileen made a tremendous quantity of chocolates for Valentine's Day, and so this is your White Day present from me and the demons."

"Goodness, you didn't need to."

"No, that wouldn't do. It would disgrace the demon king if we weren't able to thank a lady properly. —It's candy the demons particularly recommend; I put up the money, and Beelzebuth purchased it. The demons all chose the flowers together."

"Thank you very much." She can vividly picture the role division that went into preparing this, and she giggles. Keith gives her a mature, sophisticated smile and tells her she's welcome.

"I'm sure you'll be busy today. I'll take care of both Lady Aileen and milord, so please enjoy your White Day."

"Oh no, I couldn't—"

"Those are Lady Aileen's wishes as well."

Keith has been an attendant far longer than Rachel has, and she's no match for him. Smiling wryly, she thanks him once again.

White Day is special only to women who've shown courage on Valentine's Day.

However, Rachel doesn't expect much from it.

The man she's thinking of wants Rachel to be nothing more than his coworker, and he'd never tried to find out whether that orange peel had been a special touch meant just for him.

"Huh?! Ailey's with the demon king in an ice mansion... What are we supposed to do now? Do you think they'd let me in?"

"If you're with us, it should be fine. He'd never kick his security detail out. No, absolutely not."

"Yeah, if he did that, we'd kick the door down and break up his rendezvous with sweet Ailey."

"You two are really starting to seem like the demon king's guards, huh!"

"...You're getting full of yourselves. You're only guards."

"Aha. James is jealous."

"Who's jealous?!"

Having heard about the situation from Rachel, the former

student council members are heading for the mansion in a noisy group.

They've each given Rachel return presents. Delicious cookies, a handkerchief, a hairpin adorned with flowers, a simple dictionary of foreign languages. Each giver's personality shows through in his gift. Frankly, Rachel hadn't expected to get a return present from James. She hadn't even been sure he remembered her name, but apparently he's aware she exists.

Although Rachel had offered to accept Aileen's gifts for her, they'd all said they'd deliver them in person. That seems like a sign their consciences are clear, so she's only seen them off, without trying to stop them.

In contrast, all the members of the Oberon Trading Firm have entrusted their gifts to Rachel.

"Oh, in that case, please give her this! I think this music box will go really well with the ice mansion."

"Uncle Jasper here would also like to take you up on that offer. Give her this pair of tickets, and tell her to go have fun with the demon king… He can't possibly get mad about that, right?"

"Please take this perfume as well, then. Do tell her we won't be turning it into a product."

"…Put these in water as soon as you can. They just bloomed this morning."

Then they all gave Rachel the same things they were giving Aileen.

It's like they're forestalling an attack. Rachel laughs quietly to herself. Everyone's clever when it comes to navigating the demon king's feelings.

She's sure Isaac will use the same approach.

Due to this expectation, the fact that he's waiting for her in the corridor doesn't fluster her.

"Here," he says curtly, pushing a rectangular box at her.

Rachel is just on her way to leave Aileen's presents at the d'Autriche estate, so she checks with him. "Is it for Lady Aileen?"

"Huh? Why?"

"Lady Aileen is scheduled to spend the day with the demon king in a mansion of ice, so it may be best to leave return gifts for her with me."

"An ice mansion? What, he seriously made that...?" Isaac sighs in disgust, then holds the box out to her again. Before she can assure him she'll pass it on to Aileen, he says, "It's for you."

"What?"

While she's still blinking at him, Isaac looks away. Unable to hide her surprise, Rachel timidly accepts the box. "Th-thank you very much. May I open it?"

"...Go for it."

Setting Aileen's presents on a nearby console table, she unwraps the package, heart racing. Upon opening the box, she finds a necklace.

A transparent, pale blue jewel rests in a silver loop shaped like a drop of water. Is it an aquamarine? The simplicity makes its exquisite design even more apparent.

Placing the necklace on her palm, she murmurs in spite of herself. "It's lovely..."

"Glad to hear it. See you."

"What? Um, what about Lady Aileen's present? Will you give it to her yourself?"

Isaac, who's just turning to leave, stops in his tracks. "Does that mean you don't want me to?"

"N-no, that isn't what I…" Hastily, she begins making excuses, then collects herself with a start. That isn't a suitable reaction for Aileen's lady-in-waiting.

She needs to tell him more calmly.

"—Lady Aileen is scheduled to spend the day alone with Prince Claude. I don't know whether he will permit you to have any time with her. Therefore, I believe Lady Aileen will be more likely to receive it if you allow me to take it back to the d'Autriche estate."

"…Yeah?"

He gives her a significant look, but she's told him the truth, so she holds her head high.

There's a short silence, as if they're probing each other's intentions. Isaac's the one to break it. "Too bad. I didn't get Aileen anything. Yours was my only return present."

"What?"

"Look, Aileen makes me do tons of reckless stuff on a regular basis, and she owes me anyway."

In other words, their relationship has progressed beyond the point where Valentine's Day and White Day are anything to make a fuss over?

This makes sense to her, but on the other hand, she's not entirely happy about it.

"That orange peel was tasty, though, so that's my thank-you. I like oranges quite a bit, actually."

Saying either *"I know"* or *"Oh, you do?"* seems brazen, but she can't come up with a better response right away.

Either would have been fine; the important thing had been to casually acknowledge what he'd said and move on. If she'd done that, she could have kept him from noticing she'd been paying attention to his response, to see whether he'd realized she'd made his chocolates special by adding orange peel.

"See you," Isaac says, turning away. The corners of his lips have definitely risen.

I was careless...!

She'd never dreamed he'd try to sound her out this long after the fact. He's caught her completely off guard.

Besides, that isn't the only thing Isaac's left behind.

He said mine was his only return present!

He's left an incredible bombshell as well.

Leaning against the corridor wall, Rachel covers her face with her hands and groans. He's one tough customer. She does admire him for that, but it's embarrassing.

...I may not be suited to these things. Still, I have to give it my best.

After all, if she only loves and idolizes him, she's sure he'll never look at her.

"Welcome home, Lady Aileen."

"Rachel... I... I've made it back, haven't I... I've returned from that mansion alive...!"

"Y-you must be very tired. You'll want to go to bed immediately, won't you?"

"No, I'll work. If I sleep now, Master Claude is sure to appear in my dreams...! He'll close in on me with that lethal face and voice of his! I doubt I'd ever wake again!"

"I—I see... Oh, Lady Aileen, your White Day return presents from everyone are over there."

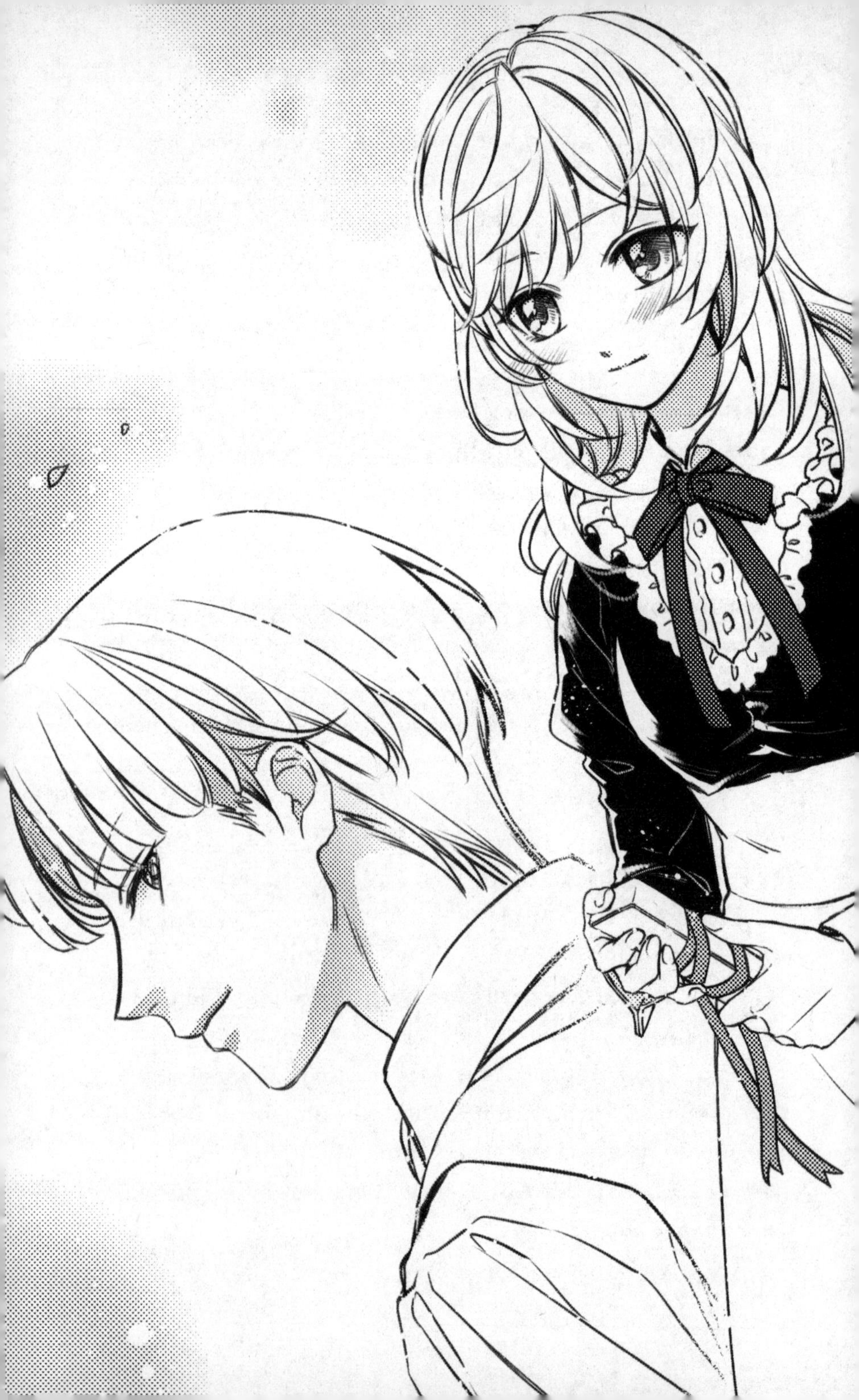

"Come to think of it, Rachel, how did it go? With Isaac, I mean."

She's wearing the necklace under her uniform, where it can't be seen. Tracing it with a fingertip, Rachel smiles at the mistress she loves and respects.

"It's a secret."

✦ Third Act ✦
What Manner of Thing Is Love?

"Serena! Why did you cancel on me yesterday?!"

Auguste's angry question echoes through the imperial castle's laundry.

Serena only gives him a cold look, then walks away with her laundry basket.

Auguste freezes up, shocked. Then he hastily goes after her. "Hey— Serena, come on."

"......"

"Why didn't you come to the dinner party yesterday? Everybody else did."

"......"

"Were you not feeling good? You could have said something—"

"Die," she tells him, glaring sharply.

He can't understand it. He promptly comes to his senses, though, and falls in beside her. "You'll never make friends if you act like that."

"......"

"I mean, sure, after all the stuff you pulled, I bet it's awkward to be around the others, but—"

"Die."

"Look, why do you keep saying that?!"

"Because you're a child who has no grasp of the subtleties between men and women, obviously!"

She's shouted back at him twice as ferociously, and he blinks, stunned. She sets off again, and he hastily runs to catch up with her.

Um, no, that's not it!

That's not what he's trying to say. He tends to end up getting emotional with Serena, and conversations just don't go well.

"It's fine that you canceled on me— I mean, it's not, but forget it. Everyone said it was only natural, and I realized I'd been in the wrong, too."

"…You did?"

Her expression is filled with suspicion, but she's finally looked at him, so he nods back, solemnly. "You and I aren't friends yet, so it would have been tactless of me to surround one girl with a bunch of guys."

"…I really do think you should die."

"Look, why do you always— No, not that! Listen! This time, let's go somewhere, just the two of us!"

Serena stops.

Auguste nearly runs into her slim back, and he hastily catches himself.

Moving as stiffly as a broken doll, Serena turns back. When she speaks, her voice seems to have a curse in it. "—What was that?"

"Huh? I said the two of us should go somewhere together… Our next days off are on the same day."

"How do you know when I have time off?"

"I had James check for me."

"Oh, I see. The cambion's gotten real full of himself, now that he's a young nobleman." She practically spits out the words, *tsk*ing in irritation. He wants to ask her not to talk like that, but he keeps it to himself.

Aileen has cautioned him about that. She said that if he wanted to ask Serena out again, self-restraint would be everything.

"...Can't we?"

He peered up at her through his lashes, using the secret technique the demon king taught him.

One of Serena's eyebrows rises, and she gazes at him for a few moments. Then, with an extremely long sigh, she gives an answer that doesn't seem as if it could have come from the same place as that chilly gaze. "All right."

"Huh?! You're kidding!"

"Actually, never min—"

"Okay! That's a promise!"

If she backs out over his careless remark, this whole back-and-forth will have been for nothing.

Auguste sets a meeting place and time without giving her a chance to refuse, and then they go their separate ways.

Several days later...

"You know, I had the feeling it would end up like this..."

Their day off is also a general holiday, and parents with children, couples, and groups of friends are streaming past Auguste. He and Serena had promised to meet for lunch an hour ago. There's a clock tower beside the shop, and the clock's long hand has already made one full circle.

Well, maybe something happened. Either that, or she got the time wrong.

Two hours pass.

...Or maybe she got the date wrong?

Three hours.

No, no, James and Kyle and Walt all told me up and down to brace myself for something like this.

Four hours.

And I'm the one who decided I still wasn't going to give up.

Five hours.

I don't know why I'm getting so worked up about this. Still, it wouldn't be right to desert a girl who was our friend for a little while...

Six hours.

Come to think of it, how come Serena's going to stop trying to become Prince Cedric's mistress if I become successful? I mean, it's fine. Whatever gets her to stop, but...

Seven hours.

Actually, how long am I supposed to wait? If she shows up after I leave, though...

Eight hours.

I'm really getting hungry.

Nine hours.

I seriously don't know when to head home.

Ten hours.

"What am I even doing...?"

Auguste gazes out over the street, which is now pitch dark. He's been crouched at the edge of a flower bed so as not to obstruct traffic to and from the shop, but the shop's been closed for ages now.

It's already close to midnight. In sharp contrast to how lively the place was when he first arrived, the foot traffic has grown quite sparse.

...It has to be okay for me to get mad about this, right?

Okay, then. I'll do that tomorrow.

Making up his mind, Auguste rises to his feet. Maybe because he's been crouched down for so long, his joints creak just a little. He hasn't trained anywhere near enough yet.

That probably goes for his heart as well as his body.

He sighs so heavily his shoulders slump, then stretches. The moon looks full tonight. He's wondering if that's why his surroundings seem so bright when he hears it.

The *click* of a heel on paving stones.

"You're still waiting? Are you stupid?"

A white skirt flares, and he catches a light, sweet scent on the night wind. Long, perfectly straight silver hair glimmers in the moonlight.

"Serena..."

"Anyone normal would have gone home, you know."

If he said her exasperated tone didn't get to him, he'd be lying. Even more than that, though... "I toughed it out, and I won."

He gives her a faint smile, and Serena scowls. "For your information, I was only passing by. I'm not here because I was wondering or anything, so don't get the—"

"Serena. For now, just be friends with me."

"Are you stupid?"

"I'm serious."

Serena falls silent, her forehead furrowed.

Gazing straight at her face, Auguste continues, "I haven't forgiven you for what you did to James, but...I do think I was making fun of you on some level. If it made you do a thing like that, because you couldn't rely on anybody, then it was partly my fault, too."

"......"

"James says that had nothing to do with it, but I can't see it that way... The thing is, I always wondered why you were so desperate, but wondering was all I did."

He'd arbitrarily concluded she probably just wanted to stand out, had arrogantly laughed it off, and hadn't even bothered to hear her side of the story. He'd known she was playing him for a fool, and yet he'd paid no attention to why she kept trying to get close to him.

Serena had been in the wrong, of course. She's done something unforgivable. Even Auguste knows that.

However.

"I could have at least listened to you. There was plenty of time."

Serena Gilbert has been declared dead, and it's probably going to be hard for her to lead a decent life.

Time can't be rewound.

He's voicing his regrets, just as they are.

"In other words, you're being smug."

"Don't put it like— Dwah?!"

She's abruptly shoved everything she's carrying into his hands, and a tower of boxes blocks his view. A round box on the very top teeters, and Auguste has to flail around to keep it from falling. "Wh-what is all this?" he yells.

"I refuse to be your friend. I'll let you be my porter, though."

"Huh?! Hey, wait—"

Skirt flaring lightly, Serena sets off. Auguste follows, still carrying her parcels. "Wait just a minute, Serena! What is all this?"

"Today's shopping. I was Lady Aileen's guard at her wedding the other day, remember? It earned me a tidy sum, so I blew it all today. I had somebody else carrying that for me until a minute ago, though. It really is too heavy to lug around on my own."

"Well, yeah, if you've got this much... Wait, you were out on the town today?! Who with?! Don't tell me you were tricking somebody again!!"

"It has nothing to do with you, does it?"

"Actually, in that case, couldn't you just have gone out with me—?"

Auguste's criticism is interrupted by a protracted, dumb-sounding gurgle.

His stomach has begun growling up a storm, and the noise makes Serena turn around. "What? Don't tell me you haven't eaten."

"That's your fault, Serena!"

"Want this?"

She holds out a waffle in a triangular paper wrapper. Belatedly, Auguste realizes that it's the source of the sweet scent he keeps picking up. *Huh? No, but "Want this"....?*

Both of his hands are full. Serena is still waiting, holding out the waffle.

In other words, this is one of those "Say 'aaaah'" situations.

He's getting nervous. Even though he's fine with snitching food out of James's hands.

Swallowing hard, he timidly leans in.

Just before his lips reach the waffle, she whisks it away.

"......"

She was teasing him. At a time like this. After she stood him up. When he's desperately hungry.

Anger boils up inside him. "Serena...!"

"Moooron."

However, at the sight of her moonlit smile, his anger just evaporates.

It isn't a mocking sneer or a flirty smile. It's a genuine grin, from a normal girl.

"Boys are seriously too easy."

"……"

"What? Are you mad? In that case, you're free to leave my things here and go home."

"…One more time." His voice is hoarse.

"What?" Serena turns back, and he says it again. "Smile one more time."

Silence falls, but he doesn't realize he's messed up until Serena's eyebrows come down.

Before he can make an excuse, she's shoved the waffle into his mouth and turned her back on him. "Boys are the worst."

He wants to say *That's not what I meant*, but the waffle is in the way.

She was cute.

But saying it would probably make her really angry. Besides, that might have only been an illusion.

Oh, man… So I'm starting from "porter"?

The road to friendship is going to be a long one. He almost sighs, but he fights it back as he heads down the moonlit street.

For some reason, his mood is good enough to make him think, *Well, I guess that's okay.*

·

Behind her, she hears humming. As always, the man makes no sense. She's made him her porter, and even then, he's humming to himself as he follows her.

He really is dumb. Dumb to the core.

It's probably safe to say he still hasn't noticed.

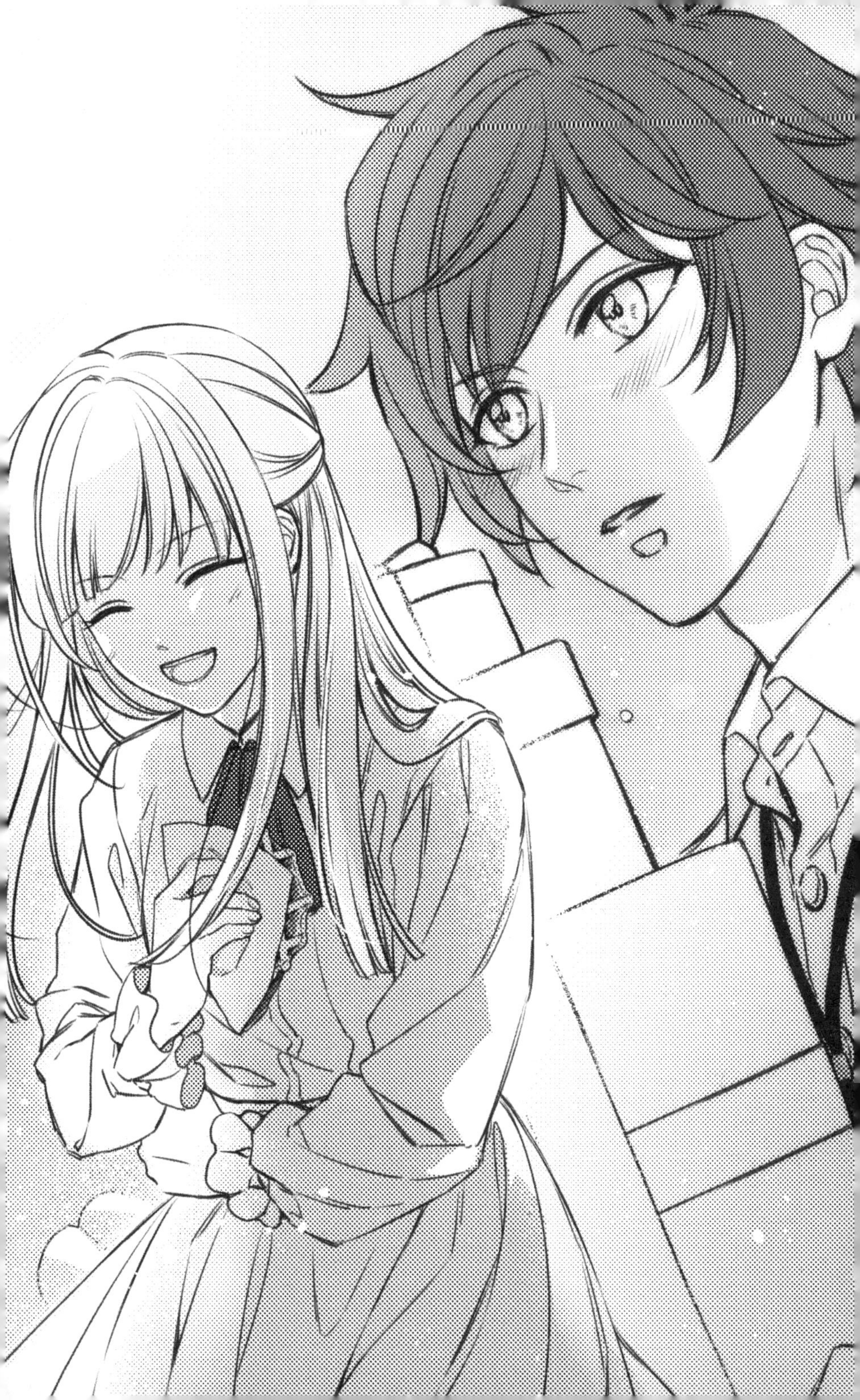

Her face is bright red, and her heart is beating very loudly.

It's from anger.

It's absolutely, positively not because he asked her to smile. It's not because he gave her that look, so unlike his usual friendly, irritating expression— A gaze that seemed to peer into the depths of her heart. It isn't because his tone held a hint of dark sweetness, and hearing it made her a little dizzy.

You simply wanted to love without being calculating, like a regular girl. You wanted ordinary days, didn't you?

The face of a nasty woman who looks like she knows everything rises in her mind. However, she threw all that away along with her life as a student, which hadn't even lasted a year.

She has no time to indulge in romance, no time to adore anyone. If she wastes her youth on stupid dreams like that, all the best men will be taken before she knows it. She doesn't want to consign herself to a life of wretchedness forever.

"Serena, be punctual next time."

"…Haven't you learned your lesson yet?"

"No."

Still, if love is something you fall into, what manner of thing might it be?

The man she'd once fantasized might be the one who gives her a carefree smile, oblivious to what she's feeling.

Love Is Something You Fall Into

This is the worst.

We have to let Aileen get away. If the demons and humans fight, we'll plunge the land into an ugly war even if the demon king does come back. We have to avoid that, no matter what.

It doesn't matter if the demon king returns when they're already in checkmate.

Everyone wants the demon king back, so Isaac thinks about what will come after that. *Minimal sacrifices, maximum effect.*

Plus someone who doesn't mind being sacrificed.

All the pawns are in place.

"…We'll send out a decoy and confuse them."

Yeah, this is the worst, and so is he.

Even he knows how awful it is to tell a girl who likes him to sacrifice herself for some other girl.

He has to do it, though.

The one who has to get away safely is Aileen.

Rachel knows that as well as he does.

"All right. Then I shall pass myself off as Lady Aileen."

He thought she'd probably agree. He'd known she might even volunteer.

Still, he's the worst. Absolute scum.

Since that's so, he thinks her response will probably be contempt or disappointment, something like that.

After all, he's telling her to die for some other girl. And yet.

"Thanks for your help."

She gives a lovely smile and nods, there in the morning light. Proudly. Kindly.

Isaac's eyes widen. He turns his back, so she won't notice he's shaken.

The worst.

He squeezes his fists, clenches his teeth. He really is the worst. He was like this with Aileen, too.

Her engagement had been broken in a truly nasty way, and even so, she hadn't cried. When he'd seen her like that, after he was in no position to tell her he loved her, it had finally hit him that he did.

In other words—he always realizes he's fallen in love at the worst possible time.

"My next day off? I'm sorry. I already have plans."

"Oh, I see."

Isaac had assumed she'd refuse, so he backs down without a fight.

With a patently artificial smile, Rachel says, "Another time, perhaps," and goes back to work. He can tell she doesn't mean it.

What other time? She's used that line to turn me down five times in a row.

Apparently, her days off are all booked up. Must be nice to be her. Maybe because she was running out of ideas, she'd spent all day holed up at home the other day. Who knew what she'd do this time?

Even though she has to know he's casually having Almond

and the others scout and check on her movements— In other words, they're blatantly probing each other.

It isn't interfering with their work. She probably doesn't want to let personal business come into this, either. Since that's so, their work is going superficially smoothly, exactly like it did before. That means he's got no complaints.

After all, a few minutes after reaching his realization, Isaac had settled on a policy of maintaining the status quo.

"It's pretty futile, though…"

For example, the moment he spots her, his eyes automatically follow her.

Grumbling, he rests his elbows on the window frame. The courtyard of the imperial castle spreads out below him. Rachel's down there, discussing something with Quartz. The basket she's holding is rapidly filling up with flowers. She's probably getting advice about decorations or the bride's bouquet. The crown prince and princess's wedding is just around the corner.

Isaac, who's escaped up here because he'd gotten sick of dealing with fashionable aristocrats, gazes down at her absently.

The wind that blows into the empty room is pleasant, and it's making him really drowsy. He's tired from running around preparing for the wedding, and a yawn escapes him. This room doesn't even get cleaned all that often, and it's on a high floor of a deserted tower. Since they're short-handed, Isaac's been press-ganged into helping with the wedding preparations, and it's the perfect place to slack off.

Rachel's discussion seems to be over; she trots away, holding her basket. His eyes follow her— It really is futile.

I've made zero progress, huh…

He's maintaining their relationship as coworkers. He's noticed his feelings but is pretending he hasn't, just the way he did with hers.

In short, it's like it was with Aileen. He's determined that that's the best, safest move. If he can't decide between attacking and retreating, it's strategic to maintain the status quo.

In any case, Isaac isn't convinced yet.

I mean, frankly, she's not my type. It has to be some kind of mistake, right? Like that thing that makes it easier to catch feelings during emergencies. Yeah, the suspension bridge effect.

Granted, if somebody asked him what his type was, he'd have a heck of a time telling them, but at the very least— Aileen had been his first love, and she and Rachel are completely different.

Rachel is shy and reserved, a follower rather than a leader. Apparently she wants to become a dashing woman, but the fact that she wants to be one means that's not what she is right now. Not only that, but she can't trick people or sell them out. Aileen was right to choose her as her lady-in-waiting.

However, as a lady-in-waiting, Rachel can be surprisingly strong, and Isaac's just a little uncomfortable with it. Thanks to that, although she doesn't do it with anyone else, she gets pretty high-handed with him so he won't realize how she feels, and she even tests him.

"...That's not cute, either..."

"Look, it's not that complicated." His thoughts are interrupted by a voice that drifts up from below. "You just need to get me a connection to the Oberon Trading Firm."

"I don't know what you're talking about."

Rachel changes directions, trying to distance herself from the wall of Isaac's building, but a man gets in front of her, blocking her way. Isaac recognizes his face, and his eyes narrow. *He's with a* company that has access to the castle. *The rumors about him aren't good, though.*

"You know them, right? At least hear me out."

"...I have work to do. If you'll excuse me."

"Don't be like that. Listen, just introduce me to one of the Oberon Trading Firm executives. Lady Aileen is Duke d'Autriche's daughter, isn't she? She's bound to have a connection to them."

Aileen is the president of the Oberon Trading Firm. However, she'd concealed that fact to avoid attracting the attention of the former crown prince Cedric, who almost certainly would've tried to crush the company. The secrecy also conveniently increased the brand's cachet. The Oberon executives' identities are still being kept secret, with the d'Autriche dukedom officially acting as the primary line of contact for the trading firm.

They're planning to create a public representative and separate the trading firm from the d'Autriche duchy in the near future. Aileen apparently intends to make Isaac the representative, but nothing's settled yet.

However, if somebody's harassing Rachel about it, they should probably hurry.

Just as he's feeling disgusted about having more work, he hears the man's grating voice. "Come on, I'm begging you. I bragged to my old man that I had an in with the Oberon Trading Firm."

"That may be, but I have no connection to the firm. In addition, Lady Aileen is the crown prince's consort. I can't grant you an audience with her."

"Please."

The man is pleading in a melodramatically humble way, but it's all just for show. Rachel probably thinks she's being very firm in dealing with him, but it's obvious he'll snap and lash out at her any minute now.

Can't the idiot evade a little better than that? Being high-handed always comes back to bite you.

That said, if he sticks his oar in, it will only complicate things. He doesn't want more trouble. Sighing, he leans out the window, looking up, and spots some crows conducting a regular patrol in neat formation.

"Hey— Hey! You're demons, right?"

"Isaac! What's wrong?"

When he calls up to them—loudly enough that they'll hear, softly enough that the people below won't notice—a crow with a red bow tie flies down to him. It's Almond.

Isaac puts a finger to his lips, gesturing for him to be quiet, then beckons him closer. Almond loves secrets; he lands on the windowsill and nods eagerly.

"That guy down there. Think you can run him off?"

"...Rachel?"

"Yeah. He's messing with her. Help her out, Captain."

"Understood. I'll take her frying pan."

"Uh, why? That's not what I—"

"You wench! I come to you hat in hand, and you still—"

Sure enough, the merchant suddenly starts shouting. *Oh man...* Isaac looks down.

Rachel has shrunk back, startled, but she lifts her head resolutely. Even though her eyes are full of fear. She's just like... Aileen.

There's absolutely no need for her to be like Aileen, and yet...

"No matter what you say, if I don't know, I can't—"

"Huhn?! What, so it's gonna take pain to get you to list— Gah!" *Crud*, he thinks, but he's already done it.

He hadn't planned to help her out himself, but...

A book has fallen from the window, striking the man squarely on the head. Writhing in pain, he looks up, then bellows at him. "What the hell?! Was that you?!"

"Uh... Yeah, sorry, I dropped that."

He's committed now; he'll have to fudge his way through. Rachel's finally noticed him, but bailing out a coworker is a perfectly natural thing to do.

Steeling himself, Isaac gives an amiable smile. "It looks like you're not hurt, though. That's great."

"Like hell I'm not! You're the Lombard Company's third son, right?! Get down here!"

"C'mon, don't get so worked up. I'll give you something better than the Oberon Trading Firm."

"Huhn?"

He slips an envelope out of his breast pocket. It's something he always carries with him, just in case. He drops it out of the window, and although the man looks suspicious, he shuffles left and right, eventually managing to catch the envelope. "What is this, a check or something? Hmph! Don't think I'll let you off that ea— ...Th-this letter of introduction... Is this real?!"

"Yeah, it's real," he assures him, his expression sober.

The man gulps audibly. Then he hastily slips the envelope into his jacket, says, "I'll be leaving now," and bustles away.

The man's true to his desires, which is a huge help. Isaac sighs with relief.

Almond cocks his head. **"What was that?"**

"An invitation to Heaven."

"That envelope… It was a letter of introduction to a high-class brothel, wasn't it?" Rachel's murmur seems oddly loud to him.

His fingertips flinch guiltily, but she can't have seen it from down there. He feigns calm. "It's the perfect way to get rid of people like that in a hurry."

"…Do you have an acquaintance there?"

"Is that something you need to know?" he asks, keeping his tone intentionally cold.

Rachel pouts. She almost looks more like she's sulking than angry.

He definitely can't let the fact that he thinks it's cute show on his face. That would ruin everything.

"No, it's nothing to do with me. No matter who you become acquainted with or how, provided it doesn't cause trouble for Lady Aileen, it's no concern of mine."

"Aileen knows anyway."

"—Does she! In that case, I've made too much of it. Thank you very much for saving me. Now if you'll excuse me."

Expressing her gratitude in a monotone that isn't the least bit cute, Rachel turns on her heel.

Relieved, Isaac drops his forehead onto the windowsill.

Almond looks back and forth between Rachel and Isaac several times. **"She hate you now?"**

"It's fine. Not a problem."

He's not completely satisfied, but the status quo has been maintained. Mission accomplished.

He doesn't put the fact that he helped her, uncharacteristically and without thinking, on his mental agenda. He also pretends not to notice that his eyes don't leave her receding back until she's out of sight.

If he was going to save her, he could have done it in a slightly more decent way.

Rachel knows she's venting her anger on him unfairly, but she can't help herself, and her steps grow rougher. Whoever Isaac spends time with, or how, it's absolutely no concern of Rachel's. She intends to become a woman who can laugh such things off with grace and composure.

At the very least, she understands Isaac belongs to a world where that sort of thing is necessary, and most of all—

...*He was dashing.*

Aaaaaagh. Writhing silently, Rachel crouches down.

Regardless of what he'd actually said, the fact that he'd kept a cool head and managed to resolve the situation really had been dashing.

No matter what sort of look Rachel turns on him, she's sure he'll let it roll right off. That's frustrating, and she wishes she could do the same.

"I bet the fact that I keep turning down his invitations isn't affecting him much, either…"

He even seems to have realized that she's making a point of refusing him at every turn. He's a truly formidable opponent. A sigh escapes her.

Even so, she's glad. There's no need for Isaac to feel guilty.

When he'd designated Rachel as Aileen's decoy, he'd made

the right choice. The fact that he assumed she'd do it if he asked is irritating; however, Rachel fell for him because he was that sort of person. She'd wanted him to rely on her.

She wishes she could at least tell him that, but she can't.

After all, she's still weak. If she confesses that she loves him and he rejects her, she can't even imagine what would become of her. The very thought is frightening.

And so, until then, she'll maintain the status quo.

I hope I'm on his mind at least a little, though.

Rachel just can't seem to take her eyes off him. She hopes the same thing will happen to Isaac someday.

However, love is something one falls into, so giving someone a good, solid push is far better than wishing.

No One Minds How Often You Fall

"This schedule needs to be reworked. There's also an error in the procedure, so I'd like the documents redrafted."

"Oh, you're right. What would you like to do with the budget for this, Master Claude?"

"It's fine as is, but tell them to make sure they have enough to cover labor costs. Some of the petitions in that box have been stamped with my seal; I'd like to have demons check on those situations."

"Maybe we could let Almond handle that."

"That sounds good. And that should do it for the morning's work. All that's left is—"

Having finished going over the jobs in his office, Claude looks up from the documents to glance at the door. Keith steps back slightly, turning to follow his gaze. The guards behind them look in the same direction.

Sapphire eyes are watching them steadily from the shadow of the door.

"...Why don't you come in already, Aileen?"

His fiancée is staring at him through a crack just wide enough for a hand to fit through. For some reason, she refuses to enter the room; he's called to her several times already.

However, she always tells him the same thing, with only half her face showing from behind the door. "Please don't concern yourself with me."

"You can say that, but, erm…"

"Let's break for lunch, Master Claude!" Unusually, Keith is the one to suggest a recess. He leans down to whisper in Claude's ear. "I'll buy you time, so hurry and get that cleared up."

"I don't think I did anything, though."

He means it.

In the first place, Aileen has only just recovered. She'd pushed herself very hard while Claude's memories were missing, and lately he's only been able to see her when he visits her sickroom. During yesterday's visit, nothing had seemed wrong, and she'd told him cheerfully she'd be able to look in at the old castle for the first time in ages.

She's looked in today, as she'd said—but "looking in" is literally all she's done.

"Don't do the impossible and get your engagement broken this late in the game. Preparing for your wedding is the reason we're so busy right now. Walt and Kyle, let's go to lunch. It's fine to leave your posts."

Inviting his guards to come along, his considerate adviser leaves the room. Walt and Kyle, whose mission is to protect Claude, follow him without objecting.

He'd thought Aileen might come in when the other three left, but apparently it won't be that easy.

Conscientiously returning the open door to its previous position, she resumes peeking in.

"……"

"……"

"…Are you still feeling unwell?"

"...No."

Her tone is unusually stiff. She doesn't seem to be angry, though.

Claude taps his index finger on his desk once, thinking. Then he calls to her, making his tone intentionally sweet. "Aileen?"

On the other side of the door, she squirms just a little.

He continues gently, in order to make it clear that he isn't the least bit angry with her. "If you won't talk to me, I can't tell what you'd like to do."

"......"

"Or should I resolve this based on my own interpretation?"

His threat is laced with a sweetness like poison, but even then, she doesn't react. Still, he can tell she's hesitating, so he waits patiently.

After a little while, an indistinct murmur reaches him. "...ember me...?"

"Aileen."

"—Do you really remember me?"

His eyes widen.

Aileen shrinks back even further behind the door, although she's careful to keep half her face visible. "You haven't forgotten me again?"

Oh. Affection fills his heart, and in that moment, she falls into his lap.

Aileen stares at him, stunned, and he wraps his arms around her, holding her close. Quickly realizing what's happened, she shrieks, "T-teleportation is cheating!"

"It's all right. I love you today, too," he whispers.

Aileen, who was about to struggle, freezes. Possibly because she feels embarrassed, she looks down and away, then begins making excuses in a small voice. "I-it isn't as if I don't believe you, Master Claude. It isn't that, really. It's just..."

"You're uneasy, aren't you?"

"N-no, I'm not. I just thought it might be better to make sure it was truly all right... I mean, the real issue is the ease with which you lost your memories, Master Claude, but even so!"

"That's true."

He nods back very seriously. Aileen seems to have collected herself; she glares up at him. "In the first place, letting Elefas deceive you was far too careless."

"Yes, there's really no excuse."

"It lost you both your memories and your magic; do you have any idea how much confusion the demons were thrown into? You are their king. Be more conscious of your position, if you would!"

The fact that Aileen doesn't point out that she was also uneasy and frightened is what's adorable about her. "Listen to me. Make sure nothing like this ever happens aga— You're laughing, aren't you?!"

"No, I'm not laughing. Can't you tell by looking at me?"

"You can't deceive me; the flowers in the vase have been growing more vibrant! You aren't sorry at all, are you!"

Even her angry expression is adorable.

If he's not careful, he feels as if he'll burst out laughing, so he gets his face under control. "I do regret it very much. I apologize."

"...I-in that case, I shall forgive you. At any rate, it's all in the past. And in the end, Master Claude, you did choose me."

She gives a proud, gloating little chuckle, and at that point, he's done for.

Covering his face with a hand, Claude laughs out loud.

Of course, Aileen is immediately furious. "Wh-why would you laugh at that?!"

"N-no. I just th-thought, you aren't very self-aware."

"Self-aware?! Master Claude, you are the one who doesn't understand the gravity of the—"

"Y-you're sulking, aren't you?"

Aileen's mouth falls open. Claude goes on, shoulders quivering. "You aren't the type to carp about things that are over and done with."

It had been the same during the incident with Cedric: Her engagement had been broken in the worst possible way, but she hadn't made a single complaint.

However, even though snide comments weren't like her, she hadn't been able to help herself with regard to Claude's amnesia. Her unease had compelled her to say that he'd been in the wrong.

How could he not find this endearing?

When he glances at her, Aileen's face turns scarlet from her neck all the way to the crown of her head. She genuinely hadn't been aware of it.

Claude tells her, sincerely and with affection, "It's all right. I fell in love with you again today."

"—I am going home!! Release me!"

Apparently her pride won't let her admit to sulking.

However, of course, he isn't going to let her get away.

"No. I'm responsible for this mood of yours."

"I-in the first place, I'm not in a mood! If you wish to be responsible, return to work!"

"What are you saying? I'm the only one who can rid you of your unease."

When he peeks into her face, speaking persuasively, Aileen says something to the effect of "That isn't true."

She understands, but she's stubborn.

That's what he likes about her, though.

"Rest assured. I'll spoil you until you melt today," Claude declares, smiling.

Aileen goes pale, then shrieks that special treatment won't be necessary.

I most certainly was not sulking, Aileen thinks, leaning limply against Claude's chest. To her chagrin, the contest had been decided in a mere five minutes.

It had been a torturous five minutes, and time enough to make it very clear that Claude's memories had indeed returned.

That's right. I'd lost as soon as Master Claude caught me.

She's begun to rather miss the purehearted version of Claude. Perhaps he'll come back? She wishes at least half of him would. Or a tenth of him, even.

However, it's true that hearing *I frightened you, I know, it's all right, I love you* over and over again has finally cleared away her unease.

That's the most embarrassing thing about this.

"I know. Since I have the chance, I'll list all the things that are adorable about you."

"That's enough, Master Claude. I'm...convinced...that your memories have returned..."

"There's no need to stand on ceremony."

"I'm not. I was wrong... In the first place, even if you do lose your memories, I'll simply have to make you mine as often as it takes."

She'd known that, and yet she'd brought up something foolish. That was what had landed her in this mess.

However, Claude looks happy, and she can't help but be slightly irritated with him. This isn't sulking. She'd just like to get a little revenge.

And so, with a spiteful smile, Aileen tests him. "Conversely, Master Claude, what would you do if I were to lose my memories?"

"You?"

"Yes. What if I cried and told you the demon king was horrifying and I wanted our engagement dissolved?!"

She can't imagine herself doing it, but it's entertaining to picture what Claude would be like if she did. Even she thinks this is rather vicious of her.

Still, Master Claude should endure at least a little trouble. I suffered a lot this time.

Would he do as she had done, refuse to give up even if she rejected him, and make her fall in love with him as often as it took?

Claude thinks seriously, one finger to his chin, and she waits eagerly for his response.

"Well, let's see…" Finally, he raises his head and gazes straight at Aileen. "First I'd lock you up—"

"Let us forget I ever asked!"

✦ Fourth Act ✦
Roxane Fusca

When she's dragged before the throne of the holy king, she feels like a prisoner.

She's certainly being treated like one.

Her fiancé—or rather, her former fiancé—had ordered two of his men to bind Roxane. Since then, he hasn't even looked at her.

She hasn't been permitted to make any excuses.

She has harassed the Daughter of God. That is her only crime.

That girl's a slave, a harem maid.

She's the holy king's possession. You mustn't pay attention to someone like that.

They extol her as the Daughter of God, but she isn't a suitable woman for you.

Do you intend to bring disgrace on the house of Fusca?

Are you constantly having trysts with my fiancé?

Know your place. You and I live in different worlds.

Roxane feels that all the things she said were correct. However, the more she said them, the frostier others became. She could see it in their eyes whenever they looked at her.

At this point, she understands it was only natural. If they called her a woman crazed by jealousy who had simply armed herself with logic, she had no way to argue.

There must have been some other way.

But I... I didn't do a thing...

"If you envy Sahra so much, I'll make you a harem maid," Ares had told her, sneering.

Those words have put the final crack in Roxane's parched love.

"King Baal. I've brought Roxane."

In other words, he's offering her to the holy king as a consort.

Giving his own fiancée to another man, as if she were an object.

Her love has crumbled away like dry sand, and now it changes into despair, drifting down and accumulating.

"Leave Roxane here. The rest of you, go."

"What? But sire—"

"You're giving this to us, aren't you? In that case, you have no right to interfere. Go."

Ares looks perplexed. Then he sighs and signals in her direction.

Roxane's hands have been bound behind her, so when they shove her away, she falls to the floor. A velvet carpet covers the marble, so the pain isn't as bad as she'd braced for.

As she hears rough footsteps leaving the room, she sees the toes of a pair of shoes start toward her.

The holy king. Baal Shah Ashmael...

The sacred ruler of the Kingdom of Ashmael.

The noblewomen of this land generally avoid contact with men who are not members of their own family. Although she knows his name, she doesn't know what he looks like. Even with regard to his reputation, all she's heard are rumors.

In the first place, even a royal consort must bow her head in the presence of this man, and she may not look him in the face unless he grants permission.

Naturally, it's unforgivable for her to receive an audience with him given her position, but all her strength has deserted her.

The only thing she can do is gaze vacantly up at the violet eyes that frown down at her and think, *They're lovely.*

The holy king doesn't get angry with her for it.

He simply looks at Roxane, who's lying there like a caterpillar.

"You've attacked the Daughter of God. No doubt this was inevitable…but they're treating you like a criminal, aren't they?"

Those words bring up a vague memory. *If I recall, Father said that King Baal was fond of the Daughter of God…*

That girl again.

In that case, he'll have no sympathy for her.

She no longer has the strength it would take to summon a defiant smile. She thinks only of her father, who was worried that the kingdom might be torn in two. Could she avoid causing trouble for him by ending her own life?

As she thinks that, she hears fingers snap.

The rope that binds her hands falls away, and she rises lightly into the air. Before her surprise wears off, she's seated on the floor.

It's magic. Or, no, it's sacred power, so calling it "magic" might be rude…

Her surprise makes her think something rather irrelevant. Once again, she looks up at the king.

Those lovely violet eyes again.

"Do you want to be principal consort?"

"What?"

She'd thought she'd cried her voice away, but she's spoken.

Impassively, the holy king asks again. "Would you be our principal consort?"

Her frozen mind begins to work again.

Ares has offered her to the harem. She'd assumed she would be used as a maid, but she is a daughter of the noble house of Fusca: If she's shown that much contempt, her father and the aristocrats around him won't stand for it.

Most of all, it would be bad if others thought the holy king had warped the class system and rules of the harem just for the Daughter of God. No doubt he would be mocked as the king a girl had rendered spineless.

Ares has made romantic advances on Sahra, a harem maid. Ordinarily, they would both have been put to death for it. However, Sahra is the Daughter of God, while Ares is a general who is very popular with the people. Executing them now, at a time when the world is anxious about the possible resurrection of the fiend dragon, would have been a poor move.

For that reason, this king has turned a blind eye to both of them.

And now he's offering her—a woman Ares has arrogantly handed her to him as a replacement—the position of principal consort.

He's trying to adjust the balance of power in the palace by putting me in that position.

If their only daughter became the holy king's principal consort, the house of Fusca's honor would remain intact.

Not only has Ares stolen his consort, but he's foisted his own fiancée onto him. It's an extremely humiliating scandal— But if that fiancée becomes the principal consort, it will be another story. No doubt people will speculate. Still, if the harem replaces the Daughter of God by acquiring a lady from the noble house of Fusca as its principal consort, no one will lose face.

It feels as if she's suddenly woken from a dream.

This man loves Sahra.

However, he's let her go and intends to make Roxane, the one who had plagued his beloved with foolish harassment, his principal consort. He's setting his own broken heart aside and putting the kingdom first.

"What do you say?"

"—Oh..."

"Either way, there's a humiliating future in store for you. No doubt everyone will assume you leaned on your family's influence and stole the principal consort's position for yourself. In addition, whether you are our principal consort or our harem maid, we will never visit you."

A principal consort in name only.

The options he's presented leave her dazed.

She can't believe she's actually being given a choice.

"What will you do, Roxane Fusca? Ares is foaming at the mouth, demanding we execute you. However, the Daughter of God betrayed the holy king, and yet she's been found innocent and released. Executing you alone would be arbitrary. We don't like that sort of thing."

Bitterness creeps into his words here and there, but even so, he speaks with the face of a king.

Even though he has feelings for Lady Sahra.

He's a fool.

If he makes Roxane his principal consort, the scandal will only continue to spread. He's taken a woman discarded by his love rival as his wife and has discarded the woman he loves. This is bound to hurt him, and even so, he's chosen what he considers the best path forward.

And yet here she is, feeling as if her life has ended over a pathetic excuse for a man.

As if...I...

As if I would end as that man's fiancée.

Gritting her teeth, she swallows down her scarred, broken love. She brushes away the despair that's drifting like sand.

She will become this king's principal consort.

It's all right if there's no love or romance there. The one thing—the only thing—she must not do is despair and end here.

After all, the man in front of her is standing all alone.

"—I humbly accept, Your Majesty. Please take me as your principal consort."

She rises to her feet, extending her attention all the way out to her fingertips, then curtsies flawlessly, as the greatest of noblewomen.

Narrowing his eyes, the holy king gives a self-mocking smile. No doubt he thinks she's a foolish woman, blinded by the position he's offered her.

That's fine. She doesn't deny it.

After all, it is true that she thought, *I would like to be your principal consort.*

Roxane remembers how Ares had looked when he heard she'd become the principal consort.

He'd seemed startled, like someone who'd been hurt for the first time.

Afterward, every time Roxane acted like the principal consort, he glared at her.

This man would one day turn against the holy king.

For some reason, she was sure of this, and she returned his glares.

I won't let you.

He is the one who is fit to be king, not you.

Such thoughts filled her mind. She thinks, absently, that she hadn't noticed the expression Baal was wearing behind her.

"You colluded with the fiend dragon because King Baal treated you coldly. Isn't that right?"

The gentle, soothing voice echoes in the gloomy dungeon.

In order to keep up appearances during her interrogation, they've allowed her to sit in a chair. Ares is seated across from her, on the other side of a small, square table made of wood.

"You were principal consort in name only. He neglected you."

He'd done so because, if he'd shown Roxane more affection than was necessary, it could have fostered ill will in those around them.

Baal had known that cordial treatment could end up cornering a principal consort whose position was already weak. Ares had once raged at him to execute her. Since there was no telling what the man might say, Baal had headed him off by giving her the bare minimum.

It had been a political decision, and entirely correct.

To think he doesn't even understand that! Oh, but I hadn't noticed, either...

The look in her husband's eyes as he'd watched her glare at Ares.

"You aren't the only one to blame here."

"......"

"Be honest with me, Roxane. The demon king took advantage of your loneliness to tempt you, didn't he?"

He probably intends that whisper as a mercy.

Out of nowhere, she thinks, *It may be my fault that this man plotted a rebellion.*

It's a terribly arrogant idea, and it makes her smile: He hadn't had the least suspicion that Roxane might fall out of love with him.

When he sees her expression, Ares smiles back in relief, as if he feels this is just like old times, so she may not be entirely mistaken.

"No."

"...What?"

"I know nothing about the fiend dragon, nor the demon king. In addition, I will not sell out Master Baal to you."

When she'd shoved Baal away by the shoulders, she'd looked her stunned husband full in the face for the first time. The hand he'd stretched toward Roxane, the hand that had fallen away, had wanted to catch something.

She shouldn't have concerned herself with a man like this. It would have been better to become someone who could grasp that hand— To have made more time to love her husband.

Although that would certainly not have been the correct course of action.

Involuntarily, her lips curve into a smile. It's a startlingly gentle smile; she can see herself reflected in Ares's eyes.

The woman who'd desperately pursued this man is gone.

"After all, I am his wife."

A shock runs through her cheek. Ares has slapped her, but he looks just as surprised as she is. Apparently he'd struck her on impulse.

Without hiding his impatience or his irritation, looking as if she's betrayed him, Ares storms out of the cell.

"We're well enough to get up."

"You mustn't."

Baal had begun saying this as soon as he opened his eyes, and she's scolded him several times already.

Like a petulant child, he's crawled out from under the covers to lie on top of the bed, arms and legs spread out like a starfish. While she looks for a blanket to spread over him, he complains again.

"Our fever's already gone down."

"No, it has not."

She drapes the blanket over him, then sets a hand on his forehead. As she'd guessed, he's still a little feverish.

After he and the demon king had gotten soaked yesterday, he'd come back shivering, then collapsed with a high fever. No doubt it's better than it was, but he's definitely still sick. He mustn't push himself.

She's about to tell him so, but Baal gets in ahead of her. "Your hand is cold."

It's childish hairsplitting.

However, he's probably aware of that. When she gives him a level stare, he sheepishly crawls back under the covers.

The relief drains the tension from her shoulders. "Rest quietly, please. Your fever was awful last night."

"...Did you nurse us?"

"Yes. We are quite short-handed at the moment."

"Ah. That's true."

Realizing his tone and expression have become those of the king, she feels flustered. Not that it shows in her face. "There's no need for you to move. All of the people you've gathered are brilliant."

"……"

"Behave yourself, if you would… Don't make more trouble for me."

Baal has poked his head out from under the covers, and now he rolls over onto his side. His fingers emerge from the blankets. "It troubles you if we don't behave ourselves?"

"Yes."

"…Are you worried about us?"

"Yes. Please get well soon."

"Who will nurse us until we do? You?"

"Yes. Because I am your principal consort."

"Ah."

Roxane is sitting on a little chair by his bedside. Picking at the red lace on her robe, Baal murmurs the word again.

As his fingertips toy with her skirts, Roxane catches his hand, attempting to put it back under the covers. However, his fingers close around her hand instead. "You are our principal consort?"

"Yes, I am. Why?" *Why would he ask something so obvious?* she thinks, but his voice is earnest, so she nods.

Pouting a little, Baal pulls his head halfway under the covers. "There wasn't enough feeling in that."

"What do you mean? Never mind that, would you release my hand?"

"Don't want to."

"Why not?"

"...That's a good question."

"You may still be delirious with fever."

"—Fine. We're beginning to see it."

"See what?"

"The fact that our conversation will never mesh at this rate, and we'll never get anywhere." Still holding her hand, Baal sits up. Frowning, she tries to stop him, but he sets her hand on his forehead and closes his violet eyes. "Roxane. We're sorry for every—"

"You mustn't." Understanding what Baal is about to do, she speaks firmly. "You must not apologize. You are the king."

Baal opens his eyes and gazes straight at her.

What lovely eyes.

They're the eyes of a king whom no one can defile, whom even the demon king can't defeat.

Oh, I'm glad.

I managed to protect this.

With pride in her heart, Roxane continues, "I merely did what was natural as your principal consort. Let me be proud of my accomplishment, if you would."

"...Hmm. That's...a good point. Well done."

Tugging her hand, he pulls her into an embrace.

She doesn't mind. She feels a restless stirring that's more than just relief.

"We're grateful to you for saving us. Thank you. You are our principal consort."

"Yes." Roxane smiles.

She feels as if she's finally ceased to be that man's fiancée. Even if she died now, she would end her life as this man's principal consort.

She is very proud of that.

"So…erm, Roxane."

"Yes?"

"In other words, uh, you don't mind remaining our principal consort."

"Yes."

"Does that mean you, um, love us?"

"No."

A few seconds pass before Roxane's honest response provokes a scream of "Impossible!" from Baal.

A Childish Love

"Since this is the perfect opportunity, let's have a little wager."

If one had said that remark had been careless of Aileen, one would have been correct. She's never played cards with another woman of her age and station before, and it's put her in high spirits.

Not only that, but the results of their games have been evenly matched so far. It was inevitable that her enthusiasm would get the better of her.

"Very well. Shall we say the loser will grant the winner a wish? On the understanding that the wish must not involve our nations."

"Yes, of course. I shan't lose, Lady Roxane."

"If I win, then, would you let me watch you kiss Master Claude?"

"What?"

The shock is so great that Aileen fumbles a card she'd been about to trade in.

"Master Baal says he would like to cuddle, but unfortunately, there are no convenient examples to use for reference... It's childish and terribly embarrassing, but I couldn't even visualize how kissing might be performed. It was quite distressing."

"C-cuddle...?"

"I believe you could provide a fine reference for me, Lady Aileen."

"……"

"That's settled, then. Thank you in advance for your assistance."

Retrieving the card Aileen has dropped, Roxane shows her own cards.

It's a brilliant hand, the strongest one possible.

The Kingdom of Ashmael is hottest at this hour, just past noon, so only eccentrics willingly work during this time of day.

The holy king and demon king are no exception: They're cooling themselves by the pool the Holy Dragon Consort has made. Technically, no man except the holy king is allowed to enter the harem. However, the harem is half demolished after the incident with the fiend dragon, and the Holy Dragon Consort is using half the property as if it's exclusively hers, so no one is going to complain.

Even in this desert country, the Holy Dragon Consort's pool is deliciously cool. The spring is surrounded by vibrant greenery, and it lies in the shadow of a crumbling building that's covered with vines. It feels a bit like an oasis surrounded by ruins, and its setting alone makes it well worth a look. This place is a particular favorite of the Holy Dragon Consort. Roxane says the only ones who can enter it without souring her mood are Baal and Claude. No doubt that's why it's completely deserted, and such a good spot to rest.

When Aileen and Roxane arrive, the first to notice is Baal, who's floating in the middle of the pool. Perhaps the Holy Dragon Consort has gone off somewhere to play; she's nowhere to be seen. Claude is sitting on the edge, dangling his feet in the water, but when he sees Baal raise his hand, he turns around.

Ngh!

The sight of him stops Aileen in her tracks.

Claude's hair is tied up in a rather disheveled way. Not only that, but he must have been playing in the water with Baal, because his light clothing is loose and rumpled. Since he's been soaking his feet in the spring, his trousers are rolled up to his knees; his shirt is undone, exposing his collarbones, and his skin shows through the wet fabric. This half-dressed state is alluring in the extreme. It would look far more wholesome if he simply stripped to the waist, like Baal.

When he scoops up a spoonful of ice cream, then withdraws the spoon from his lips, she can't seem to find anywhere safe to look.

"Aileen? What's wrong?"

"N-nothing. It's only..."

Why oh why must he be different now, of all times? She can't even look him in the face.

Claude looks perplexed. Swimming over to him, Baal climbs out. "What, are you two here to swim, too?"

"Hey, don't just steal other people's ice cream."

"You're a miser. Some demon king you are."

"You're a shameless thief. Some holy king you are."

"This little fight can wait. As a matter of fact—"

"Lady Roxane! A moment, please!" Roxane is about to broach the subject with her usual expressionless face when Aileen claps a hand over her mouth. "I-I'd like you to leave this to me."

Roxane nods in silent agreement. Clearing her throat, Aileen releases her. *Th-there's no need for nerves. You've kissed before!*

Just as she's telling herself there's no longer anything to be shy about, she realizes something with a jolt. *Wait, am I supposed to initiate this? Or should I ask Master Claude to...?*

"Roxane. Grab us those oranges, would you?"

"Dry yourself off first, Master Baal. You might catch a chill."

"There's no need for that in this heat— We said there's no need."

Roxane, who's picked up a towel from the shore and begun to dry his head with it, is being far more physically affectionate.

She has to press Claude for a kiss here, to serve as an example? What manner of torture is this?

On top of that, Claude is watching Baal—who doesn't actually seem to mind his situation—with chilly eyes, patently unamused. Under the circumstances, Aileen can't think of any words or wiles that would coax a kiss from him.

In that case, initiating it herself is better. Or rather, it's her only option.

"Master Baal. Do you have a proper change of clothes?"

"On a day this hot, these will dry if we just let them be. Do you intend to treat us as a child?"

"No, but... Don't move yet, please. You're all wet."

"D-don't bring your face so close. We told you, let us be."

"That's hardly convincing if he smirks while he says it. Am I wrong? ...Aileen?"

As Claude watches her, perplexed, she grabs his shoulders firmly, facing him straight on.

He blinks. "...What's the matter? Why the scary face?"

She simply has to do it, then run. She keeps her mind, which seems on the verge of flying to pieces, focused on that thought. Her target is his lips.

Yes, his lips. Her husband's moist, extremely enticing lips.

"Your face is red, too. Don't tell me you have heatstroke."

Claude frowns, worried, and his cool fingertips touch her

cheek. Her throat tenses in a stifled shriek and she cringes back, squeezing her eyes shut.

She's done this once, though. She's sure she can do it again.

It's simple. Keeping her eyes closed, moving decisively, she'll make straight for his lips.

"Aileen, for now, let's get you into the shade—?!"

She's swung her head down rapidly, and it connects solidly with Claude's chin.

Aileen's headbutt sends Claude right into the pond. At the sound of the splash, she opens her eyes with a gasp. "M-Master Claude! Master Claude, are you all right?!"

"I see... I'd expect no less of you, Lady Aileen. That was very educational."

"We don't know what you were supposed to be learning from that, but don't do it to us, Roxane."

"—In other words, as a penalty for losing a bet, she was supposed to demonstrate a kiss, and that's how this happened," Claude says, holding a cooling compress to his jaw.

"Yes," Roxane responds. "But Master Baal says I mustn't use that as a reference."

"Of course not. That was a headbutt. What sort of reference would that be?"

"So that really was a headbutt? It wasn't one of Lady Aileen's wiles?"

"N...no, Lady Roxane!" Aileen shrieks at the ground; she's on her hands and knees a short distance away, completely shattered. "I haven't yet begun! That certainly wasn't because I'd, erm, grown nervous..."

"Is that so?"

"Yes, it is! The real demonstration begins now—"

"Aileen."

The shadow and voice at her back make her shudder, and she flees behind a tree. "M-Master Claude, wait, please! I'm honing my concentration at the moment!"

"Bravery is all very well, but I can't have you headbutting me constantly."

Finding herself at a loss for words, Aileen peeks out at Claude from behind the tree. "Y-you're angry, aren't you...?"

But Claude isn't there.

Instead, someone catches her by the waist from behind, lifting her into the air. "If that's what you think, then don't make things harder for me. I can't use magic here."

"Wha—? R-release me, Master Claude! I haven't finished building my concentration yet!"

"You know focus isn't the issue here."

While she's struggling, they've returned to the scene of the headbutting, and Claude sets her down in front of him. He's gazing at her steadily, and Aileen averts her eyes, appealing to him. "I-I'll do it correctly this time. It will be fine. I won't close my eyes."

"I don't think that's why you lost, though."

"Please give me a chance! I can't simply back down—"

She hears a light *chu*, then realizes their lips have met.

"Consort Roxane. Will this do?"

Claude's voice is so matter-of-fact that at first she doesn't understand what's happened.

"I see. So that's how it's done. That was quite informative."

"Listen, why are you so eager to see other people's love scenes, woman?"

"As I said, as a cuddling reference."

"...Wait. We understand none of this. Explain yourself."

After Aileen has let most of Roxane and Baal's conversation go in one ear and out the other, the situation finally sinks in. She claps her hands over her mouth, feeling her face grow warm. "Wh-wh-wha...? Why?!"

"If I'd waited for you, it would have taken all day. Besides, there's no telling how many times you would have headbutted me," he adds, and she bristles.

"Th-that isn't true. I can do it when I try!"

"I really don't think you can."

"Must you take that attitude with me?! Just because you're rather used to this...!"

"It's not that I'm used to it. You're just unused to it." Claude straightens up, pulling her by the hand. "Let's not wait for them. I doubt the holy king's going to be good for anything for a while."

"What do you mean—?" As Claude tugs her along by the hand, she glances back just in time to see Baal shout, "Our wife is adorable!" and topple backward into the pond. Roxane seems flustered, but Claude is correct: She doesn't want to get mixed up in that.

They're already cuddling quite nicely! It irritates her for some reason, and she surges forward, her footsteps unsteady.

Claude seems to have picked up on Aileen's indignation. As he walks through the shade under the trees, he laughs a little. "A cuddling reference, hmm? Even though it's your weakest subject..."

"Th-that isn't true."

"When I haven't given you a single kiss since we married, and your only response was to act dejected?"

He'd noticed that? This annoys her, but giving him a reaction would be playing right into his hands.

Averting her face in a huff, she changes the subject. "I merely wanted to be of some use to Lady Roxane!"

"You're very kind to the principal consort, aren't you? There's no need to worry. She'll be fine."

"How can you be so sure?"

"It's obvious. Even if one of them isn't conscious of it, they're right in the middle of a childish love. They gaze at each other, captivated, and merely making eye contact is enough to make them blush. If you unwisely get involved, it will only make your head spin."

Thinking he may have a point there, she glances up at him. Claude is walking along, looking composed. Catching a glimpse of the back of his neck and the stray tendrils of hair at its nape, she quickly looks down. A blush steals into her cheeks.

Noticing that her steps have slowed, Claude stops, turning back. "Aileen?"

"...Am I childish, do you think?"

"Why?"

"Well... All you've done is dress differently, Master Claude, and yet I don't know where to look."

He's put up his hair, rolled his trousers up to his knees, and bared his legs and arms. He looks like an ordinary young man, not the demon king or a crown prince, and it's left her completely at a loss.

"W-we hardly ever hold hands and walk like this in Ellmeyer..."

"……"

"It really may have been too soon for me to serve as an example to Lady Roxane... Master Claude?"

Claude is silent. When she peeks up through her lashes to see his reaction, he's covered his eyes with his free hand. Averting his face slightly, he murmurs, "My wife is adorable..."

"Pardon?"

"Erm, I need to think a little. Would you wait a moment?"

"Wait"? Wait for what?

Aileen tilts her head, perplexed. Then she realizes Claude's ears have turned red.

If he hadn't put his hair up, she's sure she'd never have noticed.

Once that thought occurs to her, she gets the feeling that his hand has gone slightly sweaty in hers—and she laughs, hugging his arm.

Uncharacteristically, Claude stumbles a little. It's so precious that it makes her almost unbearably happy. "Still, I know that you can be unexpectedly childish, Master Claude."

"That's irritating." He sounds as if he's sulking, but he turns her way. He must be a poor loser as well.

As his lips approach hers, Aileen closes her eyes.

When their lips meet, the childish *I love you*s melt and vanish.

✦ Fifth Act ✦
Amelia Dark

The history of the Holy Queendom of Hausel reaches back to the age of the gods. It is a great nation in the center of the vast Rufford continent, which encompasses searing deserts and fertile forests, perilous, wintry mountain ranges, and wide-open plateaus.

The coronation ceremony of its queen is so complex that merely explaining the protocol for the various rituals requires an entire day, and since the explanation itself is extremely formal, it takes up a lot of time... And yet the essential points may be summarized quite simply: "While wearing prescribed clothes, hear prescribed congratulatory addresses from prescribed functionaries, give prescribed responses, and do these things at a prescribed time in the prescribed order."

Of course, the future queen must understand the meaning of the ceremony, so she memorizes it. However, Amelia had gotten that out of the way during her days as a royal candidate.

It's pointless.

This coronation, in which the Maid of the Sacred Sword will become the queen of Hausel, has no precedent. She can see that everyone is giving it their all. She's told that more people have come running to congratulate her than any other queen in history. Amelia mustn't watch all these things with jaded eyes, but she knows everyone is feeling more relieved than celebratory.

No one praises her for having obtained the sacred sword. They don't rejoice about it. They're relieved that she's managed to keep up appearances somehow. Even her mother the queen sighs with relief over the fact that her prediction wasn't wrong.

Even at the coronation tomorrow, she's sure she won't be the one everyone's talking about. Will her older sister Grace—the one who'd won the sacred sword first and become the wife of the demon king Luciel—attend the ceremony...?

"Amelia."

Someone calls to her, and the glass on her terrace window rattles.

Amelia had planned to go to bed early, and she is rather appalled. This is the royal palace of the Queendom of Hausel. As one whose rank is second only to Her Majesty's, she has been assigned rooms near the queen's residential quarters. They are located fairly high in the palace, and the security is far from lax.

Even so, here she is, bold as brass. Her sister is as freakish as ever.

"Grace. What is it? Surely the palace gate was open..."

Opening the terrace door, Amelia shrinks from the chill in the night wind. It's still winter. Lately, she's spent all her time in the palace—which is kept at a constant temperature by divine items—and she'd forgotten about the season.

"Oh, using the front door would have been a pain. They treat me as an honored guest for being the queen's daughter and the next queen's sister, and it's tiresome. Besides, Luciel's here... What's the matter, Luciel? Why don't you come down?"

"Huh? You said I mustn't enter young women's rooms."

When she looks up, she sees the demon king floating in midair beyond the edge of the terrace. The night is so dark it may as well be made of layer upon layer of black, but even then, his sparkling pale silver hair and red eyes seem to shine.

"Amelia may be my sister-in-law, but she is a girl, isn't she? So—"

"That's one thing, this is another. The guards will spot you if you don't hurry. You already stand out, you know."

"It's fine, I've put up camouflage. But Amelia, could I come down to the terrace? If I'm up here, it feels like I'm looking down on you two; it seems arrogant or, um, demon king-ish..."

"...Please do," she tells him, doing her best to keep all emotion out of her voice.

Shyly, Luciel alights in front of her.

"Oh good. How've you been, Amelia? The other day, it was all I could do just to explain the situation..."

The situation. He means the time when he was accused of being a demon and nearly dragged in front of a mirror of truth.

That was when Amelia had learned he was married to her sister.

"I've been worried about you ever since. I thought knowing me—or rather, being my sister-in-law—might have put you in a bind. Oh, but I heard you'd won the sacred sword! That's terrific."

"Listen, you. You're the demon king, remember? She might vanquish you with that thing."

"Ngh... B-but now no one will say she's not fit to be queen. I'm happy about that. Amelia worked so hard for a long time."

His words are straightforward, completely devoid of any falsehood, and they make Amelia's chest tighten.

Luciel gives a lovely smile. This man always has the most beautiful, heartfelt smiles. Just like her sister, who's nodding in proud agreement.

These two are the only people who will genuinely celebrate the fact that she's become queen, and truly believe she's worthy. *How ironic.* Amelia smiles. "And? What brings you two here?"

"Oh, right, that's right, I got sidetracked. Listen, Amelia. Starting tomorrow, you'll be queen. That's a rough role to take on. I doubt you'll get many chances to relax and unwind."

"True." Amelia nods apathetically.

Her sister lowers her voice, letting it fill with mischief. "So. Want to come out for one last frolic?"

"...Pardon?"

Sometimes her sister says things that defy understanding. Beside her, Luciel is nodding, too. "Well, you see, there's a festival today, as a run-up to the coronation tomorrow. I heard that cake you love so much is all-you-can-eat. Come with us!"

"'All-you-can-eat...'"

Somehow, that phrase seems to spoil all of the day's intricate ceremonial explanations.

"It's fine: I may not look it, but I am the demon king! We'll be able to fool 'em."

"...I really don't think we should be fooling them..."

"Oh, it's no big deal. I did it all the time! It's fun."

I'd appreciate it if you didn't lump me in with you, Sister, Amelia thinks, but she swallows the words.

"Come on, Amelia, let's go. This is so none of us forget who you were before you became queen."

"That's right. You're my little sister-in-law, so let us spoil you."

She nods, but is it because the embers of her extinguished first love for the demon king still glow, or because she wants to feel superior to her sister, to truly feel she's won? She doesn't know.

Fifth Act

★   ★   ★

As Luciel had said, the castle town is lit up as bright as day, and the streets are bustling and lively. The white flowers that adorn the town sway in the night wind, illuminated by the streetlamps. Fires where people can warm themselves have been kindled, and it feels as if the cold has lost its edge.

Amelia is wearing a thick cloak that matches her sister and brother-in-law's. She pulls its hood up to cover her head and looks around, her breath misting white. This is a festival in celebration of the birth of the new queen. In other words, it's being held in her honor, but it just doesn't seem real.

"They say the all-you-can-eat cake was only during the day…"

"That's what happens when you don't check into things properly. At any rate, 'all-you-can-eat' is a waste. You couldn't eat anything else that way."

"If you were there, Grace, I thought it might work out."

"What exactly do you think I am? Well, never mind. Amelia's top priority tonight. Amelia, what do you want to eat?"

The question leaves Amelia bewildered. Luciel peeks in at her from the right; from the left, Grace does the same thing. In other words, she's in the middle. It seems natural, and a little strange.

"…Anything's fine."

"That's an irresponsible answer. You're letting others make your choices for you."

Her sister's comment makes her bristle, but before she can say anything, Luciel cuts in. "With this many stalls, even Amelia's going to have a hard time making up her mind. Besides, you're the one who said we were celebrating her today, Grace. That means we need to take the lead and celebrate."

Kindly, he says it's not her fault, the way he always does. Even now, Luciel believes she's a good girl.

His kindness and trust had always saved her. Now she feels wretched for every time she'd felt saved. She squeezes her hands into fists.

"Hmm. You've got a point there. I was wrong. It is Amelia's celebration."

"Oh, the church is selling canelés. Amelia, let's have some."

"What are you saying, Luciel? We're celebrating. Meat comes first!" Grace says emphatically, clenching her fists.

Luciel grimaces. "That's just what *you* want, Grace. Amelia doesn't like that sort of thing much."

"? That can't be true. I often saw her in the cafeteria after the tests, tearing into steak—"

"Grace!"

Apparently her sister had seen her ripping meat apart with her teeth in order to vent her frustration over constantly being outwitted by Grace. She'd always acted like a sweet girl who ate like a bird in front of Luciel, so she's even more rattled than she might have been otherwise.

Grace looks a bit startled at being cut off. However, seeing Amelia's expression, she nods as if it all makes sense, then gives Luciel an oddly triumphant look. "Actually, that's right. Even if he is your brother-in-law, he doesn't need to know about that."

"...What do you mean?"

"I mean Amelia and I are close, as sisters go. Go on, get over there and buy your canelés or what have you already."

She flicks a hand at him dismissively, shooing him away, and Luciel's red eyes gleam dangerously. It's the face of the demon king, the one which had sometimes made Amelia shudder.

"It hasn't even been a year since you found out you two were sisters. I really don't think you should be acting like you know all about her."

Luciel has told Grace what Amelia always keeps inside her. It's gratifying, but at the same time, Amelia sneaks a look at Grace, concerned about how she'll react.

"I watched Amelia do her best all through the royal exam. Time has nothing to do with it," Grace declares boldly, standing tall.

Amelia hates this side of her sister. As a rule, she'd say, "Yes, that's right," while privately making fun of her, and that would be that. However, this time is different.

Irked, Luciel retorts, "In that case, I cheered her on while she was putting in all that work. We went to lots of different places together, and anyway, you fell into the demon realm and disappeared partway through."

It's Amelia's fault that Grace fell into the demon realm. She flinches guiltily, but Grace says something she completely doesn't expect. "That was because you said not to go home, and you know it!"

"Yes, but I was meeting Amelia the whoooole time, and that's the truth! That means it's not right for you to shut me out like that. I'm her brother-in-law, okay?!"

"What's that 'okay?!' about…?"

"You said you liked sweets, right, Amelia?! You ate cake with me, didn't you?!"

Luciel presses her for confirmation, looking as though he might burst into tears. Amelia nods. She does like sweets. She hasn't lied.

"There, you see?! I do know!"

"Amelia, this guy says he's your brother-in-law, so you don't have to hold back around him anymore. Those sausages over there look good. Let's go get one of those."

"My canelés come first!"

"U-um, I'll eat both, so..."

When she wearily proposes a compromise, the other two charge off to their chosen stalls as if it's a race.

As a result, Amelia's abruptly left by herself.

What on earth is wrong with those two?

Luciel had always been rather naive about the world, while her sister is as inconsiderate as ever. Will that pair be all right married to each other?

Just standing there and waiting seems rather ridiculous, so she seats herself on a corner of one of the benches around a bonfire.

No one has noticed her.

Even so, starting tomorrow, she will be this nation's queen.

She's studied and worked hard. She even dropped her sister into the demon realm. For a fleeting moment, her first love had gone to her head and made her take a risk that could have cost her the throne, but in the end, she'd even obtained the sacred sword.

...I'll be a magnificent queen.

Her hands have gone red with cold. She opens and closes them, flexing her fingers.

The chill numbs the pain, numbs her senses. It probably makes it harder to feel things like wretchedness and anger as well. That's why, even when she's walking with those two, she's able to hold on to only what's important.

"Amelia, canelés!" Luciel is the first one back; he's panting so hard his shoulders are heaving. Was this anything to get so desperate about? She's rather disgusted, but the fact he's bought drinks as well is really quite considerate.

"Thank you," Amelia says, taking the offered sweet, and Luciel beams at her. *He's like a dog*, she thinks, and the fact that she's able to make fun of him reassures her. He doesn't make her heart race anymore.

"I really am glad you've become queen," Luciel says, sounding deeply moved, just as she's bitten into her canelé. "If you hadn't, I'm sure I would have ended up at war with the humans. Grace would've gotten dragged into it, too."

In other words, ultimately, it's all for Grace. Amelia is convenient. That's what he's saying.

She sinks her teeth into the canelé with more ferocity than before. She refuses to let this emotion show on her face, or to say anything about it. Those are things wretched, weak people do.

"Grace and I actually wanted to attend tomorrow's coronation as the emperor and empress of our new country, but they said we couldn't. They told us there's no such country as Ellmeyer."

"…Was that Her Majesty's decision?"

"Probably. Since Grace is her daughter, they gave her permission to attend by herself, but she got angry and said she'd never heard of anything so stupid… So we won't get to see your moment of triumph tomorrow."

Luciel is despondent. She pities his ignorance, and inwardly sneers at her sister's recklessness.

A country where demons and humans coexist? They'll never get a thing like that acknowledged by marching it through the front door.

Since these two are fools, they must not even realize that much. The people around them are fools as well, so all they can do is fear and reject them.

Amelia alone will choose a different course. She's going to

become a person who can use anything at her disposal, even the two of them.

"When I am queen, I'm sure I'll be able to help you."

Luciel blinks dramatically.

No doubt he'd simply been telling her that they wouldn't be able to attend her ceremony. He really is a straightforward demon king.

"It may take time, of course, but please wait. I promise to aid your cause."

"But..."

"It's something only the new queen of this country could do."

The other fools could never manage it. Neither could her sister or brother-in-law, of course.

Her heart feels clear and invigorated.

This is the feeling she's envisioned: pride fit for a queen.

"Amelia! Here's one that's just off the fire!" As if to blast that refreshed feeling away, a fragrant, fatty aroma drifts toward her. She looks at her sister, feeling as if the woman has taken the wind out of her sails, but Grace's eyes are sparkling. "I had them roast it while I was at it. It's good. It's definitely going to be good."

"Amelia's already eaten her canelé."

"That doesn't matter a bit! Come, Amelia, let's dig in. We'll split it."

"Huh? Where's mine?"

Ignoring her husband's pathetic question, Grace sits down on Amelia's other side, triumphantly displaying her spoils. "I had them put mustard on it, too. It's absolutely going to be g—"

"I don't like mustard."

As an experiment, she tells her the truth for the first time.

Grace freezes up, then wilts dejectedly. "I see... You don't, hmm? I didn't know that. What have I done...?"

"G-Grace, you don't have to get so depressed. If you go buy another one—"

"I'll eat it, though. I'd never actually tried mustard before; I just assumed I wouldn't like it."

Grace looks at her, wide-eyed. It's rather gratifying, so she takes the sausage from her, holding it by its stick.

The sausage is still piping hot, and it's slathered with a dose of mustard so generous it seems like overkill. Even so, she takes a determined bite.

As Amelia chews, her sister and brother-in-law watch her from either side, holding their breath.

Even here, she's at the center. Her, and not them.

She is the center of the world.

"...It's delicious."

"—Isn't it, though?! I knew it: It's a great combination!"

Her sister is grinning from ear to ear. Amelia had always loathed her easygoing ways. However, strangely, they don't bother her now.

The two of them keep pressing recommendations on her— "This next! No, try this!"—and Amelia laughs. It's the most she's laughed since she came to the Queendom of Hausel.

While she's laughing, there at the center of the world, the sky begins to pale as if announcing a new era.

She's forgotten to write in her journal. Amelia gets through the coronation ceremony with sleep-dazed eyes, and as she makes her way toward the altar where the final succession ritual will take place, she's biting back a yawn.

Ceremonies really do make one drowsy. She suspects her sister

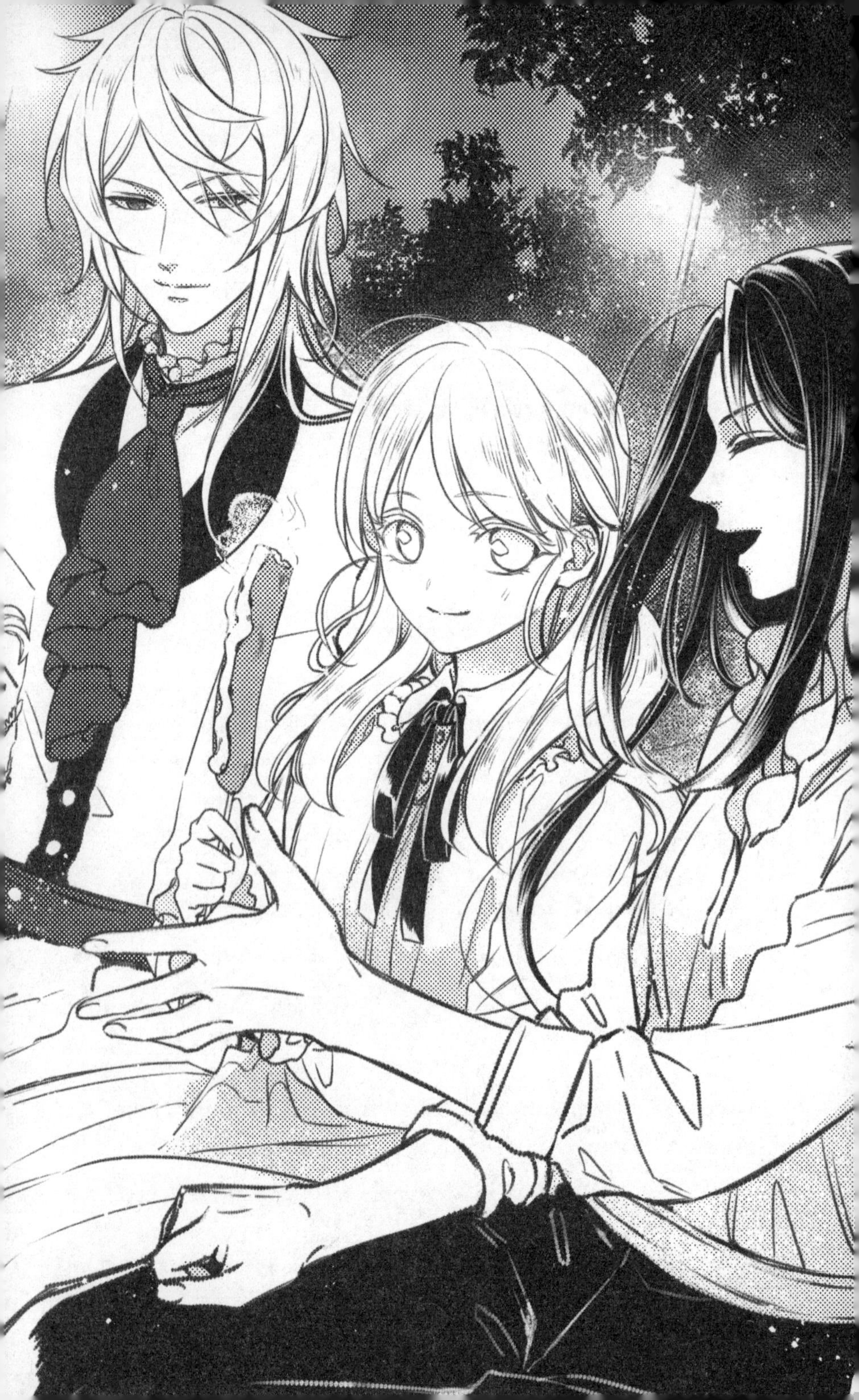

and brother-in-law made the right choice in not attending. She hears her mother ran the two of them off before the coronation, telling Grace that if she persisted in calling herself the demon king's wife instead of the Maid of the Sacred Sword, she would never be allowed to set foot in Hausel again. The foolishness of that move had appalled Amelia.

From this day on, Amelia's whims will determine the course of the world. How long does that mother of hers intend to act like she's queen?

The powers to foretell the future and see the past are handed down from one queen of Hausel to the next. Once she inherits these, Amelia will be queen.

She reaches a door which can't be seen by those who have no sacred power.

Raising her head in a dignified way, Amelia speaks, preparing herself to spin a correct destiny and future into existence.

"—Hear, O past. Open, O future. I am the maiden who inherits the regalia of saints and demons."

What the Holy Dragon Consort Saw in the Sunset

Long ago, someone had told her that when she grew up, she'd get to marry the man she loved. It had been true: He'd even given her a splendid name. With the blessing of the demon king, Mana has become the Holy Dragon Consort.

Mana isn't able to talk with her husband Baal. He's a very observant person, though, and between this and that, he understands what she wants to say. He treasures her and dotes on her.

Baal has many wives. Apparently it's a system known as a harem.

However, Mana is a great and ancient dragon, and she doesn't concern herself with the concerns of common people. It's only natural for females to flock around a strong male, and to be honest, she doesn't really understand human systems anyway.

That said, she makes an exception for one individual.

At sunset, a time of day when the land of Ashmael is dyed a blazing red, a shadow falls across her favorite bathing pool. Irked, Mana lifts her head. The only people who may enter this place without Mana's permission are her husband and the demon king, and everyone knows it. She growls threateningly, and the sandaled feet stop, startled.

"I-I'm terribly sorry. I didn't realize…"

Her least favorite woman in all the world is standing there, looking as if she's just noticed her.

She's a human female named Roxane.

She has no sacred power. No magic either, of course. If Mana got a little serious about lashing her tail, she'd probably die easily. However, the demon king has told her that she mustn't hurt people recklessly, and being a violent girl would repel her husband. As such, she puts up with it—or maybe not. She doesn't, not really.

In any case, she doesn't like the woman, so she glares. Roxane seems uncharacteristically dazed, though. Realizing that her usual irritating briskness is gone, Mana feels a little unsettled. Now that she's looking, she thinks she sees faint dark circles under the woman's eyes.

Is she tired from nursing Baal?

There had been a major battle the other day, and although Baal had come home safely, he'd collapsed from exhaustion. Mana had been distracted with worry, and this very woman had told her, "Lady Sahra is here as well. He will be fine." She's also the one who's been caring for him. Mana has spent the whole time watching from her bed, which is connected to Baal's bedchamber, so she's positive about this. During her negotiations with the demon king's country, the woman had shown such anger that Mana's tail had curled up, so she'd assumed she was fine— But come to think of it, she has seemed a little strange lately.

In particular, when the Daughter of God and that general person are with Baal, the woman gets a distant look in her eyes, just like this. Mana lies in wait, determined to get Baal to pay attention to her before Roxane does, so she's well aware of it.

In the first place, it's unusual for this woman to be dazed at all. She shows Mana more respect than anyone else in the kingdom, and the fact that she's just standing there instead of hastily taking herself elsewhere is strange.

In lieu of asking *What's the matter?* Mana twitches her long whiskers, tickling Roxane's cheek. Roxane's eyes widen. From her expression, she's finally come to her senses.

"You're very kind, aren't you?"

Of course she is. When she throws out her chest proudly, Roxane sits down on the spot. This really isn't like her at all.

"...Would that I could be so kind."

The woman has said something that doesn't make much sense. Mana blinks, and Roxane turns to her, smiling cynically. "Holy Dragon Consort, did you know Master Baal used to be in love with Lady Sahra?"

She knows. She's heard lots and lots of complaining about it. When she nods, Roxane says, "I see. You really are broad-minded, aren't you...? I can't be. I know I must be, and yet I simply can't. I have no intention of making the same mistake twice...yet when I see those three together, I inevitably remember something unnecessary. The fact that I was cast aside."

Even as Mana tilts her head, unable to make any sense of this, Roxane continues. Does this land have a custom that its people have to arbitrarily talk at Mana or they'll die?

"I understand why the harem exists. I should be satisfied with the fact that Master Baal has made me his principal consort. And yet, I've begun to think 'I hate this.' I'm not fit to be the principal consort. The idea that I may be unable to carry out my duty and will revert to being a foolish, jealousy-crazed woman frightens me..."

Hugging her knees, Roxane buries her face in them. Mana doesn't know what to do.

"...Perhaps I should return to my family home, before I do something to disgrace myself."

"Ngyah?!"

Mana has no idea what this is about, but she panics a bit. If the woman does a thing like that, Baal's bound to be sad.

After all, he likes this woman. He's always asking Mana for advice about her.

What should she do? Just as she's thinking it's probably a bad idea to just let her be, she senses a second presence and raises her head. Roxane is smiling through her tears, her face turned toward Mana, and she hasn't noticed yet.

"You may laugh and call me pathetic. It truly isn't a crime to love one's husband, and yet I can't even do that properly."

"……"

"After all, you see how it is. Master Baal has crowds of other wives, and he is obligated to father children. If I can't endure that, I should simply retire from the position of principal consort. A woman like me isn't fit to be Master Baal's wife. I know that."

"……"

"And yet I can't even bring myself to do that. I don't want to leave his side. I want to remain his wife. Not only that, but I find myself wondering if there's a way to become his only wife. That side of myself frightens me. All I think about is how to love him, and how to make him love me."

"Uh… Um, Roxane."

Roxane has been pleading with Mana with such keen sorrow in her face that she seems on the verge of tears, but at that, she whirls around.

Mana's beloved husband is standing there, covering his face with his hands. "Just…stop there for a minute, all right? Our heart can't really, um… It's a problem."

"…How long have you…?"

"We, erm, we didn't mean to eavesdrop. It's just that we knew someone had gotten near Mana, so we came to make sure it hadn't made her cross, and...uh..."

"...I shall go hang myself." Baal looks up, startled. Mana feels all her hair stand on end. Roxane continues impassively, "Thank you for all you've done for me."

"No, wait, please wait! Don't just say words we'd meant to make sure you never said again! Hey, where are you going? Mana, stop her!"

Roxane doesn't seem to hear Master Baal anymore. She tries to walk into the lake—she can't be planning to drown herself in Mana's pool, can she?—and Mana hastily catches her around the waist with a whisker and pulls her back. The woman's face is completely vacant.

"I beg you. Kill me..."

"Why are you like this, woman?! Hear us out; we'll explain everything! First, we won't restore the harem to what it was. Not during our reign, at least. We'll send the low-ranking and high-ranking consorts back to their families; those who wish to may run away to the Levi tribe as prospective brides."

Roxane blinks, and her eyes are abruptly sane again. "...Levi? Do you mean Ellmeyer's tribe of magic grand dukes?"

"Right. We hear they wish for knowledge about sacred items. Since that nation tried to shun Claude, their development of magic items is lagging. One of the high-level consorts who perjured herself with you the other day knew a lot about sacred items, remember? When we suggested she go there, she accepted. She said it sounded like more fun than withering away in the harem."

"But that will still leave several here. No doubt some of them will find it hard to return to their families."

"We'll hire them on again as priestesses who'll care for Mana. There will probably still be some left even then, and we're considering propping them up by saying that outstanding women will be given the position of consort. That much is for the sake of the kingdom. However, you are the only one who will bear our children."

Roxane's sanity seems to have finally returned. She frowns fiercely, taking a few steps toward Baal. "You must not do that. If you fail to pass on your blood, the blood of the holy king, Ashmael, will—"

"We know you know this: Children born to the consort the king favors are the ones most likely to inherit his power. More specifically, the children of a holy king and his wife who love each other."

Roxane's face betrays the fact that this had never even occurred to her. She looks utterly foolish. Baal looks happy, and that makes Mana happy, too.

"Our parents were incredibly close. They were, what's the word? Lovey-dovey?"

"Lovey-dovey…"

"Don't worry. You will definitely bear the next holy king. That was what you were talking about, isn't it?"

Even when Baal sets his forehead against hers, Roxane seems dazed. What a dense woman. Mana snorts.

"Good grief. We thought it might take a few more years. You wouldn't listen to a word we said."

"Um… Then you mean I… You'll…"

"May we visit your bedchamber tonight?"

Baal's ardent eyes aren't looking at Mana. This doesn't bother Mana one bit, though. What she's concerned about is Roxane. She

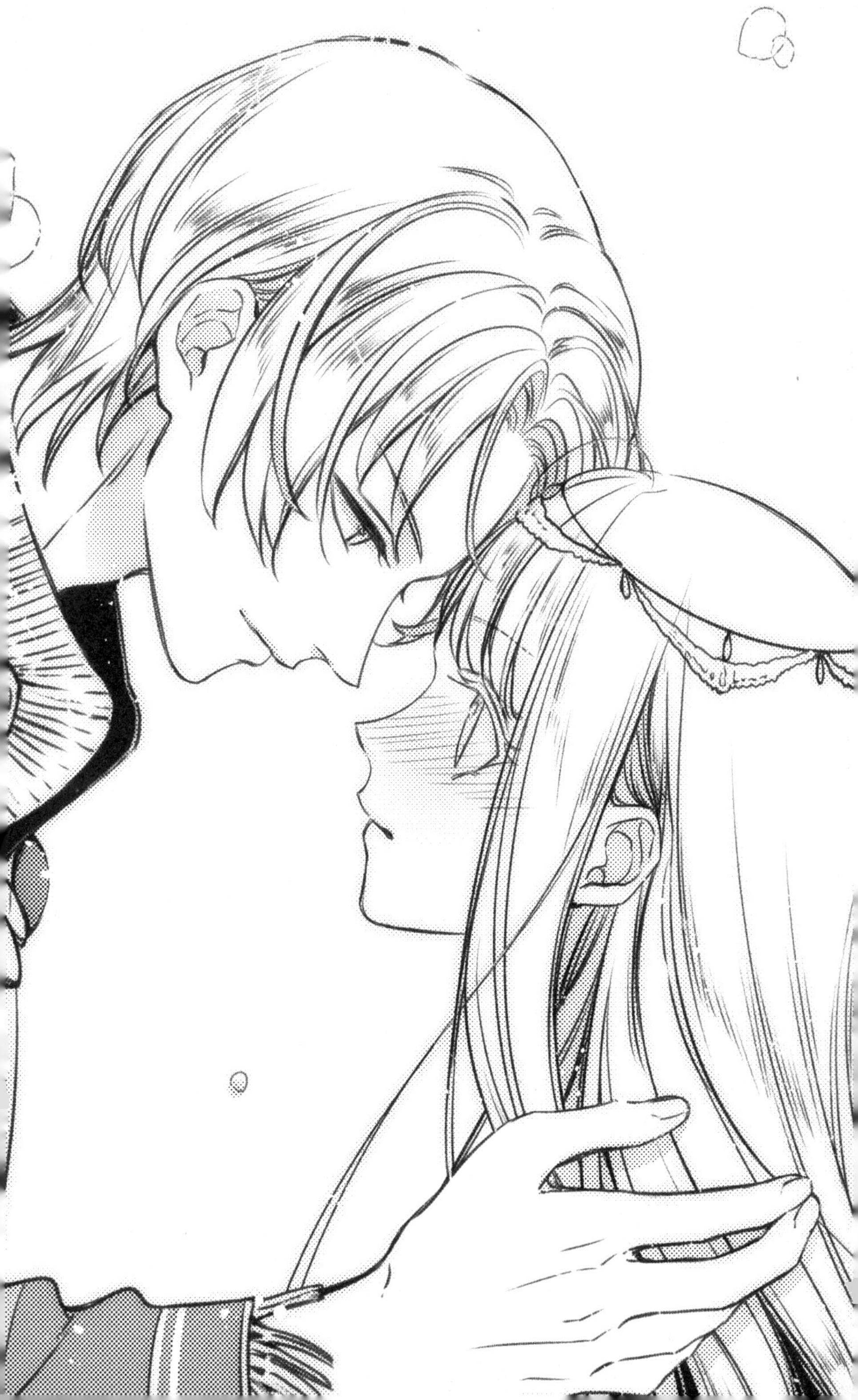

glares at her. If the woman makes Baal sad now, she'll drop her into the lake.

Roxane tries to speak, then turns bright red. Tears bead in her eyes, and she gives a small, decisive nod. Baal breaks into a grin, then kisses her.

Humans are such a bundle of trouble, Mana thinks. What needless complication. They should just love whom they love however they want.

Still, she feels she shouldn't watch Baal and Roxane now, so she quietly averts her eyes. Looking up, she sees a perfectly cloudless evening sky.

The stars are sure to be bright and clear tonight.

The Imperial Couple's First Day

When Rachel wakes, winter has transformed into spring. She's awakened rather early, but birds are already twittering, and the sun is shining brightly.

Obeying her lady-in-waiting's sharp intuition, she gets dressed earlier than usual, then makes her way to the imperial couple's bedchamber. As if to confirm her instincts, Keith is already waiting in front of the great double doors. After a brief exchange of greetings, the emperor's adviser points toward the bedchamber, smiling a bit wryly.

"The door won't open."

"It won't...?"

"Incidentally, the old castle's a riot of blossoms, and there's a rainbow over it. Since it's inside the barrier, it's extremely easily influenced. The entire imperial capital is getting spring sunshine, even though it's midwinter... I do hope the bedchamber hasn't become a meadow of flowers, but..."

"That...would be difficult to clean, wouldn't it."

However, they'll have to gain access to this inaccessible bedchamber before they worry about things like cleaning.

It's quite clear why the door won't open.

"Now then, how shall we lure them out? Should we make his guards do the Demon King Love-Love dance?"

"Do you suppose they can hear us from here?"

"I think Master Claude is listening, at least. I've been calling to him, but there's no answer. I assume this means we aren't to interrupt. Ensuring the line succession is one of the emperor's most important jobs, after all."

Keith knocks on the door, but as before, no one responds. He folds his arms. "How shall we persuade them? Today is the new emperor's important first day. It wouldn't be seemly if he skipped work or started late. One would think Lady Aileen would be telling him the same thing, but…"

"Lady Aileen… Do you suppose she's all right?"

"I'm terribly sorry, but I can't guarantee it," he tells her soberly.

Rachel thinks hard for a little while, then raises her head. Standing tall, she calls toward the bedchamber. "Good morning, Master Claude and Lady Aileen. It is time to prepare for the day. Would you please open the door, Master Claude? If you don't, I won't be able to help Lady Aileen get ready for this evening."

On the other side of the door, all is silent, but she feels as if she's made a slight impression on it. At the very least, she senses that Master Claude has begun to listen to her.

"If Lady Aileen should fall ill, you will worry, Master Claude. Please leave everything to us."

"Unlike Keith, you're fairly persuasive," a voice says from inside the bedchamber, and then the door opens on its own.

Flowers spill out into the corridor. As Keith had feared, in the space of a night, the bedchamber has transformed into a paradise of blossoms and young greenery. A sweet floral fragrance mingles with the refreshing wind, and crisp, cool air eddies around them.

"I hate to leave her, but I'll let you handle this. I was just having a bit of trouble. She won't stop crying."

On the bed in the center of the room, the emperor and demon

king smiles bewitchingly, naked to the waist. Just like that, the bedchamber is transformed into a sultry lost paradise.

"Oh, I knew it was going to be like this…"

Half resigned, Keith walks in, trampling the flowers. Rachel hastily follows, making for the bed.

Aileen is lying beside Claude. She's cocooned herself in a pure white sheet, and her face isn't visible.

"Lady Aileen."

"…Rachel?" says a rather hoarse, tearful voice. Aileen peeks out from a gap in the sheet.

Claude smiles affectionately. "What, have you stopped crying?"

"……"

"Don't be embarrassed. Show us your face, my sweet Aileen."

"……"

"Well, that's a problem. She's been like that ever since this morning, and she won't talk to me."

Claude doesn't look as if he thinks it's a problem at all. He's wearing a brilliant smile. Beautiful people have it good: He doesn't look like he's smirking. Not only that, but although it is only his upper body, he's exposing his dazzling nakedness. Even Rachel, who's grown fairly used to him, feels as if it might blind her.

"Even though she was so adorable last night."

The thought of Aileen's mental distress after being exposed to that all night long makes her want to offer up a prayer.

"Or did I bungle something?"

"That's quite enough scandalous behavior first thing in the morning, milord." Unfazed by his master's extreme sensuality, Keith drapes a long robe around Claude's shoulders.

"Scandalous? All I've done is love my wife."

"Your very existence is scandalous, immoral, and obscene. Bath first."

"I want to bathe with Aileen."

"You mustn't. If you insist on pestering her, she won't like you anymore." Keith puts Claude's arms through the sleeves, then ties the belt at his waist, working with practiced hands. Claude seems used to this as well; he looks puzzled in a melancholy way. "But if my wife won't even tell me good morning, I'll be too uneasy to go to work."

"It's your own fault. You must have done something to make her not want to greet you."

"I wonder what it was, exactly."

"—All of them, obviously!" Abruptly, Aileen bolts up in bed and lobs a pillow right at Claude's face. "I—I asked you, over and over, to please stop…!"

"But you didn't act as if you didn't like it."

"But, but, I said 'Wait' so many times…"

"Oh, I see. So that meant you didn't like it. It wasn't because you were embarrassed." Claude looks patently startled. Then he leans in close to Aileen, smiling back at her thinly. "No wonder 'everything' was all I could think of."

Rachel can almost hear Aileen bursting a blood vessel. "Why you—!"

"L-Lady Aileen. Calm down."

Aileen has raised the pillow for another attack, and Rachel catches her from behind, restraining her. At the same time, Keith grabs Claude by the scruff of the neck and hauls him to his feet. "All right, come on. It's time for work."

"Wait. I want to talk with my wife a little longer."

"It's fine. Night will come again."

Keith sends Rachel a significant look. *You take care of the rest.* Nodding in response, Rachel bows to Claude. "Please leave this to me."

"I see... Yes. All right; I'll let you handle this. Aileen."

"What?!"

"I love you. I was to blame, and I'm sorry, so please don't be angry."

Dropping a quick kiss on her cheek, Claude follows Keith out of the room.

Left behind, Aileen opens and shuts her mouth uselessly, her face a mixture of anger and shame. Then she flops back down onto the bed. Timidly, Rachel calls to her. "L-Lady Aileen?"

"—That was not normal..."

"What wasn't—?" she starts to ask, then shuts her mouth.

Turning bright red and covering her face with her hands, Aileen repeats herself, half in tears. "That was most definitely abnormal... Wasn't it, Rachel?!"

"...After your bath, let's have breakfast."

"Please, listen to me!!"

She must not listen.

She respects her mistress more than anything in the world, but even then, there are things she absolutely must not hear.

Uncharacteristically, Aileen whimpers that she can't stand; however, by noon, she's rallied completely. Having her take breakfast with Roxane seems to have done the trick. When Aileen complained, further scrambling her scrambled eggs with her fork, Roxane flatly declared, "Practice is key," proving to Rachel yet again that she is a valuable friend for her mistress. Having awakened to her mission, Aileen seems to be thinking of measures to "satisfy her husband"—or in other words, retake the initiative. She'll probably enter the bedchamber valiantly again tonight. Even if she's planning something unsavory, Rachel's job ends once she's sent her to bed. Everything beyond that can be left to Claude.

In a way, I suppose it's just like her to be so focused on Master Claude that she isn't at all concerned about the fact that the whole capital knows.

"Magic flowers on sale, with prayers that Her Majesty the empress will conceive!"

The florists are selling the vibrant flowers that have bloomed all at once with an advertising slogan that's extremely ill-mannered, depending on how one thinks about it. In addition, vegetables that can't be harvested during this season are lined up in storefronts as if the merchants are determined not to let the wave of sales escape them. The vendors of the imperial capital are a hardy bunch.

Rachel, who's come to the third layer to do some shopping and take a slightly belated lunch break, gazes at them with a smile.

The line between Claude's magic and a natural disaster is always a very fine one. The fact that the people are able to accept the results this way is probably a sign that they have a very high opinion of their new emperor. She hears the blush-worthy slogan "It isn't the demon king's magic, it's the power of love" and knows it's based in goodwill.

The weather today really is very fine. That must be why her fiancé, the person she's here to meet, is sitting outside on the terrace instead of in the café. Rachel spots him first, and her face lights up, but Isaac responds with a glower. In another moment, she understands why.

Denis, Jasper, Luc, and Quartz—members of the Oberon Trading Firm—all pop up.

"Hello! So you were the one Isaac's meeting, huh, Rachel?"

"Oh-ho, I see. That's why he's been trying to run us off."

"Let's stay out of their way. We'll be working together at the old castle later today anyway."

"...That's right. We mustn't interrupt their date."

"Forget that, just get lost! She's on her lunch break!"

"Rachel's busy, isn't she? I'm sure you want as much time alone with her as you can get, huh!"

"Yeah, I bet he does. Your uncle Jasper will take his posse and get a move on, before Cupid hits us with a fine."

"Enjoy your date, you two! It is a date, after all!"

"...Date. Isaac on a date, hmm... A date..."

"Why do you keep repeating that?! Go on, get out of here; this is partly for work!"

When Isaac yells at them, they grin and leave, trading places with Rachel.

The last thing she hears from the group is Denis's artless voice telling the cashier, "That man over there is paying for all of us."

Isaac mutters, looking worn out. "This is why I didn't want to meet outside."

"I-I'm sorry. I'll be more careful next time."

Rachel had decided to have lunch with him during her break because she'd had shopping to do in the third layer. Not only that, but this restaurant has a lunch that she's always wanted to try. Since they'd agreed to meet outside the castle for her convenience, she feels apologetic.

Isaac hates being teased. However, the members of the Oberon

Trading Firm aren't about to hold back on his account. They're particularly enthusiastic when it comes to his engagement, so Rachel is careful not to sour his mood further, but...

"...It's nothing you need to apologize for. Never mind; just take a seat and order." Clearing away the documents that are strewn across the table, Isaac jerks his chin at the chair across from his.

This is enough to make Rachel happy, all by itself. Isaac is brusque, but the consideration he shows here and there is startlingly sweet. For example, even though it's pretty late, he's waited until Rachel arrives to eat his lunch, and then he matches his pace to hers.

"Everyone's very commerce-minded, aren't they? One would think waking up to find it was suddenly spring would be a shock, but they're saying it's the power of love and making merry over it."

"Yeah, we spread that idea around on purpose. Getting a bumper crop without doing a thing sets a bad precedent. If we didn't make sure they knew this was a special occasion, then when crops were poor, people would start complaining and asking why the demon king wasn't helping."

In addition, he always thinks of things that would never occur to Rachel.

"People like Quartz don't like it when the demon king's power makes plants grow. He says it screws up his research. Most people want to go along with whatever's easiest, though. Tell the demon king not to pull this stuff tomorrow, seriously. Tell Aileen, too."

"I—I will."

"Although it might not do any good..." Isaac gazes off into the distance, and a flicker of unease crosses his face.

What does Isaac think of the fact that Aileen and Claude have become man and wife in the truest sense of the word?

He must have made his peace with it when they married, but for Aileen's sake, he'd even come up with a plan to kill the demon king. That thought makes her béchamel sauce, which had been delicious, lose its flavor.

Even though it's one of the things she likes best about him, and the reason she chose him.

"……"

"Oh, Isaac! And—"

Auguste claps a hand over his mouth after calling to him from the entrance to the terrace.

The reason is immediately obvious: Serena is with him.

However, no sooner has Serena seen Rachel than she stalks up to her. "On a date?"

Rachel isn't sure what to tell her. Isaac's pretending he doesn't know what she's talking about. When Rachel smiles noncommittally, Serena's eyebrows come together in a scowl, and she grabs her arm. "Get up. Come over here."

"Huh? But—"

"Auguste, you sit there and wait."

Leaving the bewildered Auguste behind, Serena pulls Rachel away. She looks at Isaac, but he shrugs.

Serena takes her to a corner of the terrace, pushing her into a space where plenty of empty seats and potted trees provide cover.

"Why are you dressed like you're obviously just on your lunch break?"

Reaching into her little shoulder bag, Serena takes out some lip rouge. While Rachel stands there stunned, the other girl grabs her jaw, then paints her lips for her.

"That's why you can't answer when people ask if it's a date."

'Th-that's not... I was working in the kitchen today, so cosmetics were strictly forbidden—"

"No excuses. Turn around."

Serena briskly turns her to face the other way, then starts tugging at her hair. Before Rachel has time to complain, she's bound it back with a ribbon, then pulled it forward so that it falls over her shoulder.

"Now you're relatively presentable. Do these things properly. If you cut corners, he'll look down on you."

Serena herself is wearing a white dress and a lace-trimmed cape, and her perfectly straight hair is bound back with a pretty barrette. She looks charming, trim, and tidy. However, her makeup isn't saccharine, and she isn't obviously playing the coquette. Her appearance is a concentration of femininity that's terrifyingly refined at a level undetectable to most men.

"...Does Auguste care about that sort of thing?"

"That idiot doesn't even notice. This isn't that sort of problem, though. Or, what, you don't mind if people assume you're that man's servant?"

Rachel does mind, and she meekly repents. Perhaps it hadn't been possible to change out of her uniform, but she should at least have done something clever with it. Work is no excuse to not try.

Even Serena is currently studying for the female bureaucrat appointment exam.

"Thank you."

"Just putting on lip rouge makes a difference, so don't get careless. The Oberon Trading Firm's released one that stays on for a long time and is easy to carry with you. It comes in a decent range of colors, too," Serena adds, smiling wryly.

"We appreciate your business... Um, this isn't meant as thanks, exactly, but... Please listen properly to what Auguste tells you today."

"What? Why would you put it like that?"

"It isn't something I'm free to tell you about. I suspect he just isn't sure when to bring it up. I do think you should hear it sooner rather than later, though. Pretend you don't know and cleverly draw it out of him. I'm meddling, so you're free to ignore me, but..."

"...It's advice, isn't it? I'll take it; thanks. I thought he'd been oddly quiet lately."

Her worry shows in her tone, and Rachel smiles at her. "In that case, it will be fine. Give it your best, please, and don't fight."

"You, too. Don't worry; we'll find another café."

Serena sets off first, calling to Auguste. Auguste has been discussing something with Isaac, and he looks rather subdued, but he hastily puts on a smile and leaves with Serena.

"I'm sorry to interrupt you."

When Rachel returns, Isaac's eyes widen slightly. Rachel pinches the tip of her ponytail and smiles. "Serena did it for me. She scolded me for not dressing properly for a date."

"...Oh. Huh."

He doesn't correct the word. Silently, she thanks Serena. Possibly since she's already thinking of her, she brings up the other pair, who are already out of sight. "I hope she'll be able to talk with Auguste properly."

"...She's studying for that exam, though. Shouldn't this wait until that's over?"

"But then she wouldn't have time to emotionally prepare herself. It's very hard to be angry with someone for being considerate that way, and I think he should say it now."

"...Is that how it is?"

"The worse something is, the sooner one should report it. That's particularly true if there's nothing to be done about it. Oh—Although Auguste's matter isn't a bad one."

"...Actually. About the wedding..."

The fact that he's brought it up now makes her rather tense. Her unease, which she'd thought had vanished thanks to Serena, spreads like a stain.

Resting his chin on his hand, Isaac continues in a low voice. "I told you my family's against it, right?"

"Y-yes. But, um, so is...mine..."

Rachel is the eldest daughter of a count, while Isaac is a count's third son. Neither of them has the right to inherit their family's title; however, they are both favored retainers of Her Majesty the empress. As a result, their families are quibbling, saying there must be better matches for them. Specifically, Rachel's family is recommending she marry the eldest son of an aristocratic family, while Isaac's says he should marry the daughter of a nobleman who has no heir.

Right after they'd signed their engagement contract, Isaac had predicted their families would be against it. At the same time, he'd said he'd take steps that would bring them around.

For that reason, even when Rachel's parents had disapproved, and even though Isaac has never said a single word that could be construed as a confession of love or a marriage proposal, she'd felt secure.

"Yesterday, I got a letter from your little brother."

...And yet, although Rachel had feared he might be calling it off after all, the conversation takes a completely different turn.

"What? From my...brother?"

"He sent it to me, so I can't show you what it says, but here." Isaac shows her the address on the front of the envelope, and the sender's name on the back. The letter really is addressed to Isaac, and it was sent by Rachel's little brother.

Contrary to Isaac's prediction, Rachel's brother approves of his marriage to his sister. He calls Isaac their benefactor for freeing his family from debt and rescuing his sister from an engagement she hadn't wanted. He even says that, while he's young, he's tried to persuade his parents that his sister's happiness is more important than whether or not Isaac has a title.

It doesn't seem as if any letter sent by a brother like that could pose a problem, but Isaac's expression is hard. "He says your former fiancé has proposed reinstating your engagement, and your parents are in favor of it."

"...What?"

"He has a title, and this time he's offering betrothal money. Not only that, but he's a count whose domain is in Mirchetta. That means their only daughter will be coming home someday. As far as they're concerned, it's a situation with no downside. Your brother says they're preparing to send the marriage covenant to the church."

This news strikes Rachel like a bolt from the blue. She's stunned for a moment, then comes to her senses with a jolt. "I... I-I-I've heard nothing about this! They can't just— That's far too..."

"What with cleaning up after the Queendom of Hausel and the demon king's coronation, we've been busy. We've made our reports, but that's it; we've been putting off the persuasion until later. If they think I'm short on sincerity, there's no help for that."

"No help for... I-I'll—" Rachel starts, then presses her lips together firmly. She mustn't rely on Aileen for this. If she relies too much on the influence she gets from being the empress's lady-in-waiting, it will eventually become a habit, and that will ruin her.

But what else can she do? Both Rachel and her former fiancé are from titled families. Those families may have substantial links to the church. Unless she does something, she could find herself married to her former fiancé before she even knows it's happened.

"—Since there's no help for it, for now, I put some pressure on them."

That simple remark dries up the nervous tears she's been struggling to hold back. "What? Uh, how, exactly?"

"The two guards should be handling things on the church's end, and James says he'll arrange it so the duchy of Mirchetta won't accept any surprise marriages, no matter what."

"U-um, why would Walt and Kyle... And James, too. D-don't tell me... Have you asked Master Claude for assistance?"

"Who the heck would put himself in the demon king's debt? It's just that Aileen's bound to stick her oar in if she finds out about this, and then it's a sure bet that the demon king will volunteer to play matchmaker. I just went around and asked the others to help before that happened."

This man really is clever. Rachel is impressed. He's good at indirectly cajoling others and convincing them to act voluntarily.

"...Besides, you're popular."

"Pardon?"

"Nothing. I'm just saying everybody was worried you'd get married off against your will, and they weren't about to let it happen. The demons were all screeching about how they'd go over and burn their cookies or something. A certain fiendish mage

said he'd cast a spell that would literally change their minds...
Stopping their little schemes would've been more of a pain," Isaac grumbles, and so she feels rather apologetic about it, but a variety of feelings steal warmly through her heart.

"They all support us, then. I'm glad."

"...All I'd really need to do to fix this is beg the demon king for a noble title. The thing is, I don't want to. Sorry."

His apology flusters Rachel. "Oh no, it's nothing you need to be sorry for, Isaac. After all, you have the Oberon Trading Firm, and gaining a title would create more headaches for you. In turn, it might trouble Lady Aileen, so—"

"Wrong. I just don't want to end up begging the demon king for something because of you."

He's spoken so plainly that it takes her a moment to process what he's actually said.

"It's just stupid pride. I know that, but I still... So I'm the one to blame here. As far as you're concerned, it's unreasonable. After all, it's making things awkward between you and your parents."

Isaac sounds as if he's mocking himself. The sight of him really should pain her, and yet Rachel feels her heart filling up.

Isaac is a reasonable person. If he thinks something is practical, he'll swallow his pride and get it done. If it were for Aileen or the Oberon Trading Firm, he'd beg Claude for anything he had to.

The fact that he doesn't want to do it for her means this is his pride as a man talking.

He might as well have said he'll concede Aileen, but he refuses to concede Rachel.

Rachel's tears spill over before she has a chance to fight them back, and Isaac looks shocked. "I-it's bad enough to cry about?! Don't tell me you actually want to be a countess."

"N-no. I-Isaac, you really... You don't understand how women feel."

"Huhn? What's that about? Don't be rude."

"I was worried about getting married."

Isaac freezes up. She notices it, but she feels this needs to be said. "Isaac, you explain everything properly, you carefully prepare, make sure all the paperwork is in order, and you're perfectly considerate, but sometimes it feels like you're a regulations-obsessed business partner more than anything else."

"Regulations-obsessed..."

"For example, I've sometimes wished you would say it the way Master Claude does. I don't need that much honesty, though, and I don't envy Lady Aileen. There're also times I've thought it might be nice if you were as easy to read as Auguste, but that also seems difficult to deal with in its own way."

"...You're being casually cruel here."

"I'm through with that, though. You don't need to say anything, Isaac. You're fine just as you are."

"Uh, I'm not fine with that at all..."

The sight of Isaac grousing is rather amusing, and her tears of joy threaten to turn into tears of laughter. She wipes them away, then sits up straighter. "I understand the situation. I'll thank everyone for helping to stop this later on. So...is there anything I can do now?"

"......"

Isaac looks as if he'd like to say something, but he sighs, then seems to mentally switch gears. "We'll railroad it."

"...Pardon? I'm sorry, I don't understand."

"You and I signed that contract, and the empress is our witness.

That means we don't actually need our parents' permission to get married."

"......"

The meaning of what Isaac is telling her sinks in, and she feels her face grow warm. "Um... You mean, we'd be, um...eloping?"

"We've both got work, so we won't leave the capital, but yeah."

Isaac's ever-practical attitude dampens her enthusiasm a little, but he's definitely telling her he wants to get married.

"For starters, I think we should rent an apartment or buy a house; I've picked out a few candidates." He holds out a sheaf of documents to her. These are what he'd cleared off the table earlier. "I'm fine with any of these, so go ahead and narrow down the list. If you've got any requests, let me know. We'll make sure our next day off matches and visit these places."

"Huh... Um, m-me, too?"

"We'll be living together, so yeah."

"Huh? Wait— Huh?!"

"Geez, what? Should I take that as a no?"

She shakes her head, hard and enthusiastically. Looking relieved, or maybe as if he's regained his composure, Isaac gets to his feet. "Sorry, but I'm heading out first. I've got a deal to make. I'll take care of the bill on my way out."

"Oh, but mine is—"

"Denis and the rest of 'em ordered stuff, too, so I'll write it off as a business exp— ...Is this the sort of stuff I shouldn't say?"

"What?"

Rachel is trembling so much that she hasn't picked up the sheaf of "rent or buy" documents, and Isaac thumps her lightly on the head with them. All she can see are the shadow of the papers and Isaac's hand holding them.

"I'm definitely in love with you, so relax."

"—What?"

"See ya!" he says loudly, pushing the papers into her arms. All she can do is watch him stalk out of the terrace, shoulders squared.

As Rachel looks after him, feeling dazed, the papers begin to slip off her lap. She hastily claps a hand down onto them, holding them in place—and as if it's suddenly remembered, her blood begins to flow again.

Her face flushes bright red. Hiding it with the documents, she writhes. A soft breath of wind rises into the sky, as if to carry the heat away.

Today is an impossible spring in the dead of winter. Even so, she thinks, *We'll be all right.*

♛

When Serena awoke, it had been spring. She'd thought it might not last, but even at noon, the sun still shone as if it intended to sear away midwinter. As a result, she'd had to rethink the outfit she'd picked out yesterday for today's date, which meant choosing new accessories as well. It was a nuisance. However, she couldn't cut corners.

And so, as she approaches the Holy Knights' training ground, she's wearing something completely different from what she'd originally planned. Hearing cheers go up from the training ground, she frowns.

The warm weather must have made this a perfect day to watch the knights train. She had stopped by with the vague idea that she'd do him a favor and admire how hard he was working, so she can't exactly criticize the girls who've also come to observe. That said, she doesn't want to be like that crowd of squealing fangirls.

She could leave and come back later, but there's an awkward thirty minutes left before their scheduled meeting. In the end, she waits for Auguste in the shade, in a spot where the girls block her view.

...*This is ridiculous. I shouldn't have stopped by for a look.* Come to think of it, isn't peeking at your beloved's place of work a little like spying? She does have excuses lined up—such as the fact that work and studying have kept them so busy for the past month that they've kept missing each other and have only had time for greetings, or the fact that Auguste keeps looking as if he wants to say something only to stay silent, which is awfully concerning—but...

"Oh! If it isn't Serena!"

She's been looking at her toes, lost in thought, when she hears someone she wants nothing to do with outside of work. Grimacing, she looks up to see Lilia and Sahra.

"Why are you people here?"

"The weather's lovely today, isn't it? We heard they'd thrown together a practice match between the knights and the Holy Knights, so I came to see it with Sahra. She idolizes our knights over here, don't you, Sahra?"

"Th-that's right. We don't have anything like them in Ashmael..."

"...That's fine. Lady Lilia's the problem here. What happened to your guards?"

"Well, the Daughter of God, a terribly important guest from a neighboring country, said she was just dying to see this. As the wife of the second prince, it's my job to accompany her, isn't it?"

Although the younger royal couple have been allowed to marry, they're still living in confinement. This woman is brazenly ignoring that, and this soon in her marriage. There's no point in cross-examining her, though. Today is Serena's day off, so she isn't obligated to report her for wandering around and turn her in.

"It's fine. The demon king knows aaall about this."

"Does he?"

"Well, I mean, I've still got that magic bomb on my neck. More than anything, he seems to like seeing Cedric go pale, dash over, and apologize whenever I go missing."

Apparently the demon king's got a nasty personality, too. Sahra speaks up, a little late. "What? A bomb? Guards? What is this about?! Um, when you said everybody was busy and we couldn't cause them trouble, so we should just go on our own. Were you tricking m—? A-am I causing trouble for Miss Roxane?!"

"Oh, gracious, it's fine! I'll take care of everything for you!"

"Y-you mustn't. Miss Roxane is in a delicate state right now... S-Serenaaaa!"

"Don't look at me. It's your responsibility. If you've realized this is bad news, take that woman and hurry back. If they haven't noticed she's gone yet, there shouldn't be any problems."

"I-I'll do that...!"

Sahra grabs Lilia's arm tightly; Lilia puffs out her cheeks, sulking. Still, she seems to come to terms with it quickly enough. "If I must, I must. For the sake of the league of heroines, I'll go along quietly."

"Listen you, would you stop that already? That's why you married that half-wit prince, isn't it?"

"This spring is the result. Serena understands that, not logically, but on instinct.

However, Lilia gives a significant little chuckle. "Well, I realized something yesterday. If I hang on to that *All Ages* rating, I don't have to retire yet!"

Serena doesn't have any idea what she's talking about, but she understands that Lilia's incomprehensible idea can't mean anything good for Cedric. Between that and his apologies to the demon king, the second prince's troubles will never end.

"That means you and Sahra mustn't get involved with men, either. No cuddling allowed. All right?"

"I-I'm married to Ares, so that's not something I can…"

"It's fine, I'll get you a divorce!"

Turning pale, Sahra shakes her head. Serena smacks the back of Lilia's skull. "Stop it. When you talk like that, it's not funny."

"Aww! Then will you hold out a bit longer, Serena? I know: Let's all get lunch together, now, just the three of us! I know a good place."

"We mustn't, Lilia. You're supposed to be in confinement, aren't you?! You have a bomb tethered to you, don't you?!"

"Honestly, Sahra, you're such a worrywart. It's fine; we're heroines. It'll work out somehow, if we believe it will. ★"

"I don't know what you mean! Serena, please stop Lilia!"

There are more people around them now, and Serena glances up. The solid wall of spectators has broken apart. The training is over.

She sees Auguste through the gaps in the throng. He's conferring with Marcus, apparently having some sort of meeting with the knights. However, he promptly notices her, and his eyes widen. Next to him, Marcus spots Lilia waving at him, and the blood drains from his face.

Marcus is a member of the knights, but he's also Cedric's bodyguard. Lilia's escape is a blunder so great that it might cost Cedric his head. Starting now, Marcus and Cedric and Lester, and also Julian, or was it Gilbert? —Everyone who'd bowed their head to the demon king for Lilia's sake will probably tear around cleaning up this mess. She thinks it's ridiculous, but she also feels as if it would be all right for this time to last a while longer.

After all, someday, life will change. This sort of thing won't happen anymore.

"Sorry, I've got a date."

"What?! Lucky... I wonder if Ares and I could go on an outing of some sort."

"Argh! You two are traitors! I want to leave our silly husbands behind and have a girls' day out!"

"Lilia, it's the day after your wedding! Isn't it too early for this?!"

"We'll just plan for a different time, then. Want to go to a place where they serve parfaits the size of mountains? It's not possible to eat one of those by yourself, so people can't go in there alone." She glances at the restaurant.

Sahra's eyes light up in an obvious way, and Lilia laughs. "Oh, yes, *there*. We'll meet there, then. It's a promise!"

If she uses a cheat, she can probably get permission. She wouldn't mind doing that much for Sahra, before the girl returns to her own country.

★　★　★

"And? What are you hiding? Spill it."

After leaving the café where they'd run into Rachel and Isaac on their date, Serena and Auguste have found another one. The moment they've seated themselves, Serena forcefully starts the conversation.

Rachel had said to pretend she didn't know, but the only ones who could pull that off are Rachel, Aileen, and the principal consort of Ashmael: women who are good at respecting men. It isn't Serena's forte.

Auguste is clearly disconcerted; he doesn't seem to know where to look. He starts to pick up the menu, even though they've already ordered, then stops; he's acting suspicious. After she's glared at him steadily for a while, he finally speaks.

"...It hasn't been announced yet, but...they've decided, um, unofficially, to promote me."

She'd heard about this before Lilia and Cedric's wedding. If that's all, then it's a good thing. However, Auguste's gloomy, searching expression tells her eloquently that there's more.

"It's just...they told me I'll be transferring to Mirchetta to replace the captain, Ailey's second-oldest brother...so I wasn't sure what to do."

Serena drinks from her glass of cool water. "That's fantastic." The successor to the captain of the Holy Knights. In other words, this transfer is a definite step up. "When is this happening?"

"In spring..."

"I see. Then you'll be moving as soon as my exam's over. Don't tell me— Were you not sure when to bring this up because you thought it might get in the way of my studies?"

"—Oh, um, yes."

"Don't be dumb. Well, never mind; I'll pick up the check here, to congratulate you."

"Nothing's settled yet, though. I can turn it down, so—"

"Don't be dumb," she says again, to herself as much as to him. "I told you to make a success of yourself, didn't I? If you turn this down, I won't stand for it."

"...Yeah, I guess not." Auguste's smile looks just a little lonely, but it's as easygoing as ever.

Today is only a date, and she hadn't been thinking of celebrations at all, so she promises to make time on another day. Auguste tries to decline her invitation, but she tells him that simply isn't an option in situations like this. As the sun's color deepens to red, they part ways on a broad avenue where it crosses from the fourth layer into the third.

The house of Gilbert's title is scheduled to be reinstated, but after being taken over by her uncle's family, its finances are in shambles. Under the circumstances, Serena's treatment won't change overnight. She really will be a count's daughter in name only, and her territory is still under the direct control of the duke of Mirchetta. Aileen probably intends to have James keep an eye on Serena, since he'll be the duke of Mirchetta someday. Either that, or she's planning to give the territory to Auguste as a reward once he's climbed the ranks.

In other words, this transfer to Mirchetta is the first step in that direction. Who knows if he's aware of it...

All the way to the end, he'd looked as if there was something else he wanted to say. He can't be hesitating because he's concerned about taking their relationship long-distance, can he?

She has to congratulate Auguste for this properly, if only

Fifth Act

to ensure he won't turn down the promotion. Now then, what should she give him?

What's a suitable present for a lover who's going far away in a few months' time?

Even though she's only been able to call him her lover for a few months.

"......"

For now, she decides to hurry back home and study. The important thing is putting herself on a firm footing. No matter how much time she has, it could never be enough.

I'll pass that exam on the first try, then start making a name for myself as fast as I can. I'll restore the good name of the house of Gilbert...

How many years will that take? Auguste will be advancing the whole time. Will she be able to catch up to him?

Without meaning to, she shifts from walking briskly to almost running.

She's gritting her teeth without even realizing when, out of nowhere, someone catches her arm and pulls her back.

"Let's get married!"

Auguste has tugged her around to face him, and his proposal leaves her dazed. Then anger boils up.

There he goes again, doing something random on impulse.

What good will getting married do? Is he telling her to come with him? That's not even funny. What does he think she's studying for right now— *Argh, honestly, what a pain. Maybe I should just slap him.*

Just as she raises her hand, Auguste catches both her arms. "Then I'll be able to protect you from your relatives."

She wasn't expecting him to say that, and it leaves her speechless.

Auguste goes on earnestly, "Being apart won't be... I mean, I'll be lonely, but it's not going to change how I feel. The thing is, seeing Isaac and Rachel made me think *That's not enough to settle things*. I don't have a family, so I didn't really get it, but James told me specifically what's going to happen when the Gilbert title is reinstated."

"...It won't change much. The title's practically all I'll have."

"You know that's not true. You'll end up fighting your uncle's family, won't you."

She'd intentionally kept quiet about that, but Auguste's guess is right on the mark.

"Your uncle's the sort of man who'd work you like a servant, then try to marry you off to some old man with new money as security for a loan, right?"

Serena bites her lip. She doesn't want to remember what was done to her, and she doesn't want to answer. "He won't be able to do a thing. It'll be fine."

She doesn't sound persuasive, and she knows it.

There's no way her uncle's greedy family will keep quiet. If anything, the fact that they're not making any noise now is downright unsettling.

Given that, Serena needs a way to fight back. She'll be a count's daughter and a government official at the same time, acquiring both authority and rank. In the process, she'll become someone they can't touch. "In any case, no one knows where they are, or even if they're alive or dead. Worrying about it is pointless."

"As things stand, though, I won't be able to step in. I'm just a stranger. If we're far apart and something happens to you, I may not even find out about it until it's too late. Things will be different if we get married, though. Once I've married into the house of Gilbert, I'll be able to shield you."

She shouldn't become the wife of the captain of the Holy Knights for a while. After all, unlike her, Auguste deserves an untarnished rank that's beyond reproach.

And yet, if they get engaged now— No, they mustn't do that, much less get married.

She'd end up forcing him to clean up the Gilbert countship's mess.

"I don't need a shield. Lady Aileen and her people may not talk like it, but they're pretty soft, so they're bound to help me out if push comes to shove. Don't worry about that; you just focus on making a name for yourself."

"Listen, Serena. You don't get that I genuinely love you, do you?!"

She doesn't understand; she blinks at him. Looking straight at her, Auguste goes on insistently. "Did you expect me to say 'Oh, really? Okay'?! It's not gonna happen! Don't you understand why I'm trying to succeed in the first place?! Because I want to make you happy! Because if I do it, it'll make you smile!"

"I-in that case—"

"But more than that, I love you, Serena! I want to be the one to protect you! I don't want to let anybody else do it! I don't want to give up that role, not to Ailey or even to you!"

It's a spoiled confession of love, with no logic or calculations behind it, and she has no idea how to respond.

She can't give him a cold look and ask him if he's stupid. She can't calmly write his words off as selfish excuses.

After all, this man is cheerful and seems faithful, but he

actually wants—rather cruelly—to take only what's correct and leave the rest. Serena has always been curious about how he would approach love.

"I'll do, won't I? Even you understand I'm the only one who will, really. Why are you so humble about that, when you aren't that way about anything else?!"

"……"

"I mean, if you were the type who could be honest and say 'I don't want this' or 'I'm scared' or 'Help me,' I'd be okay with waiting, but I know you're not like— Ow!"

He's started to say something nobody needs to hear, so she stomps on his foot.

"Are you stupid?! You really are! You're an utter fool!"

"—Say whatever you want, I swear I'm gonna marry you! I'll do it even if it means begging the demon king or pleading with James! Even if you don't want to marry me, I'm doing it!"

"Don't you dare! Why would you put yourself in their debt?! Oh, for the love of— You idiot! You're so stu—"

He blocks her angry, cursing lips with his own.

That way, further arguments or resistance will mean nothing— Although Serena knows they'd lost all meaning long before this moment.

"I love you," Auguste repeats, his face a breath away from hers. There's a sincere promise in his voice. She hasn't given him permission for anything, but he holds her close anyway. "Let's get married."

Something's welling up from the depths of her eyes.

She very nearly nods without thinking—but they're right in the middle of a busy street.

Putting all her strength behind it, Serena slaps him across the face. "Are you stupid?! Who'd accept a proposal that sloppy?! Do it over!"

"Huh?! ...D-do it over? I don't understand—"

"Bring a bouquet of roses! And a ring! Find a better location, and don't just say it on impulse! Stage it perfectly!"

"That hurdle seems pointlessly high!"

"It's not pointless! It's a dream of mine, all right?! I'm sorry about that! If you won't do it, then my answer is no!"

Yanking her arm out of Auguste's grip, Serena turns on her heel.

Even she doesn't know why she's spoiling for a fight.

"—Fine, I'll do it! You'll be happy then, right?! I'll make you say yes, I swear!"

She can't ask him if he's stupid this time.

An oddly impressed cheer goes up from the passersby, along with applause and encouraging calls of "Go for it!" Rubbing her eyes, which have started to tear up, Serena sets off without looking back. Auguste doesn't follow her.

She isn't running away. She doesn't need to. The matter is already settled.

After all, no proposal could ever resonate more strongly than this one.

The evening sun is shining brightly, as if to conceal her flushed cheeks. A miraculous spring has appeared in the depths of winter.

In just a short while, true spring will arrive. She's sure this one won't be a season of goodbyes.

"Practice, practice," Aileen mutters to herself. She's sitting on the bed.

Lady Roxane overcame this. I should be able to as well.

She must manage somehow. If she fails, she'll never get past the fact that Sahra gave her a curious look and said, "Huh? I don't understand the problem." The woman seems like the most childish one there, but she's actually a mature adult on the inside. Not only that, but today of all days, Rachel is muttering "Floor plans... What should I do...?" and looking distracted, while rumor has it that Serena has been proposed to and she keeps remembering something that makes her pound her fist on the table. Baal has asked Roxane out on a date, and she's blushed charmingly and gone, escorted so delicately that onlookers might suspect she were made of glass. Claude's mind is all flowers and butterflies, which seems to have changed midwinter into spring, and perhaps those feelings are contagious, because it appears spring has come early in everyone else's heads as well.

The crowning blow is Lilia's declaration. "I've decided to preserve my *All Ages* rating!" It makes Aileen want to bellow "What is Cedric doing?!" but it's hard for her to criticize given her own sorry state. She mustn't stay in the realm of *All Ages*. Even she isn't entirely clear what that really means, but the point is that she mustn't run from this.

"Master Claude, your talks with Master Baal begin tomorrow morning. Make sure you're there on time."

"I know."

Followed by a stern reminder of his schedule from Keith, Claude enters the bedchamber, and she hears the door close behind him. They're alone.

Now their time as husband and wife will begin. In other

words, it's last night all over again— Before Claude says anything, Aileen's imagination makes her leap to her feet. "I knew it, I caaaaaaaan't!!"

Bolting from the bed like a startled rabbit, she crawls under a table in the corner of the room, taking the sheet with her.

I can't! I truly can't! My heart will never last!
Last night had been better: She hadn't known what they would be doing.

Today is different, though. Aileen knows exactly what's going to happen.

"...Aileen. I don't think that really counts as 'hiding.'" Claude sounds a little appalled.

With the sheet pulled over her head, Aileen shrieks, "I know! But I can't very well flee the bedchamber, can I?!"

"So you do understand."

"Yes, I do! I am your wife, after all! But, but...!" With a pathetic moan, she squeezes her eyes shut, curling up into a ball. Then she senses a presence next to her. Claude has lowered himself to the floor.

"My wife is adorable and full of energy again today." The composure in the way he says it makes Aileen bristle. When she peeks out of her sheet cocoon, Claude is sitting with his arm on one bent knee, watching her mischievously.

"...Y-you're exhausted by my behavior, aren't you?"

"No. I just think you're charming when you overreact."

"Overreact?! You brought springtime to the capital today, Master Claude! That's a much bigger overreaction!"

"Well, whatever shall I do? It seems I've angered my wife," Claude says snidely, not looking the least bit troubled. In a fit of temper, Aileen throws the sheet over his head, hiding that irritating face.

"I believe you've grown rather perverse of late, Master Claude! You used to be more of a gentleman!"

"I must have been courting you, so you wouldn't be wary."

"What is that supposed to mean?! Are you saying you deceived me?!"

"Don't say that. What will people think? ...And that was because you'd just been wounded by Cedric."

It's the first time either of them has ever brought up her former fiancé's name so openly.

In spite of herself, Aileen's anger recedes. Poking his head out from under the sheet, Claude smiles at her. "I had to be so kind that you'd never think of him again. A perfectly natural strategy, wasn't it?"

A restless shiver runs through her. "...Y-you were concerned about that?"

"Very much so. There was no way I wouldn't be."

"B-but you never said a single word about... I-it's mean of you to bring it up now..."

"Of course. Cedric may have hurt you, but I'm the older brother he fears."

She has a bad feeling about this. Claude spreads his arms, turning his palms up. "By the way, the only time a magician reveals how a trick is done is when he no longer plans to perform it."

"...U-um. I really don't know what you mean..."

"Look at reality, Aileen. You fell for me, but I'm only a man: I get jealous, and I'll stop at nothing to make the woman I love forget her old flames."

"P-putting it that way isn't fair!"

It's a disclosure that's more embarrassing to the one who hears it. Not only that, but presenting it unpretentiously as a method of seduction is cowardly in the extreme.

When she turns bright red and yells at him, his large hands come to rest against her cheeks. His eyes are right there, endlessly spiteful, but with dark emotion lurking in their depths.

He isn't hiding it, though. He's showing it to her.

That thought sends heat coursing through her very being. The embarrassment is enough to blast away everything she remembers about the night before.

She covers her face with her hands, writhing. He puts an arm around her waist, pulling her out from under the table, and she doesn't have the strength to resist.

He picks her up, and she knows where he's carrying her, but she feels limp and weak. Even so, mustering all her willpower, she retorts, "...I—I won't fall for anything else."

"I'll look forward to that."

"I'm serious! I really mean—" He deposits her lightly on the bed, cutting her off midsentence.

"I'm serious, too, Aileen."

There's not a hint of teasing in his red eyes. They belong to a man Aileen is truly seeing for the first time.

She feels as if her heart may jump out of her mouth, but before it can, he's blocked her lips with his. His kiss is so rough that it's almost as if he's biting her; she's never experienced that before, and yet it's more intoxicating than frightening. It's the ecstasy of knowing this is for her alone.

There are many Claudes she doesn't know beyond this one. There are Aileens she doesn't know there as well. Just like the one who looks as if she's trembling now, but is actually shivering with excitement.

It's a little frightening. However.

"—Why are you smiling?"

Because you're adorable. Aileen doesn't say it, though. Instead, she smiles back at him.

Now then, let the villainess show you the wiles she'll use to tame the final boss.

You, and you alone.

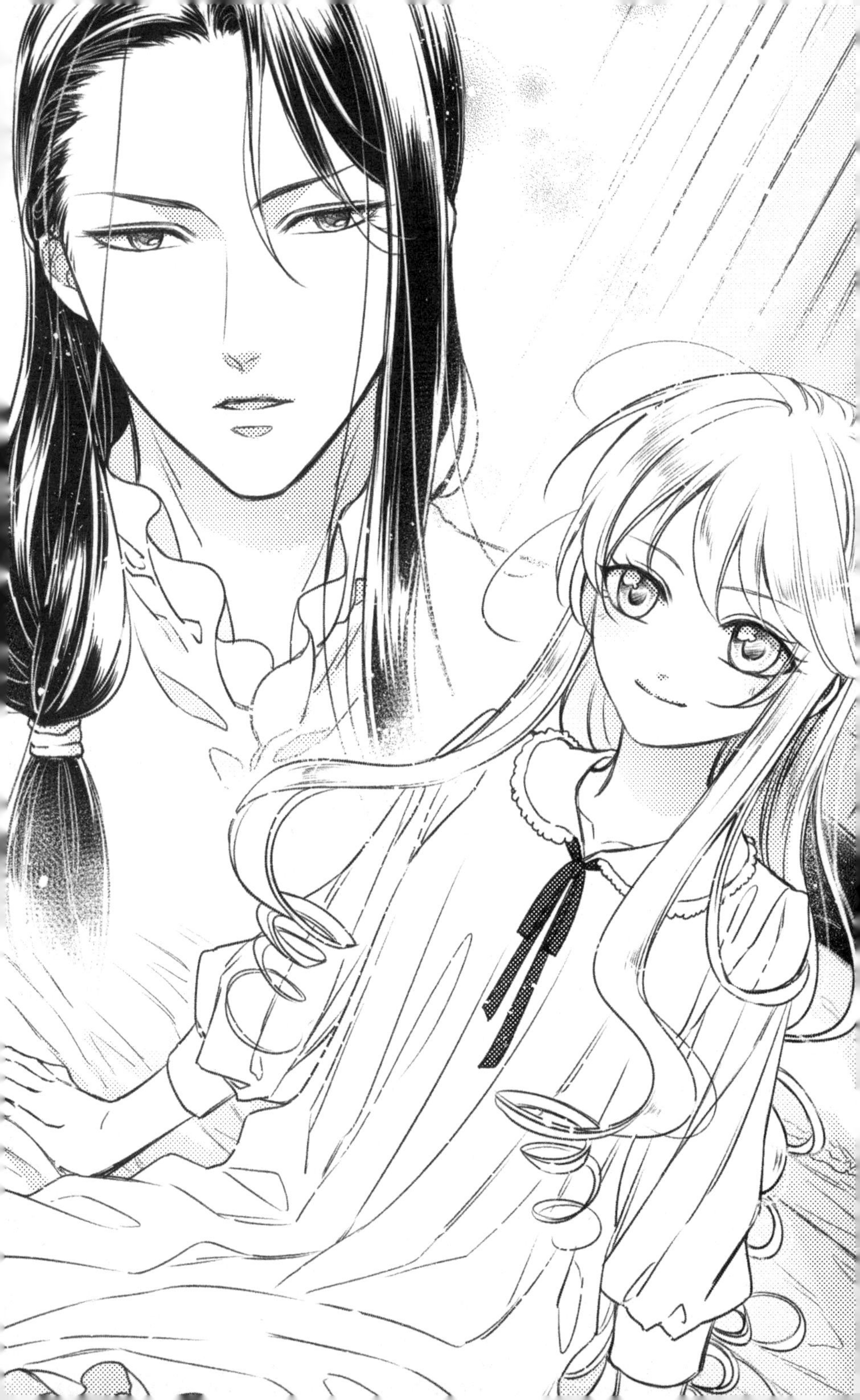

When Happiness Follows Happiness, the Result Is a Parfait

"How does one eat a parfait like this one?! Actually, why is this even happening?!"

"Oh, come on, Lady Aileen. You joined our group uninvited. These are best attacked from the top; start there!"

"Oh— Wait a moment, Lady Lilia and Lady Aileen. I'll portion it out. If you force it, it will collapse!"

"Hang on, Rachel. You work from that side; I'll scoop from this one."

"You know... Even the six of us may not be able to finish this..."

"You mustn't push yourself, Miss Roxane. If you start feeling unwell, tell m— Oh! Oh no, it's collapsi—"

As everyone cries out, the cake that's perched on the very top tumbles off. Rachel deftly catches it with a plate.

Sighing with relief, the spectators clap, and then the applause dissolves in a burst of laughter.

That's what's happening at the next table over.

"Why exactly did we reserve the whole shop for this?!" Isaac screams.

Claude tilts his head in confusion. "Well, if Aileen's going out, then I want to go, too."

"Okay, look! You're the emperor! Remember your position!!"

"Hear, hear. You're being a little too careless," the holy king says impassively from the seat next to Claude's.

"Never mind, let's divide this up. You were fond of citrus, weren't you, holy king? Here you go."

"Hey, that's considerate. Thanks."

"Hang on, Keith. Why is he first? I should be first."

"Yes, yes. I'll give you lots of strawberries, milord. And you wanted cream, right, Bel? Ares, you can serve yourself."

"Uh, right..."

The demon king's brilliant adviser expertly splits the enormous parfait into manageable portions. Isaac is clutching his head. One table over, Auguste and Walt are digging their spoons directly into the parfait—the idea of dividing it up hasn't even occurred to them—while Kyle and Elefas are yelling at them.

"You'll knock the whole thing down, you two! You're eating like pigs!"

"That's right! Everyone should be given a fair share! Oh— The melon's already gone... No..."

"Elefas, at times like this, victory always goes to the swift. Huh? You're not gonna eat, James?"

"I don't need any. Watching you people made me lose my appetite... Auguste, why did you just put a half-eaten scoop of ice cream on my plate?!"

"Huh? Well, I tried it and decided I'm not a fan of that flavor— Ow! You didn't have to hit me!"

In the end, James seems to decide that actively joining the fray is the better option, and he starts eating furiously. *They seem like they're having fun,* Claude thinks, then returns his attention to Isaac at the neighboring table.

"I wanted to celebrate Auguste's engagement, and James will

Fifth Act 241

probably go to Mirchetta with him this spring. Before that happens, I wanted our group to make a memory together."

"I mean, I get that. I'm just asking why it had to be parfaits."

"What are you saying, Isaac Lombard?! This is a battle requiring sophisticated strategy!"

With inexplicable arrogance, some fellow with glasses shouts from directly across the table. He's pretty sure his name started with "L"... He's sitting at Cedric's table, so remembering his name probably wouldn't hurt. However, lately, he's started to think he could take a cue from Marcus the "instrument" and just call this fellow "spectacles."

"Listen up! Your table and mine will compete to see who can polish off their parfait first!"

"Then hurry up and eat, Lester. It's going to melt... Cedric, you look pale. Are you all right?"

"Y-yes, Marcus... Somehow... How can Lilia eat this as if it's nothing...?"

"Some say women have a separate stomach for stuff like this, so— Oh, water, wash it down with water!"

"Stop it, Gilbert, you'll make him feel sicker. Actually, I don't feel so great myself..."

Even if he can't remember any of their names, Cedric is surrounded by people, so evidently he does have friends.

Getting yelled at seems to have left Isaac worn out, or maybe he's just resigned himself. With a sigh, he sits back down. Quartz and Luc are hard at work dividing up that table's parfait.

"Okay, Denis, here's an extra-big helping. You want an extra-big one too, don't you, Master Isaac?"

"Of course I don't; you know I'm not good with sweet stuff!"

Knock it off, don't load that up with whipped cream. This is harassment!"

"For men your uncle Jasper's age, this is kinda rough. If you could make mine mostly fruit— Oh, okay, guess not, huh."

"...Still... How do you suppose they make these?"

"Oh, I was wondering about that myself! At this level, these parfaits are basically construction projects. Lifting that dish takes both hands."

When all's said and done, they seem to be enjoying themselves. There's Cedric's table, the table James seems to have taken charge of, Isaac's table, his own table—where Keith is efficiently serving the rest of them—and Aileen's table. They're all attacking their parfaits in different ways, and it's all rather fascinating.

"This is a rare opportunity. In order to grow closer as a group, why don't we say the members of the first table to finish their parfait get to give any orders they like to the rest, provided those orders can be carried out completely within a day?"

Instantly, the restaurant goes dead silent. Even the women's table is listening, although they'd been chatting so cheerfully the men might as well as not have been there at all. The only one who readily agrees is the holy king.

"We don't mind, but you can use magic, and we can use sacred power, so our table's bound to win. The victor is already clear."

"That's true. We'll say no one's allowed to use sacred power or magic then. All right, let's give it our best."

"Uh, we haven't agreed to this yet."

Isaac is glaring daggers at him, but Claude ignores him and goes on calmly. "When we win this, I'm torn between ordering everyone to perform the Love-Love Dance or do something else."

That lights a fire in everyone's eyes.

Fifth Act

* * *

From Claude's perspective, the plan has injected a lot of life into the party. The battle is fueled by the determination to avoid obeying the most painful of orders.

Isaac tries to slip Luc a laxative. As James's group is about to finish their parfait, Lester's group sneaks some of their table's ice cream and fruit onto it. Conspiracies and treachery fly every which way in the battle to conquer the parfaits, and the winner is—

"Congratulations, Lady Aileen."

"Well, this was the only way it could end, really." Aileen gives a smug little laugh.

Isaac groans; he's pale from overeating. "I was sure the demon king's group would sabotage your group somehow!"

"Why? Who wouldn't want to make his adorable wife's wish come true?" Claude nods nonchalantly. As before, the holy king is the only one who agrees with him.

"In any case, we don't have to do stuff like this to give orders. We can do that whenever we want. We're the holy king and demon king."

"True. I don't see much value in giving orders to others. Actually, I'd like someone to give me an order sometime."

"...I'm sure I had no chance in the power struggle because I couldn't be someone like that," Cedric says, as if he feels this loss keenly.

Ignoring his strangely profound remark, Claude looks at the colorful women's table, where the victors are clapping and celebrating. "Now then, my empress. What order will you give me?"

Aileen flushes a little, then clears her throat in an affected way. "Let me see…"

His sister-in-law leans out from behind her. "Here, over here! What about reenacting the game art?!"

He doesn't know what she means, but Aileen snaps at her. "As I keep telling you repeatedly, stop doing that! If you insist, then limit your order to Cedric and the others—"

"Too late, I already gave it!"

"Oh, I see... To think you'd use your only request on something like that."

"Are you sure, Lady Aileen? You don't want to see that scene of the demon king on his knees, begging you to love him?"

"......"

For some reason, his wife falls silent. Lilia looks triumphant. From beside her, Serena cuts in, sounding completely fed up with her rambling. "Who cares about that? I don't need it. I'll settle for a purse of gold."

"For you, Serena, I recommend the scene where you make the student council members carry your purchases while you shop! With their money, of course."

"I'll take that."

"Wha—? Wouldn't that be cheating on me, Serena?!"

"Oh, be quiet. I'll be helping myself to the contents of the cambion and human weapons' coin purses."

"You've got to be kidding." Walt and the others' faces tense up.

"Unfortunately, Rachel, you're out of luck. Your fiancé is a mob character."

"Who's a mob character?!" Isaac shouts back on reflex. He doesn't notice that Rachel's eyes widen, and then she looks a little happy.

"Oh! Buuut in the fan disc, there was a scene where Serena picked out clothes for you, so how about letting the student council members serve you along with her?!"

"I—I see... Um, in other words, are you saying that Serena and I should order them to go shopping with us?"

"Why not? Anything's fine, as long as they treat you. If you're worried, mob fiancé, you could shadow them."

"Like I said, who's a mob character?!"

"For Lady Roxane and Sahra, I recommend—"

"I will allow no one to issue orders to Master Baal," the holy king's consort declares flatly, her voice cutting through the noise.

Baal seems to pick up on the ominous mood; his eyes gleam as if he's impressed. "Roxane... You are definitely our wife."

"You have a particular talent for sword dancing, don't you, Master Baal. That scene of you and Ares on that stage of flames was incredibly dashing."

"I shall go with that, then."

"Roxane?! And wait, a stage of flames? You can't mean *that* sword dance, can you? The really hot, tiresome one?!"

"I don't need Master Ares, though. Master Baal alone will do."

"What?! I need him! Please put him in."

"Sahra. That takes practice, and frankly, I don't want to—"

"I bet you'll look amazing. I can't wait to see it, Ares!"

Claude has a hunch that the artlessness the Daughter of God uses to egg on her husband isn't just foolish naivete anymore.

"That's settled, then!"

"And you? What are you going to ask for?"

"I... I'm fine. I already got what I wanted anyway!"

"...'A commoner like you, the Maid of the Sacred Sword? You can't be serious.'"

Aileen's abrupt, theatrical-sounding declaration bewilders Claude. As everyone—even Lilia—looks stunned, Aileen flashes a dauntless smile. "'Master Cedric has misinterpreted something. If that's clear, then get out of my way.'"

Crossing her legs, she gives a mocking, villainous smile.

While Claude blinks at his wife, Lilia hurls herself at her, clinging to her. Aileen is thrown off-balance by the other woman's momentum, and the back of her head *thunk*s against the wall.

"Omigosh-omigosh-omigosh, Lady Aileen, that was absolutely perfect! I love you!"

"I see, how nice for you!! Then go reenact that other scene one more time, with Prince Cedric, *and do it right.*"

"I'll do that," Lilia tells her. She and Aileen seem to share something he doesn't know about.

Still, the idea doesn't make him anxious. After all, when he glances at his half brother, Cedric has apparently picked up on the same thing he has, and his lips are pursed. That means it's probably fine.

The four who are being forced to go shopping with Serena and Rachel, and the holy king and his general, who've been compelled to practice their sword dance, will no doubt be fine as well.

At present, then, what Claude should do is...

"U-um, Master Claude. That was—"

"—You steal everything from me. I loathe you, and I adore you to the point of madness." First things first: He must kneel and beg for his wife's love, so that she won't go anywhere. "I offer up my love, body and soul, and my heart itself. In return, please, give your everything to me."

Aileen's cheeks are flushed, and she listens rapturously. Partway through, she gathers herself with a jolt, realizing that they're causing a scene.

Even so, at the end, she smiles happily and saves the demon king with her love.

Afterword

Hello, this is Sarasa Nagase.

This seventh volume in the tale of Aileen, the demon king, and their merry friends happens to be a collection of short stories. I was able to compile them in one volume and get it published thanks to your support, with the help of my former editor (who planned this volume as a parting gift) and my new editor. I hope you enjoy it.

Mai Murasaki graced this book with the cover art and its cute mini-characters, and with beautiful insert illustrations. I couldn't be more grateful. I really can't thank Anko Yuzu enough for drawing such a wonderful comic version all the way to the end. I would also like to thank everyone else who was involved with this book from the bottom of my heart.

And you, who've picked up this volume: It's thanks to all of you that Aileen and the rest have been given life in this world. Really, thank you so much. Please do continue to support them.

Now then, I hope we'll meet again.

Sarasa Nagase